Jonah sat next to her on the blanket.

A gentle breeze stirred her hair, and she tucked the loose strands behind her ear. She pulled some snacks out of her backpack.

His voice was soft as he said, "I never look at a piece of licorice without thinking about you. Still your favorite candy?"

"Still my favorite candy," Shay answered as her heart squeezed painfully.

She didn't want him remembering her favorite candy and being nice to her. Arrogant, selfish, materialistic Jonah she could handle. She could even manage bitter and sarcastic Jonah. Kind and thoughtful Jonah was too much like Old Jonah.

And Old Jonah, she reminded herself, was dangerous.

Dear Reader,

True forgiveness is one of the most difficult aspects of life for me to tackle. In fact, I would put forgiveness right up there under grief on my list of life's most extreme challenges.

Shay James has spent years grappling with a particularly cruel combination of both. And she's finally accepted that some of the things other people take for granted in life just aren't in the cards for her. She's...if not exactly happy...then at least content, and that's the most she can hope for under the circumstances.

Isn't this the perfect moment for her attorney ex—and the primary cause of her issues—to reappear in her life and turn her careful world upside down? Especially when Jonah Cedar is back in Rankins reluctantly and for reasons that might not be what they appear? Add the well-meaning "help" of family, a bit of legal trouble and the inimitable town of Rankins as the backdrop and, well, poor Shay...

At its heart, this story is about healing, self-discovery and love—love of family, friends and community—and the power of forgiveness.

I hope that, like me, by the end you'll have laughed and cried and be left cheering for Shay to allow Jonah to argue—and win, the case that could change everything for her—*A Case for Forgiveness*.

Please stop by and visit me on my new website, carolrossauthor.com.

Or we can connect on Facebook, facebook.com/carolrossauthor, or Twitter, @_CarolRoss.

All my best,

Carol

HEARTWARMING

A Case for Forgiveness

—

Carol Ross

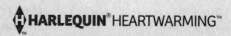

HARLEQUIN® HEARTWARMING™

Recycling programs
for this product may
not exist in your area.

ISBN-13: 978-0-373-36722-1

A Case for Forgiveness

Copyright © 2015 by Carol Ross

Printed in U.S.A.

www.Harlequin.com

Carol Ross lives in the Pacific Northwest with her husband and two dogs. She is a graduate of Washington State University. When not writing, or thinking about writing, she enjoys reading, running, hiking, skiing, traveling and making plans for the next adventure to subject her sometimes reluctant but always fun-loving family to.

Books by Carol Ross

Harlequin Heartwarming

Mountains Apart

Visit the Author Profile page
at Harlequin.com for more titles.

To Dan,
I absolutely could not do this without you.
And a special thank-you to my editor, Kathryn Lye

CHAPTER ONE

"THE SHEETS ON my bed have a *pattern* on them," the irritable little man spat out the word like one might *cockroach* at another hotel. "I *cannot* look at them. Do you understand me? My sheets need to be changed, and they need to be changed immediately."

Patterned sheets? Shay set her features to sympathetic and nodded slowly. This was definitely a complaint she'd never heard before. Hannah would be thrilled—and sorry that she'd missed it. Since she'd hired her younger sister on as assistant manager, Hannah had been keeping a list of odd guest requests. This one, Shay felt confident, would land near the top.

She softened her voice to match her expression. "All of our sheets have a pattern on them, Mr. Konrad. It's a signature feature here at the Faraway Inn." The sheets were excellent quality—super-soft, fine-spun flannel with images of tiny log cabins, bears, and moose on them, made exclusively for the inn. Shay loved them. Usually, the guests did, too.

Mr. Konrad raised his hand high and then pointed a stubby finger straight down, bringing it to rest on the marble counter between them. All he was missing was a white glove so he could check for dust. He then gestured in the general direction of her name tag. "Well, why don't you check your computer there, Little Miss Hotel Manager, and see where it says that *I* can't sleep on sheets that have a pattern on them. I have a medical condition."

"Oh my goodness, that is terrible." Shay managed to look both compassionate and remorseful as she rapidly tapped on the computer keys.

"Yes, it is—patterned sheets aggravate my vertigo. I need to sleep on only white or very, very light-colored sheets—with no pattern. My assistant called about this weeks ago and I don't understand why this concept is apparently so difficult for you people to grasp."

"I do apologize, Mr. Konrad. Somehow your request seems to have been overlooked. I will send someone up from housekeeping immediately to rectify this egregious oversight. We have some one-thousand thread-count pima cotton sheets in a light ivory shade that are as soft as butter. But they do have a small monogram along the top edge—you know where the sheet folds over? Will that be acceptable?"

"Yes, I suppose that will be fine."

"Again, Mr. Konrad, I am so, so sorry for the oversight and for any inconvenience this has caused you. Please enjoy some complimentary wine or Alaskan micro-brew here at our own Faraway Restaurant." She handed him some coupons and a business card. "If there is anything else we can do to make your stay here more comfortable please don't hesitate to let us know. My name is Shay James. I'm the owner, so you can ask for me personally if you'd like. I wrote our assistant manager's name there below mine, so if I'm not available she usually is."

Shay watched him thaw right before her eyes.

"Oh… Okay, I, uh, I will." He added a sniff and then marched away.

Shay picked up the phone and instructed housekeeping on the sheet change. She spent the next hour checking in more guests and answering the phone to take some pressure off her overworked staff. The inn was full and booked almost solid for the next two and a half months. It was only the first week of June, but they had more reservations for the summer—stretching well into fall—than they'd ever had.

After the rush subsided, she opted for a cup of coffee from the guest services station. She quickly checked that every carafe was full of their signature "Faraway Brew" and that it was steaming hot. The warm butter-and-chocolate scent drifting from the doily-covered tray reminded her that she hadn't eaten all day. She grabbed two cookies and then walked to her office, located right around the corner from the reception area.

Her cell phone rang as she swallowed the last bite. She picked up, "Hey, Em."

"Shay, hi—how are things going?" Emily was married to Shay's cousin Bering, and as president of the tourism bureau, she was responsible for enticing this attorney retreat to the Faraway Inn.

"Good, so far. We have one lawyer with an unfortunate sheet issue, but otherwise nothing too out of the ordinary or outrageous like I'd normally expect from such a large group of uptight type-A personalities."

Emily chuckled. "Sheet issue? I don't even think I want to know… But one of these days you're going to have to tell me why you hate attorneys so much."

"I don't *hate* them," she said. "They're just… so…self-important?" An unsettling image of

Jonah—her ex—popped into her head. "Uh-huh," Emily murmured in a doubt-filled tone. "Shay—"

"Emily, don't worry. I promise we will keep these people happy. What you've done for the inn—what you're doing for Rankins is nothing short of amazing and I don't want you to think I'm not grateful for all these events and conventions and tourists you've been bringing here—"

"Oh, Shay, I know that and I don't doubt your professionalism. I'm actually calling about a different lawyer—the one I know you *do* like."

"Caleb?"

"That's the one. I was just calling to make sure you remember that you're on the food loop tonight to deliver his dinner."

Caleb Cedar had been best friends with her Grandpa Gus before he'd passed away, and he was like a grandfather to her now. She made an exception for him where attorneys were concerned.

"Yep, I remember."

A FEW HOURS LATER, with homemade stew, corn bread, and a fresh-baked cobbler from the Cozy Caribou, Shay pulled up in front of Caleb's house. The large old colonial-style home stood on the edge of "downtown" Rankins right on the waterfront. Shay could see how some might deem the house a little out of place amongst the more practical and rustic buildings that dominated the town, but since it housed the only attorney in the valley the stately residence in gleaming white clapboard and brick somehow seemed right to Shay. Shay got out of her car and heard the faint sounds of a boat puttering along in the bay. She turned and recognized Crab Johnson's boat. She lifted a hand and waved in his direction and then used it to shield her eyes. It was a gorgeous early summer evening with the kind of sky so blue it made you want to take off your shoes and wade into the bay or squish your toes into a patch of lush new grass. This was Shay's favorite time of year— people recovering from winter's cabin fever, giddy with the onslaught of summer activities and the endless hours of daylight to enjoy them.

Bear, moose and all manner of wildlife were being spotted with their babies. The Faraway Inn's own resident moose, Clara, had even shown up last week with her first calf ever. At six years old, Shay had despaired of poor Clara ever being a mother—she'd begun to think that maybe she and Clara had that in common.

Shay scanned the horizon—how many lazy hours had she and Jonah spent fishing in that bay? Her heart squeezed in a way that it hadn't in a long time.

She gathered the Crock-Pot from the car and started up the sidewalk. Ridiculous, she scolded herself, to let this wave of nostalgia creep up on her now. She blamed Emily and her attorney-talk, although it was probably only natural to have thoughts of Jonah occasionally when she came here—to the house he'd grown up in. Once upon a very long time ago he may have been her fiancé, but he was still Caleb's grandson. Unfortunately for her, he would *always* be Caleb's grandson.

She knocked on the door and decided her odd feelings might be the direct result of hunger. After eating a total of two cookies all day, maybe her blood sugar was haywire or something.

Shay felt a smile forming as the door began to open. Caleb's dog, Francis, was barking madly now and she found herself looking forward to a relaxing evening with Caleb. The door swung wider, her smile melting from her face as her brain registered the sight before her…

Jonah?

She couldn't seem to make herself breathe much less speak. This reaction, she knew, was not blood-sugar related. She gripped the Crock-

Pot even as she pictured it slipping from her grasp and shattering all over the stone walkway.

"Hello, Shay." Jonah's voice came out smooth and easy, but his eyes were latched on to hers. Caleb hadn't said anything about Jonah coming home. Jonah never—well, rarely ever, came home.

She quickly calculated he'd been home a total of eight times in ten years—not that she was counting (not on purpose, anyway), and each visit had seemed briefer than the last, a day or two, or three at the most.

At first she and Jonah mostly avoided each other, then their tense encounters began to be filled with bitterness and sarcastic jibes, until they finally culminated in a conversation two years ago that had been unpleasant, to put it mildly.

Latent anger had emerged from both sides; she still seethed when she recalled how he'd accused her of taking the easy road, of being afraid to take a chance on life—on him, while she'd told him exactly what she thought of his lack of attention to his grandfather.

Nothing had been settled and Shay had been left feeling even angrier and more frustrated than before, as well as emotionally drained, and maybe a little embarrassed. And sad... There was always that underlying sadness— the grief that she was so terrible at dealing with, although she couldn't blame Jonah for that— not entirely.

But now here he was, standing in front of her looking perfectly composed and smelling freshly showered. Shay hadn't even bothered to glance in the mirror during her brief stop at home. She'd mixed the corn bread and fed the cats and then tried to give some attention to all six of them—her three and the three foster cats she'd recently taken in, while the corn bread baked. She was probably looking like a tired and rumpled mess. Was she imagining that whiff of "savvy-cat salmon grill" wafting from the sleeve of her shirt that she hadn't bothered to change?

Of course *he* undoubtedly knew that she'd been on her way over. It was so like him to take advantage of any edge, like the good cut-throat attorney he was.

"Here, let me take that for you." He reached out and removed the Crock-Pot from her white-knuckled grasp.

She was too stunned to offer any protest.

"Jonah?"

"How are you, Shay?"

How *was* she? The question sounded all laid-back and high-school-casual as if they'd parted on friendly terms last week instead of suffering an excruciating breakup ten years ago, and years of tension and animosity since.

Francis, Caleb's "maladoodle," as he liked to call the poodle-malamute mix would no longer be ignored—her tail thudding hard against the door frame as she forced her way to Shay's side. Shay reached out a hand, seeking solace in the familiar feel of her velvet-soft fur.

"What are you doing here?" she managed to ask.

Jonah's mouth curved up at the corners. "I live here, remember? Or I used to anyway. And I will be again, for a while. Come in, I hope you're planning to stay for dinner because Gramps is expecting you."

Will be again? What did that mean? Her brain refused to process what it so obviously meant.

"I told Gramps that I would take him out for dinner tonight, but he insisted on letting you bring your moose stew. He said he's been looking forward to this meal all week."

"Yeah, well, he really likes it…" Shay mumbled sheepishly and moved around Jonah. In the kitchen, a beaming Caleb waited with his arms outstretched. The look of delight on his face managed to nudge her out of her Jonah-shock.

"Howdy, sweet girl!"

"Hey, Caleb," she said as he wrapped his strong arms around her. Welcome comfort enveloped her; the sensation so like what she'd always enjoyed with her own grandpa, but different too, because she didn't have to share Caleb with her five siblings. She didn't even have to share him with his own neglectful grandson—not usually.

"How are you feeling?" Always her first question when she saw Caleb.

He pulled back, gripping Shay lightly by the shoulders as he grinned down at her. "Right as rain, now! Been saving room all day for your stew and I'm so hungry I briefly considered sharing Francis's dinner. I've got the table all set, so let's dig in, huh?"

"I, um, yes definitely," Shay said, trying to force out some enthusiasm. "There's more food in the car, so let me just—"

"I'll get it," Jonah said, and took off before either of them could say anything.

"Caleb, you didn't mention Jonah was coming for a visit."

"Well, I wasn't entirely sure about the whole thing. You know Jonah—he wasn't sure which

day he was going to be able to fly out and what-
not, so I didn't mention it. Didn't want to jinx
it—you know?" He rapped his knuckles lightly
on the cupboard door behind him and added a
wink.

She *did* know.

Every time one of Jonah's trips hadn't ma-
terialized, she watched Caleb deal with those
dashed hopes. Why couldn't Jonah understand
what his actions did to his grandfather—the
man who had loved and raised him from the
age of nine?

Caleb had given Jonah so much, and in return Jonah had taken off for the big city to
make money and buy expensive toys—and
never looked back. Well, that wasn't true—he'd
looked back exactly eight, short, pathetic times.

Jonah returned with the rest of the food and
they filed into the dining room. Caleb sat at
one end of the antique oak table, while she and
Jonah positioned themselves on either side of
him. Caleb asked a quick blessing, and then
dove into the corn bread, slicing and scooping
out portions onto their plates as if this were the
most normal thing in the world—the three of
them eating dinner together like some kind of
happy family.

Of course, it had been once…

Jonah too, appeared unbothered as he spooned thick stew into their bowls and passed them around.

Shay felt like screaming in frustration—she did not want to be here with Jonah. She knew there was absolutely no way of getting out of it now even as a parade of lame headache, stomachache, inn-emergency excuses danced silently across her tongue.

Caleb turned his animated blue eyes on her. "So, earlier I was filling Jonah in on how much you've improved the inn and how great the new restaurant is and how well it's been doing. He is as anxious as all get-out to rush up there and check it out."

Jonah looked at Shay, an amused half-smile telling her that maybe it was Caleb who was excited for him to check it out rather than the other way around.

"Apparently we are coming for the seafood buffet. Gramps said it's so popular that we have to make a reservation. Does that mean the entire town of Rankins is now having dinner at the Faraway Inn?" Jonah's voice held a touch of derision, grinding on her nerves like a set of worn-out brakes.

Caleb jumped in before Shay could comment, "Javier, that chef she hired? He makes some salmon dishes that melt in your mouth like candy."

Jonah bobbed his head and somehow managed to make the otherwise innocent gesture appear condescending. "I see. Hmm, that's... neat."

"The restaurant got a five-fork review from this fancy reporter from Anchorage. Shay offers a discount, too, for locals, and people around here think *that's* pretty neat—I can tell you that," Caleb added.

Shay wanted to kiss Caleb, at the same time she fantasized about giving Jonah a "neat" slap on the back of his head.

Instead, she shot Jonah a cool look of triumph. "I try to think first about the people around here. Like your grandfather. This community is important to me."

Jonah rolled his eyes.

She smiled at Caleb. "I'm sure the food at the inn isn't nearly as good as what Jonah gets in Chicago." It was probably too much to hope that she could discourage him from coming to eat at the inn.

"I doubt that," Jonah said. "I do miss the food here—home cooking and fresh seafood. I'm sure I'll have to double my workout when I get back to Chicago."

Shay couldn't stop herself from asking the question. "How long are you here for exactly?"

"Anxious to get rid of me already?" he teased. Caleb chuckled.

Yes, she wanted to shout. "Of course not," she returned carefully, like she was speaking to a three-year-old. He really didn't bring out the best in her sometimes. She tried again, "It's just that Caleb didn't mention that you were going to be here, so I guess I'm wondering what you're doing back in town. Are you here for Agnes's memorial?"

"Any luck finding homes for those cats of hers yet?" Caleb asked.

"Five of them, but I still have the three kittens. Agnes really wanted to keep the young ones together."

Caleb gave his head a sad shake. "I understand—Agnes was passionate about those animals of hers."

"She did so much for this community. I feel like it's the least I can do," Shay said.

Caleb directed his next words at Jonah. "Our sweet Francis was one of Agnes's rescue dogs."

"I remember you mentioning that, Gramps."

Shay raised her brows at Jonah, waiting for an answer to her original question.

"I was sorry to hear about Agnes. Story Fair won't be the same without her, huh?"

Shay gaped at Jonah in surprise and then felt a new wave of sadness wash over her. She and Agnes had started Story Fair together eight years ago. The once-a-year event offered free books for kids in a fun, carnival-type atmosphere. It was designed to foster passion for reading in Rankins' youth and had become one of the town's most-anticipated events. She hadn't known that Jonah was even aware of its existence.

She shook her head. "No, it won't." This year's Story Fair was rapidly approaching and Shay dreaded tackling the event without Agnes.

Jonah smiled sympathetically. "I'll attend the service of course since I'm here, but I've actually come home to get Gramps back on his feet."

Shay's eyes darted to Caleb. "Back on your feet? When were you off of your feet? You told me you were a *little* under the weather?"

"I may have fudged on that a wee bit."

"What do you mean?"

"It seems that… Well, you know my days are numbered here and Jonah has graciously taken some time away from his job to help me get my affairs in order. And I'm not talking about my *affair* with Mary Beth Patterson—that one I can handle just fine on my own." He chuckled mischievously at his own joke and then added, "I'm kidding about that—Mary Beth is a sweet and honorable woman and she'd take after me with a piece of her prized cast iron if she ever heard that I said that—so don't repeat it."

"Caleb, this isn't funny," Shay said, her stomach twisting with concern. "Your days are numbered? What do you mean? Are you sick? Why didn't you tell me?"

Jonah spoke up, "Shay, he doesn't mean that literally. He's going to be fine. He's going to see Doc tomorrow." Ted "Doc" Branson was Caleb's best friend and Rankins' longest established doctor.

Caleb swiped at the air. "Oh, Shay, honey, I'm sorry. It wasn't my intention to upset you. I'm sure I'll be good as new before long. There's just a little something getting me down—I'm not sure what. But right now, I'm so blasted happy that my grandson is home and that I'm sharing a meal at my very own table with my two favorite young people in the whole world. I thought I would die before I'd ever see this day again. So, no more of this downer talk—let's eat."

CHAPTER TWO

SHAY LOOKED DOWN at her bowl and then back up at her two dinner companions. Only minutes ago she'd been starving, now she felt… what? She ticked off descriptions in her head—shocked, irritated, baffled, worried…? All of the above, she decided, but especially the last one. The first three were due entirely to Jonah, and those she could get over. But Caleb? Anxiety welled within her. Did he have some secret illness that he'd been keeping from her?

It didn't seem possible that something serious could be afflicting him. He was healthy and active and sharp as a knife. He still worked in his law office most days. And when he wasn't, he was usually fishing, looking after his yard or playing cards with his buddies. He was the youngest seventy-four-year-old she'd ever known, but then again she couldn't imagine that Jonah would be here unless it was serious… Jonah could barely stand to be away from his prestigious Chicago law firm—or his cars, or his boat, or his golf clubs, or his country club—as it was.

She needed some answers, but she didn't want to possibly run out of patience with Jonah and ruin Caleb's evening.

She faked her way through dinner, picking up her spoon and giving her stew an occasional stir. When his mouth wasn't full, Caleb sported the same satisfied grin throughout the entire ordeal. He chattered about the latest news sweeping Rankins: Gary Watte had purchased a brand-new ATV with those airless, bulletproof, virtually indestructible tires; Stan Planke was building a new cabin; and the red salmon run was predicted to be a dandy.

Jonah had seconds. Caleb had thirds.

The Cedar men lingered, while Shay tried not to fidget.

When they finally finished, she couldn't get up from the table and into the kitchen fast enough. Jonah attempted to help her tidy up. It took him ten minutes to find a container and transfer the leftover stew for storage in the fridge, while she loaded the dishwasher. He eventually located the plastic wrap, managed to rip off a piece about four feet long, and then proceeded to mummify the remaining corn bread. She didn't see how it could possibly escape him that she knew her way around his grandfather's kitchen better than he did.

She dished out the cobbler, and then retrieved the ice cream from the large chest freezer in the garage. She pulled the scoop from the utensil drawer, but when she tried to dig into it, she could only scrape thin layers from the frozen surface.

Jonah gestured, silently asking if she'd like him to give it a go. She shrugged her agreement and then tried not to stare as he pushed up his sleeve and began scooping the ice cream like it was a tub of mashed potatoes and not a frozen brick of ice.

He grinned proudly and made a show of placing a perfect scoop next to each dessert.

She rolled her eyes. Jonah chuckled.

"Put the ice cream in the freezer out in the garage when you're through."

She took Caleb's dessert to him in the living room where he was now lounging in his worn-leather recliner. She took a seat on the sofa and tried to surreptitiously study him. He didn't look sick. He and Jonah had been talking and laughing like everything was fine. Caleb seemed cheerier even than his usual cheerful self, making her both sad and happy because

Jonah was so obviously the cause: the prodigal grandson returned, she thought bitterly.

But what if Caleb was trying to downplay his condition for her and Jonah's sake? She hoped Jonah really was taking this seriously…

Shay stuck it out through a half-hour of news. Her mind constantly jumping between wanting to stay because of Caleb and wanting to leave because of Jonah. Jonah left the room, so she got up and hugged Caleb, and confirmed plans to see him at the Senior Circle's bingo night in a couple of days. Yes, she told him, she and her cousin Janie would be calling numbers. Then she gathered her Crock-Pot and her bag and attempted a smooth, Jonah-less exit.

She'd almost made it to the foyer when Jonah emerged from wherever he'd gone, but not stayed quite long enough. She was sure she imagined the flash of disappointment as his eyes traveled over her form so obviously ready for departure.

"Shay, can I, uh…talk to you for a minute?"

"Um, I guess so, sure," she agreed, reluctantly.

Jonah glanced toward the living room. Shay followed his gaze to where Caleb appeared to be chatting happily into the phone. The sight made her want to cry. What would she do without Caleb in her life? He was her rock, her mentor, her pseudo-grandpa… Stop, she told herself, Caleb was going to be all right. He would see Doc and they would fix this. Doc was not only an excellent doctor, he was also Caleb's best friend and vigilant about his health.

Meanwhile, she was emotional over Agnes's death and exhausted—she reminded herself she needed to hire more help at the inn. But it seemed like she'd spent so much of the last year worrying—about Hannah, her mom, Janie and the twins, Agnes and now Caleb.

"I'll walk you out."

"Okay," she said and handed over the Crock-Pot.

They strode in silence to her SUV. Jonah opened the back door and stowed the pot. He clicked the door in place and then stared out at the water, presumably gathering his thoughts.

Shay waited with her arms crossed over her chest and didn't care in the least if she looked impatient.

Finally he faced her. "Look, Shay, I know you aren't exactly happy that I'm here…"

"Really, Jonah? Caleb is obviously ecstatic— and *that* makes me happy."

"Shay, come on—I can tell when you're

upset. I realize it's been a while, but some things don't change. I just, I…"

"I?" she repeated sharply. "As always, Jonah, you're making this all about you. I can't believe you're standing here and telling me that you think *I'm* upset because *you're* here?"

"You're not?" His arrogant smirk made her want to say something really mean—something reminiscent of their fight two years ago.

She pushed three fingers of each hand into her eyebrows, took a breath, and then released everything at once. "Jonah, I don't care what you do. Am I *thrilled* to see you? No—of course not. But my *obvious* angst is due exclusively to the fact that I'm worried about Caleb. So you can go ahead and get over yourself right now. I don't know what your plan is but—"

"Trust me, Shay, I don't want to be here anymore than you want me to be. Gramps asked me to come home—I didn't offer. He asked."

"He asked you…"

Slowly, simultaneously, they turned and looked toward the house. It didn't need to be spoken that if Caleb had asked Jonah to rush home then something was wrong—terribly wrong.

A surge of fear left her entire body tingling. Their eyes met again.

"Jonah, what is going on?"

"I'm not sure. That's why I wanted to talk to you. He hasn't mentioned anything to you about being sick or anything?"

She shook her head.

"You haven't noticed anything that might give you some clue?"

Shay thought about the times she'd seen him in the last couple weeks. "No, he had what we thought was a flu bug. It's been going around—you know a sneeze and cough kind of thing? He stayed out of the office for several days, so I signed him up for the food loop at the church. But this was supposed to be his last night for that because he was feeling so much better."

Shay gestured toward the house. "I thought he was better. I mean, he looks great, right?"

"He called me last week and asked if I could come home. I said sure, started looking at my calendar, firing off weekends that I could possibly make work but then he said... He told me that what he meant was...could I come home—like for a while?"

"I know he misses you, Jonah, maybe he just wanted you to visit or..."

Jonah started shaking his head, and she realized how silly that sounded.

"He also said there was something he wanted to talk to me about."

Jonah's composed features were at odds with the rigid tension emanating from his body. Jonah could be difficult to read, undoubtedly a valuable trait as a lawyer, but something that had always been frustrating for her. But she could see now that he was worried. She had known him very well once, and even though years had passed, maybe Jonah was right that some things didn't change—not enough anyway.

"What?" Shay stared at him, waiting. "What is it?" she repeated, impatience seeping into her tone. "What did he want to talk to you about?"

"That's just it, Shay. He hasn't said anything yet."

Her mind began whirring with possibilities. "What are we...you—I mean. What are *you* going to do?"

"Come on, Shay," he said. "*We.* In this, at least, we can be a *we*, right? Gramps is closer to you than anyone else—except maybe Doc. And that's what I wanted to speak to you about. I know I'm not your favorite person in the world, but I guess I'm asking for your help in...figuring this thing out."

As much as she wished otherwise, she felt

his words working on her as easily as he'd manipulated that ice cream. In spite of her disapproval of his lack of attention toward Caleb, she knew he loved his grandfather. Caleb was the only family Jonah had in the world. In direct opposition to Shay who had both parents, five siblings and a close extended family.

"Of course," she said without hesitating. "Jonah, yes, anything I can do. What time is his appointment?"

"Doc said he has a full day tomorrow, so we're going in early before he opens."

"Okay, if something is wrong with him, Doc is the obvious place to start. Call me after you see him, okay?"

"Absolutely. As soon as I know anything I'll call."

JONAH KICKED UP his speed as he approached the road leading to the Faraway Inn. Instead of calling, he'd decided to go for a run and tell Shay the news about Gramps in person. Running eased his anxiety like nothing else, even though the exercise didn't seem to be helping much now.

Doc and Gramps had holed up in his office for nearly an hour this morning while Jonah sat in the waiting room and tried not to let his anxiety-ridden imagination get the better of him. Then Gramps had come out and announced that Doc was sending him to see a heart specialist in Anchorage—in three weeks. Amazing how a few weeks could suddenly feel like an eternity.

Upon returning home from Doc's, Gramps said he needed a nap and then promptly disappeared into his room. This caused further angst for Jonah because Gramps didn't nap, other than dozing off occasionally in his recliner during a ball game—if that counted—and even then it had to be a pretty dull game.

Now, each stride seemed to heighten Jonah's anxiety as it took him closer to his ex-fiancé—to the woman he had once believed would be his wife and the mother of his children.

Shay…

Seeing her the night before had absolutely tied him in knots. It was difficult to believe that he and Shay had ever believed they could share a life together. She wanted this… Jonah looked around at the rugged countryside that surrounded the remote town of Rankins. Mountains with jagged, snow-covered peaks dotted the skyline, while thick green forest stretched for-seemingly-ever. The view on his other side was of a raw, picturesque, island-dotted coastline with the town of Rankins perched on the shore of a small bay.

Sure, it was postcard pretty, but it was just… nothing. For as far as a person could see, even with binoculars from the ridge on the outskirts above town—the ridge where the Faraway Inn sat. Shay's Faraway Inn. The inn that had ultimately meant more to her than he had.

Jonah had wanted—wanted still—a high-powered law career, skyscrapers, noise, a penthouse apartment, impractical cars that didn't have four-wheel drive and snow tires. And yes, he wanted to be successful, make money, and enjoy these finer things in life—the things he knew his late father had wanted for him, too.

Somehow Shay always made him feel like his aspirations were some kind of mortal sin.

The sight and sound of a vehicle going by and then making a u-turn didn't really register until a horn honked behind him. He looked over his shoulder.

"Jonah?" Shay's cousin Bering shouted from the window of the mud-spattered black pickup idling toward him.

Jonah jogged back toward him. "Hey, Bering! How've you been?"

Bering pulled over, then hopped out and stuck out a hand. "Fantastic, actually." He added a befuddled kind of head-shake as if he couldn't quite believe it himself.

Jonah gripped his friend's hand. "Yeah, hey, congratulations—in person—on your marriage. Looking forward to meeting your wife, Emily, right? Sorry I couldn't make it for the ceremony. Gramps told me all about it."

"I bet he did. And forget about it. I didn't expect you to come all the way home for it, buddy. But thanks for the uh…the gift. I'm sure Emily sent you a thank-you and all that."

Jonah grinned. "You're welcome for the… gift, Bering. I'm glad you're enjoying…it."

"Oh, boy, yeah—we are using the heck out that…thing." Bering looked guilty as he added, "Sorry, Jonah—I don't even know what…"

Jonah laughed. "I don't remember what I got for you either, Bering. My assistant took care of it for me."

They both chuckled, and Jonah realized how good it felt to share a joke with a friend. He didn't have friends like this back in Chicago. Coworkers, colleagues that he admired, but no true got-your-back kinds of friends like Bering.

"Man, it's good to lay eyes on you though," Bering said. "Glad to see city life isn't making you soft. How long are you in town for?"

"Not sure yet. A few weeks at least."

"That's great. We'll have to get together. By the way, have you heard yet that I'm going to be a dad?"

Jonah felt something wrench hard in his chest. He was happy for his friend of course; it was just being here so close to Shay where he was inundated with these thoughts of their almost-life together that had him feeling a bit envious, he told himself.

"Congratulations, Bering! That's amazing."

Neither he nor Bering were much for social media, so over the years they'd mostly kept in touch via the occasional email or phone call— usually on Bering's part. Suddenly, Jonah felt a little guilty about that.

Bering dipped his head in the direction of his pickup. "Hop in, I'll buy you breakfast at the Caribou. I'm meeting Tag and Cricket and some of the guys."

"That sounds good, but, um…I'm not quite finished with my run." Not to mention that Shay's older brother, Tag, would be less than thrilled to discover he was back in town.

"Ah, I get it. You headed up to see Shay?"

"I am, but not for the reason you're probably thinking."

"I wasn't thinking anything." Bering shrugged, but he appeared to be fighting a grin.

Jonah stared at his feet for a few seconds. Maybe it would do him some good to talk to Bering. And he definitely wouldn't mind seeing some of the guys. He looked back up. "You know what? Breakfast sounds great."

"So, if Mr. Takagi calls—or shows up—tell him that yes, he can absolutely check in early. His suite is ready and he could be arriving at any time because he's flying in on his own plane. And you will personally help Mr. Takagi put the koi in the tank and get him anything he needs, okay? We will also be feeding the fish and monitoring the water temperature et cetera, per Mr. Takagi's instructions. You've read them, right?"

"Yes, but Shay, they are goldfish. How difficult can this be?"

"Hannah, they are not mere goldfish."

Hannah tipped her head and gave Shay a doubtful look.

"For your information—these fish are worth thousands of dollars. There is one that could sell for over ten-thousand alone. It has a rare lipstick pattern."

Hannah snickered. "Lipstick pattern, huh? I don't even want to think about how that came to be."

"Hannah, this is serious."

"I know." Hannah nodded, her face now a solemn mask. "I do know, so in my ongoing quest to constantly improve my customer service skills, I am going to assure Mr. Takagi that I will win him as many goldfish as he wants at the next carnival to come through Glacier City. You can get six Ping-Pong balls for a five-spot, and as you're well aware, my accuracy at the fish frenzy is renowned. And, as a special bonus—for Mr. Takagi only—I can arrange for these fish to all have Hannah James's personalized Ping-Pong pattern."

Shay sighed, dipped her head and pinched the bridge of her nose. Then she looked back at her sister and met gold-brown eyes that were a close match to her own, except Hannah's were now filled with laughter.

"In spite of your lame attempts at fish humor here, you are going to follow all of these instructions, right?"

"Of course," Hannah said. "But remind me again why *we're* going to have the giant gold-fish trough out back."

"We have to keep these fish alive until Mrs. Milner gets her pond and atrium finished. There was a delay in the construction, but Mr. Takagi could only transport the fish now—and he insists on transporting all the rare koi himself. If she didn't get them now then she would have to wait months for another opportunity, which would add the complication of the winter weather. Mrs. Milner asked if we could keep them here because she doesn't want them at her house with all the noise and mess of the construction going on."

Hannah stared back at her and Shay could tell she was trying not to crack a smile.

"Go ahead and say it," Shay said.

"Okay, I'm thinking about how Bud and Cindy—our goldfish? The ones I won at the school carnival in fourth grade? We had them for nine years in a glass bowl in the middle of the coffee table. Mom and Dad raised six kids in that house. Mittens drank out of the bowl daily and I wasn't exactly religious about changing the water." She chuckled. "Remember that time Seth knocked the bowl over and Bud and Cindy were flopping around on the floor? Mittens swatted Bud around a couple times like he was a cat toy and I was sure he was a goner. But I scooped them both up and dropped them in Tag's glass of water." She laughed for a few long seconds.

Shay stared back at her blandly, brows arched—prompting her to get to the point.

"I'm thinking the goldfish will be fine, Shay."

"Hannah, listen to me, if you are going to operate your own place someday—like you tell me you might like to do—then you have to go above and beyond for your guests." Owning her own hotel had been Hannah's latest idea in a long list that she'd been compiling during the months of her recovery.

Shay reminded herself to have patience. Hannah was still trying to deal with having her life's work—her identity—snatched away from her. It had been just over a year since the accident—and the end of her professional skiing career. Her body had healed for the most part, but Shay knew it would be a while before the rest of her completely caught up.

"It's part of—"

Hannah interrupted. "Shay, I'm kidding. I'm ready for the fish. What is *wrong* with you, today? You always—well, almost always, think I'm funny."

Shay stared at her sister, anxiety fluttering in her stomach. Maybe it would help to talk about it. "Don't say anything to anyone else, okay? I'm waiting for Jonah to call. Caleb—"

"Jonah!" Her voice shot up in tone and volume. "Jonah is here? He's in town? In Rankins?"

"Yes, to all three of the exact same creatively crafted questions," Shay answered drily.

Hannah flashed a knowing smile with an exaggerated nod. "I get it."

"Get what?"

"Why you're all testy and irritable."

"Hannah, no, I'm not. Jonah doesn't have anything—"

Hannah held up a finger. "Hold on just a sec." She grabbed her phone and tapped out a text. Then she looked back at Shay. "Continue."

"I'm worried about Caleb. He had an appointment with Doc this morning."

"Doc? Well, of course you're worried about Caleb, too, then. But that's not what's going on right now. Because when you're worried you look like this—" Hannah made a ridiculous tight-lipped face that Shay was almost certain she had never made in her life.

"And you get quiet—not snippy. I know. It's Jonah."

Shay narrowed her eyes at her little sister.

Hannah met her look and added a one-shoulder shrug daring Shay to dispute her claim.

"Really?" Shay said. "You *know*, huh? Can you tell what I'm thinking now?"

Hannah winced. "I can actually, and I don't

think it's very nice to mind-talk to me like that. I would never mind-say something like that to you."

Hannah reached down and picked up her phone, which had let out a buzz. She looked at the display and grinned. Her fingers flew over the screen again.

"You know I hate it when you text and talk to me. And what are you smiling about?" Shay realized then that her voice did have an edge to it—best to work on that, she told herself, before she inadvertently unleashed on a guest.

"Oh, I'm just excited that I was able to scoop Piper. What do you think is wrong with Caleb? I thought he was getting over that bug. Did he have a relapse or something?"

Shay looked at her quizzically. "Piper?" Piper Davidson was a friend of Hannah's and the younger sister of Shay's friend, Laurel. Laurel owned the *Rankins Press*, the town's newspaper. Piper wrote the "Happenings" column in addition to being the biggest gossip in town.

Hannah seemed pleased with herself. "I texted Piper asking if she knew that Jonah was back in town, and she texted back saying that she hadn't heard that yet. So, yay—scoop."

"And this is news, why?"

"Come on, Shay. Jonah coming home is kind

of a big deal. Small-town boy goes off to the big city, has tons of success and makes piles of money. He's good-looking, he's a bachelor, he owns a '69 Boss 429. I can guarantee you that everyone will be talking about this."

"You know what kind of car he drives?" Shay heard Hannah's phone buzz again, no doubt Piper with a follow-up question. She hoped it didn't involve her. After all, it'd been ten years since she and Jonah had broken up, Sometimes though it felt as if it was only yesterday. She and Jonah had been friends throughout their childhood, and it had seemed inevitable when they'd started dating during their senior year of high school. They'd gone away together to the University of Alaska and earned their undergraduate degrees. Jonah proposed soon after he'd found out that he'd been accepted to Yale Law. They'd come home to Rankins to enjoy one more carefree summer with plans to elope in the fall before they moved to Connecticut. Life was as perfect for Shay as it had ever been—before or since.

But then, as that summer was drawing to a close, her world began to unravel.

Shay's Grandpa Gus died and left her the inn. Shay had spent much of her childhood working at the inn with her grandfather and while it was her dream to have her own hotel one day she hadn't expected it to be the Faraway Inn.

Shay had been touched and honored and hadn't felt like she had any choice but to stay in Rankins and take over the business. Grandpa Gus had taught her so much, showered so much love and attention on her. She owed it to her grandfather—to her family, to continue the inn's success.

Jonah and Shay had been left with two different dreams—two different lives—that couldn't possibly merge. Hannah asked, "Do you have any idea what's wrong with Caleb?"

"No, I...no idea..."

"I really hope he's all right, Shay. You know I love him, too."

"I do know that, Hannah." The entire James family adored Caleb.

"So, how did it go when you saw Jonah? Was there weirdness? Or was it like old times?"

"Okay, Hannah, you're my sister and I love you, but can we not talk about this? About Jonah? I'm anxious for Jonah to call, but it's *only* because I'm waiting for some news about Caleb—"

Hannah interrupted, "I can help you there." Hannah held up her phone so Shay could see the display. "Jonah is at the Cozy Caribou having breakfast right now with Bering and some of the guys. So, I'm guessing that Caleb must be fine or else Jonah wouldn't be…"

Every vein in Shay's body seemed to throb at once. Jonah had said that he would call her after Caleb met with Doc, but he was hanging out at the Cozy Caribou instead? Having breakfast? No doubt chowing down on a pile of biscuits and gravy. How was she supposed to help him if he didn't keep her informed? Why had she been so foolish as to think that he had changed even one bit in this selfish regard?

Shay stood up. "I have to go. Can you handle things while I'm gone?"

Hannah nodded. "Sure. Go kick some lawyer butt. But before you go—that Adele person called again."

"Adele?"

"Yep." Hannah looked down at the paper in front of her. "She called last night, too—twice. I told you."

Shay shook her head, vaguely recalling the conversation. She'd been so distracted after the evening at Caleb's she didn't remember the details. "Did you get any details?"

"I tried, but she said she only wanted to talk to you. She said it was very important."

"I don't know anyone named Adele. Did she say what it was about?"

"Nope, but I think she's from Utah. I recognize the area code."

Hannah would recognize the area code for Utah—she'd spent a lot of time there in her ski-training days. Probably something to do with a reservation. Shay was continually surprised by how often guests thought only the manager could handle their special requests.

"Can you put her name and number on my desk? I'll call her back later. I don't have time right now."

"Will do, but when you get back we need to talk about the staffing issues in the restaurant."

"Have you had a chance to look over the applicants for the server positions?"

Hannah grimaced. "I have, but there's not a lot to choose from there. Kyla Randle applied, but we know she was fired from the Cozy Caribou for stealing from the till. Randy Baxter applied, but Shay, he hasn't showered in three years. There are a few other applicants with literally no experience and/or dicey references—Crystal Scower is a known meth dealer from Glacier City and this other guy who just got out of jail because of some brutal animal cruelty charges."

"Nope. No way on that last one. I'd rather hire the drug user—but seriously, her name is Crystal and she deals meth?"

"Yes, and I agree—you know what Agnes used to say—if a person isn't kind to animals then there can't be much for kindness in there at all."

"That's the truth. We're having open interviews on Friday, so maybe someone will show up then."

Hannah looked doubtful and Shay felt the same. This was a problem. She was also short at least one more maid and a front desk person. But the restaurant was the most pressing problem. She and Hannah were picking up the slack, but it was becoming increasingly difficult with the tourist season officially upon them.

Shay had not only expanded and remodeled the dining room; she'd hired a professionally trained chef, Javier, who had overhauled the menu. Shay had been skeptical when Javier had introduced a few of the dishes—like honey-glazed salmon and halibut with mango chutney. She would have lost a lot of money betting that the men in this town would never eat "fish with jam," as her friend Cricket Blackburn had taken to calling the dish.

The Faraway Restaurant was now quite a

bit more upscale than Rankins' other two eateries—the Cozy Caribou and the Top Rock Café. This didn't include the Donut Den, but her sugar-addicted cousin-in-law Emily was the only person she knew who considered a donut a proper dinner.

Shay hadn't realized there were quite so many people in Rankins hankering for a fine dining experience. Well, fine dining Rankins-style consisted mainly of changing out of your work clothes before grabbing a bite, but still the restaurant was filling a niche she hadn't expected.

"Don't worry—we will figure this out. I need to go, so let's recap quickly—what are you going to do with the fish if Mr. Takagi shows up?"

Hannah looked skyward and slowly tapped a pink-polished fingertip to her pursed lips before pointing it at Shay. "Lightly bread and panfry?"

"Hannah—"

"Shay, chill—seriously, you need to lighten up. I've got this. You can leave the expensive lipstick-kissed koi in my capable hands."

Shay wasn't so sure about that, but she picked up her bag and headed out of her office. She had more important matters to attend to, because family trumped everything in her life—

even the inn. And she considered Caleb family,
so if Jonah thought she hadn't been thrilled
with him last night…well, then he hadn't seen
anything yet.

CHAPTER THREE

THE SUN SHONE bright amongst a smattering of high, fluffy clouds and from the Faraway Inn's ridge-top location Shay could see the entire town of Rankins below. The Cozy Caribou's distinctive red roof stood out like a beacon in the heart of its quaint downtown. Normally, on a day like this, she'd soak in the sight, be grateful for the sheer beauty of this place she was lucky enough to call home—but not this morning. Because now, instead of the lovely view and the drive down the hill calming her anger, the time only managed to rile her further.

Breakfast? With his buddies? Shay felt her blood pressure spike anew. Jonah had said he would call her as soon as he learned anything, but he had opted for breakfast instead? Unbelievable...

Shay marched into the Caribou, her eyes sweeping the place until they latched on to the table where Jonah sat, sure enough, shooting the breeze with a bunch of his old *compadres*—

Bering, Cricket Blackburn, Gary Watte, Steve
Howard and—Tag? That was a surprise. Could
her big brother finally have let go of his animosity toward Jonah? It seemed unlikely. Like
her, he'd probably been blindsided. Unlike her,
he was too polite to make a scene.

As she headed toward the table, she heard a
few greetings and comments in her periphery.
She offered only quick replies.

Jonah jumped up from the table as she approached. "Shay, I was going to—"

The table went silent as she interrupted
smoothly, "Can I talk to you for a minute?"

"I—"

"In private."

All eyes were on her, every mouth shut. Tag
asked a question with his eyes and Shay conveyed with a look that yes, she was fine.

Jonah nodded.

She pivoted and headed toward the back of
the restaurant and into the area that served as a
bar in the afternoons and evenings. The section
was closed now and darker than usual in the
normally bright space, but she could feel that
Jonah was close behind her. Maddening how
she still felt so much where he was concerned.

When she was sure they were out of earshot
she turned and faced him. "Well?"

"Shay, calm down. I—"

"Calm down? Why wouldn't I be calm, Jonah? Oh, right, because you're here eating breakfast with your old posse while I'm up at the inn, concerned and waiting for you to call me with news about your grandfather?"

He opened his mouth but she began firing off more words before he could respond. "Look at me." She pointed at her face. "See these bags under my eyes? That's because I barely slept last night. The inn is crazy busy, I'm short-staffed, and I have a guest bringing in valuable live koi that we have promised to take care of— but none of that really matters to me right now, Jonah, because *I* am worried about Caleb. You remember him? Your grandfather? The man who, outside of my own father and possibly my brothers, is the single most important man to me in the entire world."

"Did you say koi?" Amusement danced across his face and that spiked a fresh surge of annoyance.

"Yes," she snapped. He didn't deserve an explanation.

"Okay... Shay, listen—I was going to call you, but I left my phone—"

She tipped her head down and tapped on her forehead, trying to rein in her temper. "Just tell me what Doc said. That's all I really want to know anyway."

"He didn't say anything definitive. He is sending Gramps to a specialist. His appointment is in three weeks."

Her eyes shifted upward, connecting with his. "A specialist? What kind of specialist?"

"A cardiologist in Anchorage."

"A cardiologist? What…? He doesn't have a heart condition, or any family history of heart disease." She didn't care that she was informing him of this like he didn't already know his own grandfather.

"He had some abnormal test results and Doc wants Gramps to follow up with a doctor in Anchorage."

"What tests? And you didn't think this was important enough to share with me? After you specifically asked me yesterday to help you out with this? We were going to be a 'we' where your gramps is concerned. Isn't that what you said?"

Jonah stared into her eyes, and even in the dim light she could see the intensity shooting from their depths—pleading with her to listen. And there was some anger there, too, which she didn't think she deserved, although she supposed she could dial it down a bit. She'd clearly gotten her message across.

She remained silent, waiting for his explanation.

"Yes, that is what I said. And that *is* what I want. Shay, I am sorry. I was on my way to see you... When we got home Gramps went into his room to take a nap. So I decided to jog up to the inn and talk to you in person."

"A nap?" Shay repeated. "Caleb doesn't nap."

He pointed at his shoes.

Her eyes drifted down, taking in Jonah's faded Yale blue t-shirt, gray shorts—and running shoes.

"I was doing that very thing when Bering pulled up behind me, stopped his pickup, and asked if I'd like to join him and some of the guys for breakfast. I agreed, thinking that I'd give you a call on the way over, but Bering didn't have his phone with him. I'd left my cell phone behind—I don't like to take it when I run—back in Chicago it's the only time I have any peace. But, I was going to call you—" he paused and lifted one hand that held a phone, pointing at it with the other "—with Cricket's phone."

Shay stayed silent and admitted to herself that this all seemed plausible. The men in this town liked to gather together any chance they had—in packs—like playful dogs.

"I am sorry, okay? This town… It makes me crazy… How did you even know I was here anyway? I've only been in the place for maybe fifteen minutes—I haven't even got my breakfast yet."

Shay felt her temper deflating slowly like a sad helium balloon. "Okay. I know what it can be like here, with the gossip sometimes, and—"

"No, I should have called you—immediately. I forgot what this town can be like."

Small-town life was something that had always bothered Jonah. Shay didn't like the gossip either, hated when it turned cruel or nasty, but she loved this town, loved the support. The strong sense of community in Rankins was constant—something she felt all the time. She thrived on that—giving it as well as getting it. And knowing she could count on that support comforted her like a warm blanket.

"Do you forgive me?"

She exhaled a tired breath. "Yes, of course. And I'm sorry, too. I just want to figure out what's going on with your gramps. This is really scaring me."

His hand came up toward her shoulder and

Shay anticipated his touch. But he lowered his arm instead, tucking the hand into his pocket.

"So, you're admitting that you lost your temper?"

"Don't push it, Jonah."

He was grinning at her and Shay wished he would stop. A grinning Jonah had gotten her into deep trouble once upon a time. She immediately banished the memories.

If she were honest with herself, she knew she was going to be facing this situation with Caleb on her own now, at least until he consulted with the heart specialist.

Her brain began buzzing with possibilities, some of which she voiced aloud. "So, when are you returning to Chicago? Will you fly back and meet us in Anchorage for the appointment? I'll have Tag fly us—or Cricket if need be. Do you think I should stay with Caleb at the house until then?"

"No, actually, um…I'm not leaving."

"What?"

"Remember I told you last night that Gramps had something he wanted to talk to me about?"

"Yes."

"Apparently there are some issues with his practice, too."

That knocked her back for a moment. "With his practice? What kind of issues?"

"He has quite a backlog of work and he's asked me if I could take a look at some cases while I'm here. Help him sort through them and catch up. So I figure I'll be here at least another month."

Shay frowned. They both knew that Caleb was meticulous where his practice was concerned. "A backlog? I don't know anything about this either. I could have found someone to help him. I've told him for years he needs to hire a paralegal. And I love Betty, but she's not a paralegal. Don't get me wrong—she's a great typist who knows her way around a legal document, but a paralegal could give him a hand with some of the more technical stuff."

Jonah took a step closer and lowered his voice. Shay knew he would never want anyone to hear them talking about Gramps not being on top of his game.

"I had a quick look last night. It's kind of odd because some things are absolutely perfect—classic Caleb Cedar legal perfection. But then, there are others that are just a mess."

Shay tried to wrap her brain around what he was telling her. Caleb mentioned cutting back once in a while, spending more time fishing and less time "fiddling with the law," as he liked to refer to his practice, but she knew he'd never really retire. He loved the law as much as Jonah did.

He'd been so proud when Jonah had chosen to follow in his footsteps, and he'd been downright giddy when Jonah had been accepted to Yale, his alma mater. Ironic that it was one of Caleb's proudest moments that had marked the beginning of the end of her and Jonah's relationship.

Still, one of the biggest differences in her mind between Caleb and Jonah was that Caleb loved other things, too, besides the law—and not just things that could be bought. Caleb loved life.

"So…maybe he is feeling worse than he's been letting on. What should we do?"

Jonah raised a hand and squeezed the back of his neck.

His movement combined with her own ill-timed inhale resulted in a blast from the Jonah-scented past. He smelled like citrus and sweat and cedar trees. Bittersweet memories stabbed her in the chest—the pain located right in the middle of her heart. She squeezed her eyes shut and Jonah mistook the action.

"Hey, I'm worried, too. But I don't think

there's much we can do until we know more—other than keep an eye on him, right?"

She opened her eyes. "And I think it's important for us to stay positive, because although he says he's fine—this still has to be scary—even for someone as strong as your gramps. My mom went through some of this last year—heart attack and then bypass surgery. It was terrifying."

Jonah nodded. "Thank you, Shay. I can't tell you how much this means to me. Your help and everything you do for him... I—"

Shay wondered...did he just not hear the *me's* and *I's*?

"—know this isn't about me. You love Gramps as much as I do. And he loves you—probably more than he does me. Hell, you certainly deserve his love more than I do."

Well, she thought as her eyes traveled up to meet his again, that statement was a nice surprise, and strengthened her hope that he shared her level of concern.

Jonah's lips turned up into a grin, one side higher than the other. Her stomach tightened and then stirred with anxiety, because he was reminding her too much of the boy she fell in love with—too much of the man she used to love. Too much...Old Jonah.

"That's not true, Jonah. It's that I'm the one who's here." She broke eye contact and tried to focus on the giant moose rack hanging on the wall behind him. "We'll figure this out. I'm not going anywhere—you know that."

His eyes somehow lured hers back in again. But now they were hard and flat and she was a little startled by the change in his expression.

"Yeah, that much I do know, Shay. I learned that a long time ago—the hard way."

His tone was bland, but she felt the words like a sharp bite. She took a step back—his bitterness toward her a welcome reminder that she was bitter, too.

Goodbye fond memories and heavenly man-scent and good riddance. He blamed her and she blamed him. That was it, in a nutshell, and she certainly was in no mood to rehash old relationship issues that would never—could never—be solved.

She sighed. "Whatever, Jonah—let's just stay focused on your gramps, okay? Your breakfast is probably getting cold, so I'll let you get to it. I have to be back at the inn anyway. You're bringing Gramps to bingo, right?"

"Oh, yeah, I can't think of anything I'd rather do with my time than play bingo. Gramps said the entire town is atwitter with talk of the record-breaking jackpot." His mocking pretty well summed up his feelings about Rankins. "And, gosh, there are *hundreds* of dollars in prizes." He worked in one of his eye-snaps. "Does he not know how long it takes me to make hundreds of dollars back in Chicago? A matter of minutes. Bingo isn't exactly my thing, Shay."

Shay's jaw fell open. "Jonah, sometimes people just do things because they're fun, without giving a thought to much else. People enjoy spending time together for the sake of nothing more than that. You've been in town for about twenty minutes and you can't at least go along and pretend to enjoy something— for your gramps's sake? Did you know your gramps never even keeps his winnings? He always donates them back to whatever cause is being played for."

"I…" He let out a frustrated groan. "That really did sound bad, didn't it?"

"Yes, it did."

"I'm just… I'm out of my league here, Shay."

Out of his league?

"You grew up in this league, Jonah, remember? And you used to kind of like it. At the very least—you liked some of the people. And you know what? Many of those people still think

highly of you and some of them consider you
a friend, although why that is I don't know because I'm almost positive you don't deserve
it. But right now there's a whole table of them
waiting to have breakfast with you, so before
you head back there, you might want to rethink
that condescending attitude. People will catch
on, Jonah. And they won't like it."

She turned to leave.

"Shay, wait." Now he did touch her, reaching out and grabbing her elbow, but she had no
problem shrugging him off this time.

He pushed his fingers through his wavy
black hair, making it look messy and frustrated,
like she felt.

"Look, you're right. I'm sorry. It's not that
I think I'm better, it's just being here again—
like this…it makes me feel off-balance." He
inhaled a deep breath and then exhaled a sigh.
"Of course I'll go. Gramps is excited about it."

Shay watched him, waiting. It was a pretty
good apology, *but*… "And…?" she drawled.

He grinned—a sheepish, boyish grin and she
had to resist its sneaky attempt to sweeten her
mood.

"And, I will have a good attitude. I will do
my best to have fun at bingo with Gramps."

She gave him a short, single nod of satisfaction. "Good. I'll see you there."

"THAT WAS A terrible cast." Doc clucked his tongue, his lips twitching in amusement.

Caleb yanked on his fishing pole. "Don't you think I know that? That's why I'm reeling back in."

Doc chuckled. "Okay, don't get all riled up now. But you are a little off your game—you have to admit that. This is the third time you've casted and that last one only went about four feet. You sure you're all right?"

"Yes," Caleb snapped, "for the third time. I feel fine."

"I'm not talking about your health. Is something else bothering you?"

"Something besides this piece-of-junk reel my best friend gave me for my birthday, you mean? No."

"That's operator error where that expensive, state-of-the-art reel is concerned and you know it."

Caleb snorted.

Doc executed a perfect cast. "You're positive? Nothing is bothering you?"

"That's what I said."

"That's your official statement? You're ready to sign it?"

Caleb moved to face him. "Doc, you been nipping at the schnapps already this morning? It's not even close to noon yet, and that would be early even for you. If you've got something on your mind I wish you would spit it out. I feel like I'm sparring with a cagey client here—and I'm not working today, remember?"

"That reminds me—how did you get out of the house? Where did you tell Jonah you were going?"

"I told him I needed a nap, asked him to turn off the phone and not bother me before noon. Then I climbed out the window."

Doc belted out a laugh as he slowly worked the lure toward the boat. "You climbed out the window?"

"Yep." Caleb's lips curled up with the threat of a smile.

"Till noon, huh? That's not a nap, that's a whole night's sleep."

"You know I'm not a napper, Doc. Why don't you tell me how long they usually last?" Caleb bit his line in two and stowed the flasher along with the lure he'd been using in the tackle box.

Doc shrugged. "Mine are usually an hour

or two at the most. But let's get back on track here."

"I didn't know we were off of it."

"So, you're not feeling the slightest bit guilty?"

Caleb didn't answer and Doc finally, blessedly, remained silent as he shifted things around in his tackle box.

All that could be heard was the soft lapping of the water against the side of the boat. An eagle sailed overhead and they both looked skyward to watch it. Caleb didn't know a soul who could stop themselves from pausing to watch a bald eagle fly by. Then he tied a favorite lure to the end of his line.

Eventually he answered, his tone taking a serious turn. "It doesn't matter. I'm committed. There's no turning back now."

"Well, I don't like it, Caleb. I'm feeling guilty. It's dishonest, and I'm not a dishonest person."

"What have *you* done to feel guilty about?"

"Besides lying to Jonah about what we're up to today?" Doc fiddled with his own reel for a few seconds and then, instead of casting again, he laid the pole across his thighs. He leaned his head back and stared up at the clouds.

Caleb followed his gaze and marveled at the

luscious blue of the sky. Alaska in the summertime, he thought, as he let the sheer beauty of it soak into him—there was nothing like it in the entire world. He used to take weeks off every summer so he and Jonah could enjoy as much of it as possible.

Jonah used to love summers here—fishing, hiking, biking, exploring…surely, being in Rankins now would make him realize how much. And hopefully before this thing was through his grandson would realize some other things, as well.

"Shay," Doc muttered. "That's the thing. That's what I feel bad about. I understand what you're trying to accomplish as far as Jonah is concerned, but I feel guilty about deceiving Shay. I didn't think that through when I agreed to this. At the risk of waxing poetic— that woman is a shining example of all that is right with this town. She doesn't deserve to be dragged into this. And I don't like being a part of causing her any more pain."

"Yep, she is a shining example. And, yes," Caleb confessed, "I'll admit that has been poking at me a bit, too. But I'm not doing it on purpose, Doc. That girl is like my own granddaughter. I promised Gus if anything ever happened to him that I would watch out for her." Emotion clogged Caleb's chest.

It took a minute before he could speak, and when he did he let pride fill his voice. "Gus would be so proud of her, Doc. With what she's done with the inn—it looks like something from a darn magazine now."

Gus had loved all of his grandchildren, but Shay had been a little extra special to him. Her love for the inn was one reason certainly, but Caleb always thought it was her personality that so closely mimicked Gus's that had truly stolen his heart—kind, thoughtful, generous to a fault, but feisty, stubborn and strong-willed at the same time. It had stolen Caleb's heart— and Jonah's, too, once upon a time.

Doc smiled wholeheartedly. "Every time I go there I think that same thing. I imagine that ole Gus is smiling down on her every single day. But that's what I'm saying, Caleb. The devotion Shay has for her family...well, she showers it on you, too. And you're sure lucky to have it. But now, well you know she's got to be worried plum out of her mind."

"Come on, Doc, you think you can make me feel any worse than I already do? I know all of that—everything that you said. I do. But I can't very well admit all the facts to Jonah, can I? He would never forgive me. He would hightail it back to Chicago faster than this lure can spin." Caleb held his fishing pole aloft and gestured at the shimmering metal on the end of his line. "And then where would I be?"

Doc nodded his head, puzzling over the situation. "I guess that's true enough. I only wish there was some way you could do all this and let Shay know."

Caleb let out a sigh. "Yeah, I wish that, too. But I just have to believe—I *do* believe, Doc, that what I'm doing is for her. In fact, if I'm being perfectly honest, it's almost as much for Shay as it is for Jonah. And the truth is I'm not going to live forever. That is a fact, and even as painful as it may be, it's one my grandson needs to accept—and I'd prefer it to happen sooner rather than later. You know what I mean?"

He cast again and this time his aim was spot on.

CHAPTER FOUR

"B-2," Shay called out.

"Bwahh-eeek," the ancient microphone squealed back at her. Probably still upset, Jonah surmised, after being left behind by Elvis on his last tour.

Jonah caught Shay's gaze and winced with exaggeration. She narrowed her eyes at him and then shouted the sequence again sans microphone.

He chuckled and stamped the appropriate space on his card.

You have got to be kidding me, he thought. No one back in Chicago could conceive of this if they saw him now. His firm billed seven-hundred dollars an hour for his time, and here he was sipping blue-raspberry punch and playing blue-light bingo at the VFW Hall, which also housed other activities for the Rankins Seniors' Circle. According to Shay, people did this so they could "have fun" and "spend time together."

He'd promised himself, and Shay, that he would be on his best behavior, but she couldn't stop him from thinking about his life in Chicago. Couldn't stop him from thinking about his car—his beloved '69 Boss 429—garaged and waiting for him... In spite of wishing otherwise, it was going to be a while before he was driving his favorite car again. He stamped another place on his card and continued his cynical meandering—why on earth would he want to solve complicated legal cases and, *stamp*, drive a near-perfect car when he could play bingo?

"I-20," Shay called out. *Stamp...stamp*. He reached across the table with his dauber and marked Gramps's card. Shay had informed him earlier when she was helping him get set up that his ink-stamper-thing was called a dauber. He'd opened his mouth to make a sarcastic retort and then shut it firmly when he'd caught her warning look.

Although—he glanced up toward the front of the room again—watching Shay do her thing did make the experience a bit more palatable. He had a difficult time not watching her—a problem he'd been plagued with since about the sixth grade.

He grinned at her again and held up his card,

pointing with exaggerated excitement at his almost-bingo. She glared.

Jonah reached across the table and stamped Gramps's card as he was too busy flirting with Mary Beth to pay attention to much else. He noticed the B-4 spot still blank on Mary Beth's card—that sequence had been called a while ago. And so had N-32… Apparently Gramps's moves were working, he thought with amusement, continuing to eye Mary Beth's incomplete card.

He couldn't stand it. *Stamp, stamp* and… *stamp*. There, all caught up.

"What did she say?" Bernice Threck whispershouted the words across Jonah toward Erma Neville.

"N-42," Erma yelled back. "Bernice, why didn't you wear your hearing aids?"

"Because I'm trying to get Teddy to notice me and how attractive do you think I would be with those things hanging out of my ears?" Bernice looked to Jonah for confirmation. "Right, Jonah?"

Jonah presumed that by "Teddy" Bernice was referring to Doc, who was seated on the other side of her and at least appeared to be keeping up with his card.

Jonah realized that both women were waiting for his response. He opened his mouth to say he knew not what; thankfully he was interrupted by Erma.

"A sight more attractive than those fishing lures you've got hanging from your ears right now," Erma muttered.

Jonah took a drink of his blue-raspberry punch, relieved not to be drawn into the exchange after all.

"What?" Bernice shouted.

"I love to fish," Doc chimed in loudly. No hearing devices from that quarter either, Jonah hypothesized.

Erma hollered again, "A lot more attractive than having to shout, I'd say."

Bernice shook her head with disgust. Her long, dangly earrings made such a loud tinkling sound that Jonah had no idea how she could hear anything but that, hearing aids or no.

She yelled into Jonah's ear again, "Well, that's ridiculous, Erma. There's not a lot that isn't more attractive than having gout."

"B-6," Shay called loud and clear. Jonah looked up and caught her watching him. Her lips were tugging upwards in that way they did when she was fighting a laugh. So, she thought his predicament was funny, huh? He responded with a look of desperation. She turned and coughed into her hand and Jonah thought it a fairly believable attempt at covering a laugh.

He chuckled. Okay, so yes, he had to admit that he was kind of having fun. He glanced over to where Gramps was now officially canoodling with Mary Beth and decided that sight alone would make a little suffering worthwhile.

"B-6," Shay repeated, but not quite as forcefully. Jonah wanted to believe it had something to do with his nonverbal teasing.

"Beef stick?" Bernice yelled. "Are they selling beef, too? I love those things—especially the caribou ones. Don't you, Teddy?" She batted her fake lashes like a 1940s film star. "Erma, will you run and get one for me and Teddy to share?"

"Beef stick," Erma muttered with a huff. Then she shouted at Bernice, "She said B-6 not beef stick, Bernice. And no, I will not."

Then she glanced at Jonah. "That's it—I'm outta here. This is embarrassing and I'm not talking to her anymore, unless she goes and gets her hearing aids. She's out of control. And you can tell her I said so."

Someone yelled "bingo" from a table behind them as Erma testily gathered up her cards and moved to a neighboring table. Bernice didn't notice, her entire body tuned in to Teddy at this point.

Jonah thought this whole spectacle was a little out of control. It was bad enough that Shay had guilted him into being here, but she could have warned him that it doubled as some kind of geriatric singles event.

"I-17," Shay began calling a new game. Someone must have fixed the vintage mic because the sound was much better—and even louder.

The crowded room seemed to hum with a current of excitement. Apparently, there was nothing like a rousing game of "blue light bingo" to raise community spirits. Jonah had no idea what the "blue light" signified, but he was now playing four cards because Bernice had pretty much ditched hers too, to listen to Doc recite a list of fun facts about gout that was way more information, in Jonah's opinion, than anyone not currently suffering from the disease needed to know.

"Excuse me, sir, but you're clearly in violation of the house rules."

Jonah looked up to see Shay's sister, Hannah, toss a stack of cards on the table.

"What?"

She settled next to Jonah. "I believe there's

a three-card limit. And the way you're stamping away over here—I may have to report you to the bingo police."

Jonah smiled. "That might be a blessing at this point." Jonah inked up his dauber then held his ink-stained hands aloft.

Hannah laughed and began stamping her card in an attempt to catch up with the current game.

"What in the world are you doing here?" Jonah asked.

"Uh, playing bingo," Hannah drawled, pointing out the obvious. "Is the smell of all that ink getting to you there, counselor?"

"No. I mean *why*?"

Hannah raised her brows in a way that spoke clearly of her disapproval—and reminded him of Shay.

"Because it's a great cause and because I can—I'd never played bingo in my entire life until a few months ago. Can you imagine that? I've been missing out and besides, did you not hear that the blue-diamond pot tonight is one-hundred and twelve dollars?"

"Why is everything blue?" Jonah asked waving one hand across the tablescape and holding up his cup of blue raspberry punch with the other. The plastic table cloths were blue, the centerpieces on the table held little vases of blue carnations and baby's breath, and strings of blue lights were twinkling here and there around the room. Even the ink was blue.

Hannah looked puzzled. "I have absolutely no idea. Maybe it's Mrs. Wizencroft's favorite color. She can be a real dragon lady, runs the Seniors' Circle like it's the Marine Corps."

Jonah laughed. "It's great to see you, Hannah. Gramps told me you were back home. How are you holding up, not being able to ski?"

Hannah reacted with a look like he'd poked her in the ribs with a stick.

"I'm sorry—was that not okay to ask?" *Stamp, stamp.*

She grinned. "No, actually, it is. It's just that no one ever asks me that—except Shay. They ask me how I'm doing or how I am, but no one ever asks me about skiing. I think people are afraid that I'm going to break down and start bawling all over them or something." She tipped her head, looking thoughtful for a second. Then she added, "Which I might. And it feels…how much time have you got?"

Jonah pulled his brows up and made a tsk-ing sound. "No time, actually, I'm super…" He stamped Bernice's card. "Duper." He reached over to stamp Doc's card, who had apparently exhausted the subject of gout, but was now whispering loudly in Erma's ear about lupus. "Busy," he added as he then reached over and stamped her card.

Hannah made a big show of protesting. "Well, skipping over the accident and the ensuing realization that my career—my life— was over?" She nodded as if giving herself permission to continue. "Okay, so, skipping over all that and in addition to trying to forgive the drunk driver who almost killed me, I'm learning to enjoy life in a different, more content-based way—as my expensive sports psychologist terms it. Not that I wouldn't ski competitively again if I could—without risking messing up my body forever, because I would. But the cool thing is that I'm learning and trying to accept, that skiing doesn't define me as a person."

"That's...awesome, Hannah." And it was. Jonah could only imagine what that kind of recovery entailed. Hannah had been skiing since she was four years old. Even Jonah had to admit that when he thought of Hannah—he couldn't picture much else but her on a pair of skis.

"Yep, it is."

"How are you doing that?"

She belted out a laugh before commenting,

"Slowly, painfully, and with extreme difficulty. Kind of a 'two steps forward, one step back' kind of thing. Shay has been amazing, of course, giving me a job and a place to live and tons of unconditional sister support."

Her tone was light, but Jonah could hear the pain still lurking in her voice. He wasn't sure what to say. He stamped his card, and his adopted cards, and struggled to come up with something profound.

Hannah was smiling at him, warmly. "Shay's right about you, isn't she?"

He let out a chuckle. "Probably, but in what way are we referring to specifically?"

"About your lawyering, specifically—how important it is to you. You can't even begin to consider what your life would be like if you couldn't be an attorney, can you?"

This was true, he thought, and Shay had certainly accused him of putting too much importance on it in the past. But the part he'd never understood was how his focus on his career was so different than how Shay felt about the inn. He'd asked her about it when they'd had that fight a couple years back, but she'd only looked at him like he was the biggest fool on the planet.

He looked up at Shay now. She was such a

force in this town. If it was possible to person-ify a place, Shay did so with the Faraway Inn. She *was* the Faraway Inn, and how ironic he thought, that the word also described the nature of their relationship; Jonah and Shay—so far away—too far away from each other in every sense that really mattered.

"I'm sure your sister couldn't imagine her life without the Faraway Inn either." Jonah could hear the defensive tinge in his tone.

Hannah's chuckle had him thinking that she could hear it, too. "That's where you two have some common ground then, isn't that right, counselor?"

"Common ground?"

"Shay thinks she wouldn't be who she is without the inn and you probably think you'd just shrivel and die without the 'attorney at law' tacked on to the end of your name. Common ground."

Shay was staring at him again. He met her eyes and felt a shot of awareness course through him because she was smiling at him—that dazzling dimpled smile that used to leave him dumbstruck. He smiled in return, and had to correct his previous thought, because they weren't so far away in all the ways that mattered—just the ones that would allow them to ever be together again.

Hannah had started talking once more. "…but if there's one thing I *have* learned from my experience it's that true happiness is not about what you do for a living, there's a lot else besides work, right? That's what Dr. Vossel keeps telling me anyway. And I'm trying my hardest to believe it."

Jonah stared blankly at Hannah, taken aback by her statement, not sure if he agreed, but certainly not wanting to disagree in light of everything she'd been through.

Jonah looked around in bafflement as some in the crowd began making a "quack, quack" noise. Then Shay called out something that sounded like "clickety-click."

Hannah grinned, then reached over and stamped the O-66 space on his card.

"O-66," she explained and then yelled, "Bingo!"

SHAY ANNOUNCED A short break and then dabbed the sweat from her brow with a tissue.

Janie handed her a glass of cold punch. "Looks like Caleb and Mary Beth are getting pretty cozy."

"I noticed that. It's sweet, huh? They've been spending quite a bit of time together lately."

"Bernice is gunning hard for Doc."

"I could hear that, too—all the way up here."

They shared a chuckle.

"Jonah only takes his eyes off of you long enough to stamp an entire table's worth of bingo cards, which surprisingly doesn't take him long at all. It's like he's a veteran."

Shay grinned. "You can't tell but his eyes are pleading with me to come and save him."

"Save him?"

"Yeah, I kind of, um, encouraged him to come tonight."

"Ah," Janie said with a quick grin. "I see. Well, he should be here. It's not going to kill him to spend a night out with his grandfather."

They both watched Jonah extricate himself from the table where he'd been sitting for the last hour. Shay had to give him credit for sticking around this long.

"I think he's heading over here. Are you going to—save him, I mean?"

Shay turned to fiddle with the bingo cage so Jonah couldn't read her lips. "Not. A. Chance."

Janie snickered.

"As a matter of fact—I think we both deserve to go home early tonight. Or even better, Janie, how about a drink at the Cozy Caribou? Text our good buddies, Laurel and Emily, and see if we can meet up."

"But I'm supposed to call the numbers next."

"Oh, Janie, my dear, sweet cousin-slash-friend—watch and learn."

"Good evening, ladies," Jonah said as he approached them.

"Hey, Jonah," Janie said.

"Hi, having fun?" Shay asked.

"Yes," he said sarcastically. "I can only think of about eight-thousand things I'd rather be doing."

Shay frowned.

"Hey," he continued with a laugh. "I'm here, aren't I? And I have been stamping away over there like a madman in case you haven't noticed. I'm probably going to end up with carpal tunnel."

He'd obviously intended to goad her.

"I can't believe I'm saying this, but I am kind of having a good time."

His smile seemed entirely genuine, and Shay felt her insides begin to melt along with her resolve.

"And Gramps is loving it."

She considered aborting her plan.

"I also find it highly amusing that this is what you choose to do with your free time."

That comment shifted her right back into action.

"You think it's funny that we donate our free time to the Seniors' Circle, where the money earned here tonight goes to the hospital's home hospice outreach? For hospice care like your nana had before she passed away."

"Shay, I was joking. I'm—"

"Why can't you believe it?" Janie interrupted.

Shay answered for him, "Because he's a rich and important attorney in Chicago and a community game of charity bingo in his Podunk hometown is far beneath him. He's been spending the entire evening thinking about how much money he's losing by being here and wondering how lonely his car is at home without him."

Jonah's jaw tightened, but Shay noticed he didn't deny it. "Well, I think the important thing is that I'm here."

Shay applauded. "Praise for Jonah for spending time with his grandfather."

"And you know Shay, you don't have to be so—"

"Honest? I know, it's a fault."

Janie's eyes widened, and then she tried to hide a smile. "I'm just going to go use the ladies' room before my, uh, shift." She pointed and walked away.

"I thought we were going to try and get along," Jonah said, crossing his arms over his chest. "For Gramps's sake?"

"Yeah, well, you started in with your snarky comments."

"Why are you so touchy tonight?"

"Look, I'm sorry, Jonah. I—"

"You know, disliking something doesn't mean you think you're superior to it—it means you don't like it. I don't like Japanese food either, but I don't think I'm superior to the country of Japan."

Okay, he had a point there—sort of, but that was irrelevant. She needed to change her tune if she was going to get the rest of the night off and, more to the point, take the big-city attorney down a peg or two.

"Yeah, Jonah, you're probably right. I'm just stressed, I think. Worried about your gramps, worried about Hannah, I've got staffing issues at the inn, and I'm…tired."

She saw the flicker of surprise in his eyes at her attitude change. Then his shoulders sunk slightly, his face softened as his hands slid into the back pockets of his jeans. She knew sympathy when she saw it.

Reel him in, she told herself—nice and easy.

She reached over and slowly started spinning the basket that contained the little colored balls. They began tumbling over one another. There had been a call a few years ago for an electronic bingo machine, but Shay was glad the Seniors' Circle had opposed the upgrade. To her, bingo just wouldn't be the same without the metal basket full of wooden balls making that distinctive clacking noise. The sound also served to alert the troops that the time had come to pipe down, which they were beginning to do already.

Shay leaned over and casually announced the pattern for the coming round. She slowed the rotation of the basket until a ball released and rolled down the chute. Then she reached over and plucked the ball from the little cup where it landed. She picked it up…and made a sound of despair as it slipped through her fingers, landing on the floor and bouncing out of sight. Half of the crowd let out a collective groan, most of the other half looked around in bewilderment, while a smattering of flirtatious yell-talking continued.

Jonah bent to look for the ball while Shay took a step back. After a few seconds Jonah reached down and then promptly stood, proudly holding the ball aloft like a hard-won carnival prize.

"Oh, Jonah, thank you," she said with relief. "Can you go ahead and read it?" She blinked and squinted and pointed at her eye, motioning that she had something in it.

Jonah obliged. "N-35," he cooed into the microphone. "N-35."

"Shoot," Shay said when he glanced over at her again. She bent to her knees. "Now I dropped my contact. Would you mind calling the next number, too?"

"Uh…sure." He nodded and then reached over and began spinning the basket. "Like this?" He slowed the rotation until the next ball clicked into position.

"That's great," she gushed. "You're a natural."

"N-31," he called smoothly. "N-31."

Shay crawled farther away as Jonah went ahead with the next sequence and then the next. Finally, she rose and scurried over to where Janie waited by the door with their coats and bags.

"Masterful," Janie said with a giggle as she handed over Shay's belongings.

"Thank you." She executed a quick bow. She looked at Jonah and watched his face transform

from bewilderment to understanding as he realized what she was doing. He narrowed his eyes
menacingly as Shay gave him two thumbs up.
She added a wave over her shoulder as she and
Janie strolled out the door.

CHAPTER FIVE

JONAH LOOKED AROUND Gramps's office with the same degree of bafflement he had ever since he'd arrived. He'd spent the last few days hanging out with Gramps and trying to get a sense of his overall health. He would seem fine one minute and then the next he'd appear tired or weak. His appetite was good; they'd gone out for dinner a couple nights ago where he'd seemed as young and energetic as ever, just as he had at bingo.

Doc had been over to play cards twice and their gin rummy sessions were as heated and jovial as ever. Gramps had been working in the yard yet taking a lot of naps, and two of the days he'd slept for hours.

He'd confessed to Jonah that he didn't feel up to spending any time in the office, so Jonah had begun sorting through the files on Gramps's desk, which was a mess—also very unlike him. He'd always advised Jonah that the trouble it took to keep things neat now saved precious time searching for important details later. Appearances suggested to Jonah that Gramps hadn't been following his own advice. That concerned him, too—as did one of the case files Jonah had found near the bottom of a pile.

"Gramps?" he called into the other room.

The office of Caleb Cedar, attorney at law, was located inside Gramps's house with an outside entrance for clients. This had been an ideal set-up when Jonah was growing up because he'd been able to hang out there while Gramps was working, yet still enjoy the comforts of home.

Jonah had been nine years old when the small plane carrying his parents to Anchorage for a wedding had crashed. Jonah was supposed to have been with them, but he'd begged to be allowed to stay home with Gramps. His parents had acquiesced and then, less than three hours later, they were dead. Jonah had never recovered from the opposing emotions he'd felt as a child—felt still, even though his rational brain begged him to be rational about these feelings.

He felt both guilty about not being with his parents and relieved that he hadn't been at the same time. The conflicting emotions were a heavy burden for a child to bear. And then later, after he'd read his father's journals, his expectations had piled on their weight as well. His father had desperately wanted Jonah to "get out of Rankins," to achieve a level of success and security that he'd wanted for himself, but had been unable to attain. Jonah had been striving to do that his entire adult life.

Jonah was aware of how lucky he was that they'd been living with Gramps at the time of his parents' death, and now that he worked as an attorney himself, he fully understood the sacrifices Gramps had made by taking on the parental role. But Gramps had never made Jonah feel like he was sacrificing anything. On the contrary, he'd always made him feel like he was the most important part of his life.

And Jonah had loved his time with Gramps— still loved it, and Shay was right, back in those days he had loved Rankins, too. Of course, he had also loved Shay.

"What is it, my boy?" Gramps stuck his head inside the office door. Francis came in and flopped over onto Jonah's feet. Jonah gave her a quick belly scratch while she gazed up at him with love-struck eyes.

"We seem to be missing some paperwork for the real estate dispute between Will Traeger and the town of Rankins."

Gramps stepped in the room, rubbed his chin

and turned a slow circle. "Let's see, um…" After spinning a couple times, he stopped and placed his hands on his hips. He bobbed his head in the general direction of the desk. "You rifled through that pile there already, did ya?"

"I did."

"Huh." Gramps's face contorted with confusion.

And, Jonah also realized, he still loved everything about this office—the books crammed tightly into the floor-to-ceiling shelves, the stacks of files, the sound of Gramps's keyboard clacking—even the smell of the paper he consumed by the truckload. He especially loved to listen to Gramps talk about the law. To this day, Jonah considered his grandfather's legal brain the sharpest he'd ever encountered. He was so proud of the admiration and respect his gramps had earned in Rankins, and the thought of his reputation suffering now was nearly unbearable.

"Could you have given it to Betty so she could type up some documents? And it looks like it may need a title report."

Gramps snapped his fingers. "Betty, yes—that's a possibility. Why didn't I think of that?"

Jonah stared at his grandfather, emotion flooding through him. He loved this man with all of his heart, and the thought of something being wrong with his health now, when Jonah had been away so much these last years, made him sick—literally made his stomach ache. He really hadn't intended to be absent so much, but his job in Chicago was demanding and time-consuming. He didn't like coming back here, that was true, but Shay was right when she said that he didn't have a viable excuse for not making more time for his grandfather. A surge of guilt welled in him; he shouldn't have to wonder if Gramps knew how much he meant to him.

Jonah reached over and picked up the phone. He took a second to unwind the twisted cord; he couldn't remember the last time he'd used a phone with a cord.

"What's Betty's number?"

"Just hit the button there on that speed dial doohickey. Her number is right below yours."

Jonah couldn't help but notice that Shay's number was a spot above his own on the doohickey, just under Doc's.

She'd ambushed him at bingo the other night. Clever, if a bit harsh, but maybe he'd deserved it after the way he'd insulted her. He hadn't meant to insult her. And he supposed she had a point about his attorney attitude—his confidence, for lack of a better word, might not have quite the same effect in Rankins as it did in Chicago. In Chicago his attitude earned him respect. He could see how in Rankins that same self-assurance might result in some disdain—certainly where Shay was concerned anyway.

"Betty, hi, it's Jonah Cedar. Caleb's grandson… Yes, I am, thank you. How are you?… Oh, that's great."

Jonah chatted with Betty for a few minutes, about her husband, Crab, and their kids and grandkids, her quilting, Crab's garden…until finally he got around to the reason for the call. He was relieved to hear that she did indeed have the paperwork.

Ten minutes later he hung up the phone and turned toward Gramps. He smiled inwardly as he thought of how valuable that chunk of time would have been to him back in Chicago where his schedule was constantly overbooked and clients were billed to the minute. Rankins time was an altogether different animal.

"She's got it?" Gramps asked.

"Yep, she's got it. She said she'll drop everything by in a couple days. She said you told her you didn't need it until next week, but she'll get right on it."

Gramps gently punched a fist into his open

palm. "That's great news. Did she say what Crab has been up to?"

Jonah nodded absently as he consulted the list he'd made of the most pressing matters pertaining to Gramps's workload. "She did. Apparently, he's over that bad cold he had, his garden is going to be their best ever, and he's been seeing some reds around the mouth of the Opal."

Like Gramps—and a lot of people in this town—Crab loved to fish. And when the fishing was good it often took priority over just about anything else, including any emergency that wasn't literally life-threatening.

"Reds?" Gramps belted out the word.

Jonah looked up and there was no mistaking the yearning stamped across Gramps's face. Now he felt even worse. He shouldn't have mentioned fishing when Gramps clearly wasn't up for going out.

"Yep, that's what Betty said."

Gramps moved toward the window.

"You okay, Gramps?"

"Sure, yeah…reds already, huh? This is just the first of them, not the main run, but still, they're in a little earlier than Doc and I predicted."

"Happens sometimes," Jonah muttered. Jonah

hadn't been fishing in way too long. He and Shay used to fish together all the time. *That* he definitely missed—the fishing, not Shay. Okay, maybe Shay a little, too, but the way things used to be; kicked back in the boat, sneaking kisses when the fish weren't biting—and when they were, or sometimes not fishing at all but just holding the girl he loved in his arms while they made plans for the future.

Fishing held only good memories—with Shay, with Gramps, with Bering, even with Tag— before things went south in their friendship. There was nothing like fishing and there was nothing better than a good fish story either— maybe one would help cheer Gramps up.

"Gramps, remember that one year the silvers were running up the Tilachuk River and we went—"

Jonah turned to see the tail end of Gramps heading out the door. "Gramps? Where are you going?"

"Oh, um, you know what, son? I'm going to go lay down. I, uh…I could use a nap. Course if you need me here, I can stay." Gramps busted out a loud yawn, patting a hand over his open mouth.

Jonah felt that already familiar simmer of worry begin to boil again.

"No, I'm fine here, Gramps. That's a good idea—you go and get some rest. I've got plenty to keep me busy for the next few hours."

"Thank you. Sometimes this, uh, thing gets a hold of me and I just need a little rest."

"Of course, yes, Gramps—you go."

"Do you mind if Francis stays here with you? I don't want to lock her up in my room with me."

Francis peered up at Jonah like she knew she was being discussed. He scratched her neck and she stretched to make it easier for him to reach the sweet spot behind her ear.

"Yeah, no problem. I was thinking about taking a walk along the waterfront later and I planned to bring her along anyway. Now she'll get me out the door for sure."

Francis wagged an enthusiastic tail.

Gramps smiled in gratitude. "You know what, Jonah? I like the thought of us doing something together—like old times."

"I'd like that, too, Gramps."

"I'll talk to Doc and see if he thinks it would be okay if we went out fishing. What do you say to that?"

Jonah nodded. He didn't see what that would hurt—a leisurely troll in the bay—especially if Doc went with them.

"Sounds fun," he said and realized how much he meant it.

Gramps's face lit with a bright smile.

Jonah smiled back, thinking how great it was to see that twinkle in his eye.

"Gramps—one more thing—you've got an appointment with Gary and Ingrid Watte today. Do you want me to wake you up for that or call and reschedule?"

"Shoot. I, uh, I forgot about that one. Um, let me think a sec."

"What's going on with Gary and Ingrid?"

"Divorce."

"Divorce?" Jonah couldn't believe it—the Wattes had been married for an entire decade. He knew precisely because he remembered their wedding day—often. The event had taken place toward the end of summer, a couple weeks before Shay's grandfather had passed away, before she'd inherited the inn, and before things had so epically fallen apart.

But then, on that night with the air filled with the scent of forget-me-nots, Jonah had held her in his arms as they'd danced at the reception and he'd known without a single doubt and in the depths of his soul, that he would love her for the rest of his life. Shay's lips had tasted like the licorice candy he'd bought for her earlier that day after he'd stopped and ordered her engagement gift.

The gift that he'd designed knowing she would love it—the gift that their talented artist friend Kella had painstakingly crafted, but that he'd never had a chance to give to Shay. The gift that had inadvertently become his accessory instead of hers.

"The Wattes. Hmm, it's a crying shame."

"It is," Jonah said, unconsciously placing a hand over his pocket where he usually carried that accessory. His naiveté had indeed been shameful. "Sometimes love turns…impossible, huh, Gramps?"

"Sometimes," Gramps agreed with a single short nod. "But lots of times it's the people that are in it that are kind of impossible, don't ya think?"

He and Gramps had never discussed the breakup. He'd always assumed that Gramps had understood that he and Shay had had to go their separate ways, but what was he saying here? That the split had been *his* fault? Jonah definitely did not want to have a conversation about his and Shay's failed relationship now.

"You're probably right…to a degree."

"Mm-hmm," Gramps agreed without really agreeing at all.

"Do you want me to talk to them?"

Gramps beamed. "Would you do that?"

"Sure, if they don't want me to handle this initial consultation, I'll just reschedule."

"That's a dandy of an idea. Thanks, son. I sure do appreciate all you're doing for me here. I hope this thing—whatever it is—doesn't keep me down for long."

Jonah watched as his grandfather shuffled through the doorway. His black hair was now speckled with gray but still thick and wavy, his body still trim and wiry, but suddenly he seemed all of his seventy-four years, and Jonah fought the fear that tried to claw its way in. Shay was right—they had to stay positive.

He forced himself to concentrate on the now neatly stacked paperwork in front of him. He'd forgotten how challenging small-town law could be—there were such a variety of issues to tackle, unlike back at his firm in Chicago where his cases sometimes felt like "same song, second verse."

He picked up a billing statement and looked it over; reminding himself that while legal work here might be more diverse, it was definitely not as lucrative.

The "mail truck" caught Jonah's eye as the ramshackle jeep pulled to the curb. He watched

Ralph Simpke hop out and hustle up the sidewalk. Jonah rose to intercept him. He didn't want him ringing the bell and setting Francis off while Gramps was trying to rest.

He opened the door. "Hey, Ralph."

Ralph had been a transplant from the lower forty-eight nearly thirty years ago. A reformed alcoholic, he also led the weekly AA meetings in town and was a constant source of energy and inspiration for anyone who might need an encouraging word.

"Jonah! Good to see you, buddy. I heard you were back in town." Ralph reached out a hand and Jonah was reminded again of how different a simple handshake was in Rankins—strong and full of feeling—like a form of punctuation.

"I am for a bit. You look great, Ralph. How've you been?"

And that was a loaded question in this town.

Jonah enjoyed catching up, but again couldn't seem to stop himself from mentally counting the billable time as Ralph discussed his ongoing battle with red squirrels nesting in his cabin, his recent hernia operation, and a harrowing visit to the proctologist—the details of which Jonah hoped wouldn't keep him up that night. Roughly three-hundred would-be dollars later Ralph handed over an envelope.

"I've got an official-looking letter here for Mr. Caleb Cedar, Attorney at Law—needs a John Hancock."

"All right, thanks, Ralph. It was great to catch up." Jonah scrawled his signature on the card attached to Ralph's clipboard.

"Sure thing. Looking forward to seeing you around, Jonah."

He resumed his seat behind Gramps's desk— a gorgeous wooden antique made of Pacific Yew that Jonah had found at an Anchorage online auction, and had shipped to Gramps after he'd received his first big paycheck. Gramps loved the desk and Jonah had loved giving it to him. Jonah enjoyed spending his money on Gramps, felt like it was something he could do to let Gramps know he was thinking about him even though they were so far apart. But now he found himself wondering if these kinds of gestures had been enough.

A law firm's return address on the letter caught his eye. What business could Gramps possibly have in Utah? Ancillary probate maybe? Definitely something he could handle, but he didn't have any more time than that to ponder because he saw Gary and Ingrid Watte walking up the sidewalk. He got up and let them in.

In spite of the pinched look of pain on her face, Ingrid appeared as lovely as she had in high school—and way too young to have three children. Her flower-printed dress swished around her ankles and her long blonde hair was twisted into Heidi-style braids. She greeted Jonah warmly, but her cornflower blue eyes were red-rimmed and seemed to be on the verge of tears.

Gary appeared to have somehow grown even larger than he'd been at their wedding, but not muscle-turned-flab as happens to many former college football players. More like muscle turned concrete. Jonah guessed he might be tending toward baldness because his head was now shaved, but it worked on Gary; he reminded Jonah of a bodyguard or an ultimate fighter.

They exchanged greetings and reminisced like only people who'd gone to school together can. Jonah eventually got around to explaining that he was helping Gramps out for a while, but if they wanted to wait for him to return that would be fine.

Gary and Ingrid exchanged a look and then Ingrid spoke, "We're okay with you handling this for us, Jonah. We trust you. We'd like to do this as amicably as possible, anyway, to save as much money as we can. And spare the children any fighting—" She broke off on a swallowed sob.

Jonah softened his tone. "That's a really good idea. Divorces can get very expensive. If you guys can agree on a settlement it will make things much easier, faster and cheaper."

Ingrid shot Gary an "I told you so" look and Gary said, "Ingrid, I never said it wouldn't work—the only thing I said is that I don't want a divorce."

"You should have thought about that before you humiliated me."

"Ingrid, I've told you dozens of times that it didn't mean anything. What happened with Lucille was an accident. It was stupid and thoughtless on my part and I've apologized a hundred times."

"Lucille Brock?" Jonah asked.

Gary's pained look confirmed the answer.

Uh-oh, Jonah thought. Lucille Brock. With her almost-too-generous lips, doe-like eyes, and plenty of body in all the right places she'd always reminded Jonah of a vintage pin-up girl. He had never been interested because, of course, she wasn't Shay, but plenty of men were.

"You had a crush on her in high school,

Gary. And she looks exactly the same now, if not better, so don't pretend like you don't think she's attractive."

Gary lifted his massive arms above his head and then brought them down with enough force to crack a coconut. "I had a crush on you, Ingrid. I've been in love with you since the eighth grade. Lucille had a crush on me."

"You know how I feel about her," Ingrid said and then looked at Jonah. "She is the biggest flirt in town and she shares clothes with her teenage daughter—not that that would really matter if her daughter dressed appropriately—but she doesn't. She dresses like her mother—who looks like a...a...tramp."

Ingrid turned back toward her husband. "Why did it have to be you, Gary? There were lots of other guys there."

"We've been over and over this, Ingrid. I was closest. It lasted a matter of minutes and that was it."

"Yeah, but she was wearing one of those dresses she prances around in and she had it hiked up around her neck. And a red thong! Wynona saw the whole thing."

"I'm sure it wasn't around her *neck*...her waist maybe. Wynona exaggerates."

Ingrid's jaw dropped as she glared at Gary.

Jonah wouldn't have been surprised to see fire-balls shoot from her glossy blue stare. He realized the thought was irrational, but he was grateful they were trained on Gary.

After several long seconds she swiveled toward Jonah again. Jonah tried not to wince.

"Can you see he isn't taking this seriously?"

Jonah wasn't sure what to say.

Gary answered for him, "Because it's not serious—it's ridiculous."

"My feelings are ridiculous?" Ingrid repeated incredulously. "Did you hear that, Jonah? I think that pretty much sums it up, don't you? My husband and that tramp in front of half the town, but *I'm* being ridiculous?"

Gary's beefy fingers were gripping the arms of his chair so tightly Jonah couldn't understand how they managed to remain attached.

"It wasn't half the town, it was a few of the guys."

"And some of their wives and Wynona—hardly a few," she added. "And the tramp."

It was Gary's turn to look at Jonah. "And there you have it—she's divorcing me because Lucille Croft dresses inappropriately. Is that one of the choices on the paperwork there, Jonah? Reason for divorce—Lucille flirted with husband and she dresses like a tramp. Go ahead and check that box for us and we can get the paperwork started."

"Uh…well, infidelity is certainly a reason, Gary, if that's what this is about? Is, um…that what this is about?"

Gary's face bloomed in angry shades of pink and purple. A vein bulged in his forehead along with the muscles in his neck. He stood up like he was going to storm out, but then sat back down again.

Ingrid began crying softly.

Jonah silently welcomed himself home to Rankins and wondered what in the world he'd signed up for.

CHAPTER SIX

THERE WAS SOMETHING familiar about her, Shay decided as she emerged from the Faraway Restaurant's kitchen and spotted the woman standing by the hostess station. She tilted her head to look up, probably admiring the gigantic open beams that ran along the ceiling. They *were* pretty spectacular, if she did say so herself. Shay had designed the dining room, and was extremely proud of how the new addition had turned out.

Oiled and polished wood beams cut from Alaskan yellow cedar were spaced along the length of the A-shaped room, which was twenty-three feet from the floor to the highest point in the ceiling. The beams, each decorated with beautiful and intricate carvings, soared up to the point where they were secured to a much larger ridge beam. Her talented artist friend, Kella Jakobs had done all the carving.

Shay turned her focus back to the woman, who now seemed drawn toward the view, which wasn't surprising. The views at the Faraway Inn were stunning and eventually enticed everyone.

Because of its ridge-top location, from nearly any spot at the inn you were offered a generous slice of breath-taking scenery; white-capped mountains, a vast expanse of wilderness, a picturesque stretch of the Opal River, or a truly stunning panorama of the bay and coastline. Every room had a view of something—summer reservations were made up to a year in advance for specific rooms and arguments were waged over which held the most spectacular vista.

"Hannah?" Her sister was walking by with a basket of napkin-wrapped silverware. "Who is that woman standing by the hostess station? Black skirt, purplish shirt, with the long brown hair?"

Hannah peered in that direction. "I'm not sure, but she reminds me of someone. Like an actress or something? She's pretty."

"I was thinking more like someone we know."

"Hmm. I hope she's here for an interview though because she appears completely normal." Shay smiled. "There's no one else listed for an interview today, but I'll go talk to her and see."

The woman stilled as Shay approached, her smile frozen in place.

Shay reached out a hand. "Hello, how are you?"

The woman's grip was warm and firm, if slightly clammy.

"Um, fine. You're Shay, right?"

"Yes, have we met?"

"No, we haven't. I'm Adele Mason. I recognize you from your photo on the Faraway Inn's website." She patted a hand on her skirt. "Sorry about the sweaty palm. I'm really nervous."

Shay gave her what she hoped was a reassuring smile. "I understand. Don't worry—it's a quick interview. We're pretty informal here at the Faraway Inn. Do you have serving experience?"

"Excuse me?"

"You're here to interview for the server position, aren't you?"

"Interview…?" She stared at Shay for an awkward moment and finally said, "I'm sorry. *Interview*. Yes…"

Shay repeated, "Do you have serving experience?"

"What?"

"Waitressing? Have you been a waitress before? A server? We're not supposed to call waitresses, waitresses anymore, are we? A fact which I find kind of silly. I worked as a waitress all through college, and never expected anyone to call me anything but that. What's wrong with being a waitress, I say. I loved it. You do have experience, right?"

She let out a surprised chuckle as if the meaning of the question finally dawned on her. "Yes, actually I do, but—"

"Did you bring a résumé?"

"No, I didn't. I'm not—"

"References?"

"No, my situation is kind of complicated… I'm from out of town and I'm afraid I'm not as prepared as I'd like to be. I'm actually…" Her words trailed off and she suddenly reminded Shay of a frightened kitten. "I don't know what I'm doing here. I mean, I *know*, but…"

Shay's heart went out to the woman because it was obvious to her that Adele had come from some kind of a difficult situation. And Shay was both familiar and sympathetic with difficult situations.

"It's okay."

"It's okay?"

"What I mean is—you don't have to tell me." Shay gave her another warm smile. "This is Alaska. People come here for all kinds of reasons and we generally don't ask a lot of questions if they don't want to answer them.

Whatever your story is, as long as you're not being chased by the FBI or hunted down by U.S. Marshals then we're good. If it's a psycho ex you're running from though, I've got your back."

The woman seemed beyond your typical job-interview nervous, which of course only made Shay curious about her past. But Shay meant what she said—she wasn't one to judge and she wasn't going to probe her with personal questions. Didn't we all have our issues? Our secrets? Shay certainly did and she appreciated that her family and friends loved her in spite of the former even as she planned to maintain an unwavering death grip on the latter.

"Nope, no marshals, no agents and no exes—well, none that I know for sure are truly clinically psycho, but—"

Hannah sidled up with a warm smile and introduced herself, interrupting whatever Adele might have added. She complimented Adele's lavender top and colorful, gem-encrusted shoes and Shay watched her relax under Hannah's smooth small talk.

Apparently she'd been the one making the lovely Adele nervous if her demeanor with Hannah was any indication, which was odd because usually she was great with people.

Maybe because she was the owner and Adele was seeking a job? That seemed possible, although Shay had to admit there was also something special about Hannah's charm—when she chose to turn it on.

"So, how much experience do you have?" Hannah revisited Shay's earlier question.

"Um, let's see…about eighteen years."

"Eighteen years!" Hannah exclaimed. "Shay, did you hear that? *Years* of experience. So, have you worked in busy restaurants? Cafes? Diners? Dives? Roadside pie stands?"

Adele let out a chuckle and said, "I think I've worked in all of the above at one time or another—except the pie stand. Although I have worked plenty of county fairs and craft shows. I can dip a mean corn dog and serve up a steaming hot funnel cake with a smile, even in one-hundred degree heat."

Hannah and Adele shared a laugh.

Hannah placed a hand on her hip. "Okay, so switching gears now. Tell me, what's your stance on kittens and puppies?"

Shay could tell that Adele was trying not to look at Hannah like she'd lost her mind. "Um, I love them. I have a dog—a schnauzer mix. He was a rescue dog. He has some issues, but I adore him. I drove up here all the way from

Utah so I could bring him and he wouldn't have to fly. He doesn't like to be crated."

"Poor baby," Hannah said sympathetically. She then leaned over and sniffed the air next to Adele. "And that's a lovely perfume you're wearing."

Hannah might be laying it on a bit thick, but Shay couldn't help but say a silent prayer of thanks. Finally—someone with experience— who smelled nice and didn't harm puppies or kittens, and hopefully didn't steal or do drugs.

"Thank you."

"And what did you say your name is?"

"Oh, I don't think I said it—to you, I mean, but it's Adele. Adele Mason."

"Wait," Hannah said with a snap of her fingers. "Utah. You're the person who has been calling the inn, asking for Shay."

Adele nodded, and Shay saw it again—that look. Like a flash of panic. Shay was certain that Adele was hiding something, which only made her want to help even more.

"Yes, that's me."

Shay felt terrible—she'd totally forgotten those phone messages from Utah. The "Cedar stress," as she'd begun referring to Caleb and Jonah in her mind, was truly distracting her.

Jonah had been texting and calling, keeping her updated about Caleb. And of course Shay wanted updates, but that's all she wanted. Somehow their conversations kept traveling off onto other subjects. Each time, in spite of her silent vow not to let it happen, their discussion seemed longer and never focused solely on Caleb.

"Adele, I'm so sorry I haven't returned your calls. I'm not normally such a flake, I promise." Shay inhaled a deep breath and blew it out. "I admire the fact that you came here to see me in person, so how about this? We'll skip the interview, even though Hannah has already done most of it anyway, however unconventional it may have been."

Hannah shrugged a shoulder as if to say "but I got the job done."

And indeed she had.

"Can you start tomorrow? We'll throw you in with the wolves—so to speak—and see how you do. If things go well—and I mean that both ways—for you and for us, then you're hired no questions asked. You provide me with your particulars, whatever they may be. No judgments or reference checks on my end and we'll go from there. How does that sound?"

"Great." Adele smiled at her again and there

was no mistaking that it was genuine. "Thank you, so much."

Hannah couldn't contain her excitement, probably due in large part to the idea of lightening her own workload. But Shay couldn't really blame her for that. They'd all been working extra hard, and no one more than her and Hannah.

Hannah said, "I have a good feeling about you, Adele Mason from Utah."

ONE CRAZY DAY at the inn seemed to follow another, but Shay was grateful for the chaos which had kept her mind engaged and distracted from speculating about Caleb—and thinking about Jonah, except when he texted her like he'd done two seconds ago: Hey, can you call when you get a sec?

She happened to have a free moment and was feeling better about her employment woes. Hannah's instincts seemed right on where Adele was concerned. She'd picked up on details quickly and already seemed as if she'd been working here for years.

Shay had also hired another maid for the inn and three more employees at the restaurant. Including Vince—wonderful Vince—he had been summer help the year before. He'd grad-

uated from high school a month ago and had
been hired on a fishing boat for the summer.
Unfortunately, seasickness had plagued him,
waylaying his commercial fishing plans. Shay
was disappointed for him but more than happy
to put him back on the payroll.

Now, if only she could get some respite from
worrying where Caleb was concerned. That
appointment with the specialist couldn't come
soon enough. She hit the talk button and waited
for Jonah to answer.

"Hi," he said. "That was fast. How are you?"

"Fine," she said. "What's up?"

"I hate to bother you but do you have any
idea what could be wrong with Gramps's washing machine? He insisted I call. He said you've
helped him fix it before."

"Was he trying to wash Francis's bed again?"

"Francis's bed? Hold on. What Gramps?"

Shay could hear muffled conversation and
then, "He says it's not off-balance. I was the
one using it actually."

"Did you trip the breaker?" Shay hoped not.
She could fix a lot of things, but she really disliked working with electricity. She knew her
fear of fire was irrational, but that didn't mean
she could make it go away.

A fire had burned the original Faraway Inn

to the ground. Her grandpa Gus and his brother Eli had barely escaped.

Jonah's tone took on an edge of concern, "Don't worry, Shay, it's not the breaker."

"Huh. Well, that machine can be a little temperamental." Shay looked at her watch. She had a couple errands to run in town anyway. "Okay, I'll be there as soon as I can to take a look at it. Ask him if he needs anything from the pharmacy."

She waited again while Jonah relayed the question. "He says he could use some more of those things you've gotten him for his teeth? I hope you know what that means because I don't."

"I do. I'll see you guys in a bit."

Shay hung up and went to tell Hannah she was leaving.

Quick stops at the hardware store, the pharmacy to pick up her mom's prescription, then the bakery, and she was soon pulling up in front of Caleb's house. She texted her mom to let her know she'd be swinging by with her medication later. Then she grabbed the packages and tried to be brave.

She dreaded seeing Jonah again. Things had been okay since bingo, but she knew that was why—because she hadn't seen him. They'd only exchanged calls and texts.

"Caleb?" she hollered, walking in without knocking because she knew they were expecting her.

"Shay, there you are. Thanks so much for stopping by. Darn washing machine—I was hoping we could figure it out like last time."

"No problem." Caleb looked good, maybe a little tired, which concerned her because Jonah said he'd been napping a lot.

She handed over the bags. "Here are your flossers and a loaf of that honey wheat bread that I told you about—that Lilah's been baking at the Donut Den? I thought you might like to try some for your peanut butter toast."

Caleb smiled. "I sure would—especially with these little gadgets to get the peanuts out of my teeth. Thank you, Shay."

Jonah strolled in, a dark sheen of whiskers covering his jaw, black hair ruffled, jeans attractively faded, Chicago Cubs T-shirt hugging in all the right places. Exactly how much stew and cobbler would it take to make him fat? she wondered.

But his annoyed scowl was even better than a paunch at reminding her of how unattractive he could be. In fact, annoyed ranked right up there with condescending smirk in that department.

"What's going on with the washer?" she asked Caleb.

"I'm not sure. Jonah put in a load of clothes and a while later it just kind of sputtered to a stop."

She looked at Jonah. "Did you drain the water out?"

Jonah crossed his arms over his chest, looking a bit defensive.

Shay imagined he hadn't been thrilled with the idea of calling her in the first place. This used to be something they joked about—her superior mechanical skills.

"I didn't have to because it happened near the end of the spin cycle. I'm not used to these old agitators. I have one of the front-loading machines now. I've been trying to talk Gramps into replacing this ancient piece of junk with one of those but he won't hear of it."

Shay flicked her eyes up toward the ceiling impatiently before turning them back on Caleb. "Obviously Mr. Moneybag's solution would be to buy a new one.

"I realize, Jonah, it's been a while since you've lived here, so I'll refresh your memory. We don't generally get rid of things around here just because there's a shiny new model available. We're proud of the use we get out of the things we have. Unlike you folks, who fall for those marketing ploys thinking something newer is going to be better—we don't. We like to fix things and then brag about how many miles we get out of something before we *have* to buy something new."

Caleb grinned at her proudly. "I was just telling him the same thing."

"Yeah, well, you know what they say about a fool and his money."

They laughed together. She glanced at Jonah who was biting his cheek. She couldn't decide if he was amused or irritated.

"Let's go take a look." She headed for the laundry room, the Cedar men following close behind.

"I don't see anything obvious," Shay said a while later after she'd removed the agitator and the drum, checked, cleaned and lubricated all the moving parts she figured could be causing a problem. Then she carefully reassembled the appliance—Jonah handing her various tools as needed.

"The motor looks fine and sounds fine when I turn it by hand. There was some debris under the drum, but that shouldn't make it quit like that."

"Huh." Caleb scratched his head.

"Do we order one from Bradbury's?" Jonah asked. He sounded eager as he brushed his palms together for effect. "I'm guessing they don't stock washing machines—especially not the front-loading ones."

Shay scowled. "I know your credit card is burning a hole in your pocket, but let's turn the thing on first and see what happens. You never know with these machines. Sometimes just moving things around and cleaning off the parts can help. Or maybe something was jammed under the drum and dislodged when I removed it."

Jonah muttered something that sounded like, "my money isn't what's burning a hole in my pocket."

"What?" Shay asked sharply, assuming he was making a joke at her expense.

"Nothing—never mind, but I think I'll go get my shoes on and grab my wallet just in case. And we might as well get you a new dryer while we're at it, huh, Gramps?"

He stood there looking proud of himself like he'd actually done something wonderful, besides offer to spend his money.

"Let's try firing her back up like Shay suggested first. I need to plug her back in though." Caleb disappeared behind the washer for a moment. "Okay, let's do it."

Shay pulled the dial, and prayed.

The machine surged to life and then proceeded to smoothly continue through the cycle without a problem.

"She's really spinning now," Caleb said. "And she's not making that clinky noise like she was before either." He patted the machine, and winked at Shay. "Not bad for an old piece of junk, eh?"

"Not bad at all," Shay agreed. Then she looked sideways at Jonah and waited for a response.

Jonah sighed, but Shay could see he was fighting a grin. "All right, already—you guys win—for now. But we'll see how long this tired heap of metal lasts. And next time, I'm buying you a new one, Gramps. No argument."

The phone rang and Caleb hurried toward the kitchen to answer the call.

"Nicely done, but of course I'm not surprised. Do you still do all the maintenance at the inn?" Jonah opened the washer and began stuffing in the still-wet clothes from his earlier attempt.

"Most," Shay answered, irrationally pleased by the compliment. "What I can anyway. Tag is really handy, too, as you know, so he helps me out sometimes, and then I have a guy I can call—and of course an electrician."

Jonah turned and leaned against the washer. "It seems like there's a lot that could go wrong in a place like that."

"You'd be amazed," she said and then proceeded to tell him about the time the electricity went out and the generator wouldn't start.

"Thank goodness we have that giant fireplace in the lobby. Thirty-some guests huddled around singing campfire songs and telling stories until Bering and Tag, hours later, could bring in another generator and get it hooked up."

"How did people handle that?"

"Guests are generally so nice—I actually received a couple cards thanking me for that wonderful evening around the campfire. I think the experience was hardest on me, as I tried not to lunge for the extinguisher every time someone put another log on the fire."

They were both laughing when Caleb reappeared. He looked from her to Jonah and back again, a pleased expression on his face.

"Sorry to duck out on you guys, but I've

gotta run. Shay, thanks again for fixing the old girl."

"Run?" Jonah asked. "Where?"

"I've got a thing I forgot about."

"What thing, Gramps?"

Caleb scratched his cheek and Shay tried to decide if he looked embarrassed or confused. Her stomach tightened with a fresh bout of anxiety. It wasn't like Caleb to forget. Anything. Ever.

"I, uh, I promised Doc I'd help him put together his new deck chairs."

"Oh, I don't remember you mentioning it."

He pointed a finger at Jonah. "I just told you I forgot. I've been doing that a bit lately, haven't I? Probably just age, huh? I made a batch of cookies earlier and put on a fresh pot of coffee, so you two enjoy." He turned and hustled out the door.

Shay reached down and scratched Francis's snout. Neither Shay nor Jonah spoke for a long moment.

Then he looked up and whispered, "Please don't let him be getting dementia or Alzheimer's."

"Jonah, I'm sure it's not that." She said the words but her thoughts had already taken off in that direction.

Without speaking they moved together toward the kitchen. Jonah poured two cups of coffee and slid one cup across the countertop toward Shay where she now sat on a stool. Jonah leaned a hip against the lower cupboard. A plate of Caleb's famous oatmeal raisin cookies sat untouched between them.

"Have you noticed anything like this before? Gramps forgetting things?"

"No. Never." Shay wanted badly to reassure him.

"This wouldn't be that big of a deal except combined with the state of his office it's... You haven't noticed anything out of the ordinary lately?"

"No, I... No."

His tone had a new level of intensity. "Shay, this is important. Think. You haven't noticed him forgetting things? Losing things? Missing appointments? Anything like that at all?"

"Jonah, no," she answered with an edge to her tone, too. "Don't you think I would have said something if I'd noticed anything like that?"

"I do, but..."

"But what?"

"He's not a young man anymore. Have you considered that maybe you may not have picked up on something this subtle? Being around, all the time, you might not be able to see the situation as clearly as I do—" His words, his tone combined, with an already high level of anxiety, to ignite her temper. "Hold on there. Let me get this straight. You're saying you have a better view of your grandfather's life from three-thousand miles away in Chicago than I do—from right here in Rankins? I am well aware of the fact that he's aging, Jonah. I have parents, too, that I watch out for. I look out for everyone in my life."

Jonah held up his hands, palms down in a conciliatory gesture. "Okay, all I'm saying is that I think we need to analyze this from every angle as objectively as we can and—"

"You know what, Jonah?" Shay slid off the stool, her heart pounding so loudly in her head that it seemed she could barely hear her own voice. So she made it louder. "I'm sorry if I'm not an unemotional robot like you who can visit my grandfather every year or two for about twenty minutes and be okay with that. How dare you march in here and treat me like a defendant on the witness stand, and accuse me of missing something this important? He has not been forgetting things, Jonah. On the contrary—he reminds me of things on a regular basis."

"Shay—"

"No, we're done. This conversation is over. I have to go. I need to get back to the inn."

CHAPTER SEVEN

"Ms. James, may I speak with you for a second?"

Shay froze at the sound of Mr. Takagi's voice. The man had a manner of speaking that always made him sound angry, even when he wasn't, although right now she feared he might be. She plastered on a smile and turned toward him, her scalp prickling with anxiety.

"Of course, Mr. Takagi." *Please don't let Hannah have killed off any of the goldfish.*

Mr. Takagi had arrived as scheduled. Hannah had checked him in, and over the following days she had taken care of everything Takagi-related—getting him settled in their best suite, setting up and then transferring the fish to their temporary home, and driving him out to visit Mrs. Milner to tour her new atrium and pond.

Hannah had been continually assuring Shay that everything was going well. And she'd been relieved to allow Hannah to handle it all, thinking that she already had enough to deal with herself. Now she feared the ramifications of that decision even as the guilt welled up for laying so much responsibility on Hannah.

"I would like to discuss your sister, Hannah."

Shay looked at him expectantly and opened her mouth to begin apologizing.

"Your sister is an absolute treasure, Ms. James. I have never seen such a sharp mind or such a hard worker in one so young as Hannah."

"Oh? Why, yes, thank you, Mr. Takagi. She is indeed. And she does…work very hard." That last part was true. Hannah did work hard. Her time training to be a professional skier had instilled a work ethic that was translating beautifully into the business world, even if she might need to take things a smidge more seriously sometimes.

"She is an asset to your business, Ms. James. And I hope you realize how valuable she is. I have never seen anyone take to the intricacies of caring for the *nishikigoi* in the sense that she has."

Shay could see Hannah grinning at her over Mr. Takagi's shoulder.

"I am so pleased to hear this, Mr. Takagi."

"Your sister could easily become a breeder."

"A breeder?" Shay repeated carefully.

"Yes, the *nishikigoi* require a special touch to produce high quality offspring. Hannah has the touch, and if you are not careful, Ms. James, I may try to lure her away."

He laughed, Hannah laughed, Shay chimed in mostly out of relief.

"You can be sure that I will reward Hannah for her efforts, Mr. Takagi."

Mr. Takagi bobbed his head. "I am very glad to hear this. She truly deserves such a reward."

Hannah smiled and began speaking, her tone a perfect mix of respect and admiration, "Shay, *nishikigoi* have the most interesting history. It's absolutely fascinating. I've typed up a fact sheet, laminated it and placed it by our temporary pond in the courtyard so that our guests can truly appreciate them, too."

Shay was impressed by Hannah's pronunciation of the Japanese word, not to mention her newfound devotion to ornamental fish.

She nearly choked at Hannah's next statement.

"It seems difficult to conceive, doesn't it Shay, that some people believe these exquisite creatures are simply glorified goldfish? When, in fact, the two fish were developed from entirely different species of carp."

"Mmm, yes. It certainly does, Hannah."

"Did you know the *nishikigoi* is a symbol of love and friendship in Japan?"

"I did *not* know that. How interesting."

"Yes, it is, and Shay, Mr. T has generously gifted me one—a *showa sanke*. I have told him he is too generous but he insists."

Mr. T? Shay swallowed nervously and tried to remember what she'd just been told. Hannah was getting a pet fish? "A *showa sanke*?"

But apparently the pronunciation wasn't quite right because Hannah spoke the words again.

"*Showa sanke*—yes, she is incredibly beautiful with black, white and red markings. She looks like a calico cat." Hannah glanced at Mr. Takagi and added, "Only much prettier and so much better behaved."

Hannah and Mr. Takagi started to giggle and then burst out laughing. How nice. Apparently, Hannah and "Mr. T." were now sharing private jokes.

"Mrs. Milner has graciously offered to let me keep it in her pond. Isn't that wonderful?"

"Yes, it is…just…wonderful. Mr. Takagi, you are too generous to my little sister. Thank you so much."

Mr. Takagi bowed. "It has been my pleasure. I feel so comfortable leaving my precious brood here in her more than capable hands."

Hannah was flashing a brilliant, guileless smile at Mr. Takagi, and in that moment Shay could not have been prouder—or more relieved. Hannah really did seem to be recovering—getting back on her feet. Shay was happy the inn had been able to play a role in this; to give Hannah a job and help her find some direction in her tipped-on-its-head life.

The inn had done the same for her once and Shay didn't think she'd ever stop being amazed by the blessings it continually brought into her life and into the lives of others—security, knowledge, friendship—apparently even expensive Japanese fish.

She couldn't begin to imagine what the future might hold.

"THANK YOU FOR agreeing to see me, Mr. Cedar, on such short notice. I know you're probably very busy."

"No problem at all. It's a pleasure to meet you, Ms. Mason. I'm Jonah Cedar, Caleb Cedar's grandson. Please call me Jonah. Like my grandfather, I'm also an attorney, also licensed to practice in the state of Alaska. I'm helping my grandfather with some of his cases at the present time as he's currently indisposed."

Jonah studied the woman in front of him and

felt a twinge of curiosity and something else… familiarity? Had they met? He didn't want to ask because that sounded like such a pick-up line, and he wasn't interested in her in any romantic way. He was guessing she was around his age and she was pretty—not Shay-pretty, but definitely an attractive woman.

"Right."

"You're new to Rankins?"

She smiled and nodded. Circles beneath reddish-tinged eyes and a tightness around her mouth suggested she was also tired. Jonah felt a twinge of pity. He was worn out, too, and he'd only been in town for a little over a week.

"Well, welcome. I'm not a permanent resident, but also like my grandfather, I graduated from Yale Law. Now I work for a firm in Chicago—or normally I do. I'm on a leave of absence right now because of my grandfather's health, but here's the name of my firm if you want to check me out." He handed her a card. "Or you can call your attorney and have him check me out. I should be capable of helping you in whatever legal matter you are here to consult my grandfather about."

"I was hoping to meet with Caleb Cedar because he's familiar with the…um, my family here in Rankins."

Jonah smiled reassuringly. "I see. Don't worry, my grandfather is available for consultation if necessary. He can bring me up to speed on anything I need to know."

She stared at him and Jonah had the feeling she was assessing him, trying to decide what to do.

He waited in silence.

She finally nodded. "That sounds fine."

"Okay then, Adele, what can I do for you today?"

"I'm not sure where to begin. My attorney in Utah sent a letter to your grandfather, but I don't know if you've seen it."

Jonah didn't recall seeing a file with her name on it, then he remembered the envelope that Ralph had delivered the day he'd met with Gary and Ingrid.

"Utah, you said? I do recall an envelope being delivered a few days ago."

Jonah rifled through the basket where he'd been placing the mail. He fished it from the stack and held it aloft. "This must be it. Things have been a little hectic around here and I haven't opened it yet. Do you want to go ahead and give me a general idea of what this is about?"

"I guess you could say that I'm here to stake a claim."

Jonah frowned thoughtfully. "What do you mean? Like a mining claim?" Jonah had never dealt in mineral law before but the idea of tackling something new always excited him.

She laughed and the sound surprised him. It didn't match her voice. It was a low, throaty sound and it sort of reminded him of… Could he not stop thinking about her for more than two minutes?

"No, it's more like a family claim."

"I'm afraid I don't understand. A family claim?"

"Yes, I'm hoping to find a place for myself in the James family."

"The James family?"

She cleared her throat. "Yes, I've recently learned that I'm the only child of Eli David James, which makes me related to the James family here in Rankins. And, I believe, that also means I have a claim to a share of the Faraway Inn."

Jonah's brain began to whir; Eli James had been Gus James's brother. He'd heard Shay talk about Great Uncle Eli, but as far as he knew Eli James had been a lifelong bachelor until his death some years ago. Although that didn't mean he couldn't have had a child. But Jonah had no idea how that would mean this woman was entitled to any portion of the inn.

"Uh-huh." Jonah took a letter opener and sliced through the end of the envelope. He slid the contents out and began reading.

Estate law was not Jonah's specialty, but the phrase "unknown heir" burned through his brain. According to the letter, the property Gus had built the Faraway Inn on had originally belonged to his parents, Isaac and Viola James. Upon their death the property had passed to their three sons—Gus, Eli and Lyman.

There was also a copy of the Faraway Inn property deed showing the owner to be Shay James, et al. Jonah knew that ambiguous "et al." meant that somewhere down the line another name had existed on the deed for the property—an interest in the property that had never been legally removed.

This indeed meant that someone, and possibly Adele Mason, could essentially claim partial ownership to the inn. How much, or the value of the share, Jonah had no idea.

But there was no question this was going to be a legal mess to rival any he'd ever encountered in Chicago. And how could Shay...?

Shay.

This couldn't possibly be true. If this was

true Shay would be devastated. The inn was everything to her.

Jonah tried desperately to think this through. He scrutinized the young woman sitting across from him who suddenly seemed like some kind of beautiful, unlikely villain from a spy movie.

"You said your name was Adele Mason?"

"Mason is the name I go by because that is—was—my mother's last name. I didn't even know that 'James' was on my birth certificate until a few months ago when my mother was dying. Since then, my attorney and I both spent a good deal of time researching my father's life, including his time here in Alaska. And I..."

She continued to speak about her research while Jonah listened and managed to hold on to his composure. He stared into Ms. Mason's amber-colored eyes and suddenly realized why she looked—and sounded—so familiar.

Jonah's entire body went cold—a blast of frigid Alaskan air could have warmed him as the conclusion soaked into him that Adele Mason looked like a James. She could easily pass for one of Shay's sisters—or a cousin. Could this really be possible? Possible, yes, but he wasn't about to accept her words at face value. And he wasn't going to allow Shay to give up even one square inch of the inn without a fight.

"So, as I'm sure you can imagine, I don't know where to begin. I'm not sure how to introduce myself and then—"

Jonah interrupted, "I'm going to have to stop you right there, Adele, and let you know that neither I, nor my grandfather, can help you. We are both too personally involved with the James family to fairly represent you in this matter."

Adele frowned. "I understand that, but I'm not asking you to represent me. I have an attorney in Utah. Since I was coming to Alaska, my attorney suggested I contact your grandfather for help and also to possibly avoid some of the legal hoops. My father and his brothers knew your grandfather well, so my attorney was hoping through that connection we could expedite this whole process and avoid the court thing… Do you think that's possible?"

Her expression appeared innocent and hopeful but Jonah saw something else there, too. Fear? Hope? Greed? He wasn't sure but his instincts told him it was the latter. He was too used to liars and schemers in his line of work to fall for a good acting job.

"I'm not sure. What is it that you want—

that you think you are entitled to—exactly?" Jonah asked the question even as he dreaded the answer.

Her gaze flicked away nervously and then landed somewhere on the top of Gramps's desk. "I understand this is a difficult situation and I can assure you that I'm not looking to cause undue problems for Shay James or for the rest of the James family. I'm here in Rankins to claim what is rightfully mine. I'm not sure what that might be at this point. That's what you attorneys are for, right?"

She topped her speech off with a light shrug and Jonah felt his distrust growing.

How in the world was he going to break this news to Shay?

Jonah was careful to keep his expression bland and his tone neutral. "Mm-hmm, I'm also going to let you know that I will be representing Shay in this matter, whatever that should entail. So maybe we should table this conversation until you can have your counsel present and I've had a chance to consult with the James family."

Jonah studied her as he waited for a response.

"Okay." Adele sighed and then shook her head in dismay. "Well, this isn't working out quite like I hoped, but thank you for your time. How much do I owe you for today?"

"There won't be any charge for this consultation."

A flicker of surprise lit in her eyes. "That's extremely generous, but I'd like to pay."

Jonah insisted. "Not necessary. Have your attorney contact me and we'll proceed from there."

He picked up a pen and leaned back in his chair. He tapped the pen slowly on the desktop in front of him, even as his mind took off at full speed.

He needed to call Shay. No, he needed to handle this in person. He would call her and tell her he was on his way up to the inn. Then he would break the news, and reassure her that he would fix this for her. Whatever it took, he would personally see to it that this woman would not steal the inn from her, which was funny because there had been a time in their lives when a part of him had wished the inn didn't even exist…

Adele tilted her chin as if considering an important point. "I think… Yes, one more thing before I go?"

"What's that?"

"I'd just like to confirm with you that the

attorney-client privilege covers our meeting today?"

Jonah felt a rush of unease. This was true. He couldn't talk to Shay about this matter if Adele didn't want him to. "You don't want me to discuss this with Shay? Or facilitate this with the family in any manner?"

"Thank you, but no. Not at this time. I've decided that I'd like to talk to the family myself first."

He calmly watched Adele Mason take her leave even as panic washed over him; he was going to have to keep this knowledge from Shay until this woman was ready to reveal her identity and intentions.

He felt his frustration build as Adele Mason walked out the door and down the sidewalk. She climbed into an older model, faded blue four-door sedan. It seemed to take her an inordinate amount of time to start the car, but finally it jumped forward and then crawled away from the curb.

Jonah leapt into action. He immediately went online and ordered a title report for the land where the Faraway Inn was located. Then he made two phone calls; one to Niles Gadget, a colleague who's a specialist in estate law, and the other to Frank Hill, a private investigator he occasionally employed back in Chicago.

He might be prevented from revealing this situation to Shay, but he would be prepared for the instant that changed.

CHAPTER EIGHT

SHAY'S EYES SWEPT the dining room for Caleb and Jonah as she reassured herself that all was running smoothly. King crab legs and jumbo prawns were sitting on ice. Halibut had been chopped, lightly battered and deep fried, and fresh salmon fillets were coming off the grill at regular intervals. Shay thought she could probably charge for the delicious aroma alone.

The restaurant was filling fast as the Saturday seafood buffet shifted into high gear. She felt a twinge of alarm—it wasn't like Caleb to be late—especially for dinner. And Jonah was always prompt.

Hannah had been right about Jonah's return to Rankins causing a stir. It seemed everyone was talking about him, and most of the buzz was good from what she'd heard. Even though Shay tried not to participate in gossip, she couldn't help but hear the talk—between Laurel, Laurel's sister Piper who was the town's champion gossip, Hannah, and even Janie, she seemed to be continually bombarded with Jonah-news. Bering and Jonah had rekindled their friendship, so even Emily was dropping his name into their conversations.

Shay had heard through this rather reliable grapevine that Jonah had already been tackling some of Rankins' stickier legal matters, including convincing Will Traeger to drop his suit against the town. She hoped the rumor about Gary and Ingrid getting divorced wasn't true. Shay felt certain Jonah's achievements were being exaggerated. He'd been in town for two weeks.

They hadn't spoken since she'd stormed out of Caleb's house the week before. As the days passed, Shay had begun to feel worse and worse about her reaction. She knew in her heart that Jonah's intensity—for lack of a better word, came from a place of love. Jonah loved his grandfather and in spite of the lingering issues between her and Jonah, she needed to remember that. She needed to keep the situation with Caleb separate from the problems between her and Jonah, they both needed to keep Caleb front and center, and she needed to apologize.

Just when she was ready to abandon her search and head back toward the lobby she felt a tingle start on the back of her neck and then tiptoe down her spine. She braced herself and turned.

"Shay," Jonah said, his blue eyes seeming to lock hers to his with the aid of some magical magnetic force.

Shay wanted to look away, she really did… But it was like looking at the ocean's blue horizon on a perfect sunny day, there was too much to see with only a glance. And she realized that he seemed happy to see her.

She felt a smile form on her lips. "Jonah, I was just looking for you guys."

"I thought you might be. I saw you scanning the room. Gramps told you six-thirty and it's closer to six forty-five. I'm sorry—he's outside talking to Doc. He asked me to come find you and see if we could eat a little later?"

Shay felt that now too-familiar rush of worry. "Does it have something to do with his condition?"

"I don't think so. They were talking about fishing when he sent me in to find you."

"Oh…well, that's good then, I think."

He looked concerned as he asked, "Is this going to mess up your reservations?"

"No, since it's the buffet tonight we have a little more room to maneuver than normal. Hannah is at the hostess station, so she'll know to hold Caleb's table. Jonah—"

"Shay—" He started to speak at the same time.

"You go," she urged.

"I want to apologize for what happened the other day. I didn't mean to imply that you aren't watching out for Gramps. I was a little freaked about the whole memory episode. My imagination ran away with me and I didn't mean for it to come out sounding like an accusation. Maybe I... Maybe there is a little too much attorney in me sometimes."

Shay felt a rush of relief that he wanted to patch things up, too. "I understand, Jonah— I do. I want to apologize, too. I overreacted. I know I need to keep in mind that you're as worried as I am."

He nodded, his eyes searching her face. His expression still seemed odd—full of remorse but tense at the same time.

Shay felt guilty for adding to what must already be a constant source of worry over his gramps. She was worried also, and being at odds wasn't going to help.

"Jonah, it only seems normal for the stress to get to us, right?"

"Yes, I'm sure you're right about that. But

Shay, I really want things to be different between us—you know? At least while I'm here and we work all of this…stuff…out."

"Different?"

"Better, I mean."

He was standing so close now that Shay could smell his sweet, cedar Jonah-smell and memories of "better" nearly brought tears to her eyes.

"Less tension and antagonism," he added. "You know—try to be more of a unit."

She swallowed but her throat felt dry. "A unit?"

"Yeah, a unit, a team—like we used to be. For Gramps's sake."

"I'd like that."

Jonah blew out a breath. "Okay."

"Okay," she echoed. And then tried to lighten the mood. "So, we've agreed that you're going to quit insulting me, interrogating me, and just generally irritating me and or making me angry?"

He tipped his head back and laughed and the boyish lightness that transformed him made Shay's heart soar, snippets of childhood, teenage, college memories flashing in her mind's eye.

"I'm going to try. But I can't guarantee anything with regards to the irritation aspect. I've always been pretty good at that where you're concerned—even before we broke up."

"Yeah, well, you were always just as good at defusing my temper, which I admit can be a little quick to ignite. I guess we both have some things to work on."

"Fine by me," he said with a grin.

"Me, too," she returned.

"And… I've been wandering around looking things over. Gramps wasn't exaggerating—this place is spectacular."

"That is so nice of you to say, Jonah."

"It's true. Shay, I want you to know that I'm really happy to see that you've made your dreams come true. I know how excited you were when Gus left you the inn, but I also know you were torn by wanting your own place. You've put your own stamp here, though. You've kept enough of what made the Faraway Inn so special from the first, yet you've clearly managed to turn it into your place at the same time."

His compliments and his understanding of what she'd wanted to accomplish somehow soothed her, reminded her of what she did have, what she'd worked so hard for all of these years as she'd tried to find some way to replace the memory of him—of them—with something that didn't hurt so much.

"Thank you, Jonah. That means a lot. I…it's been a long road and a lot of hard work, that's for sure. We're still dealing with some of the bugs from the expansion and remodel this last year. But I'm really pleased with how things are going overall. And I think Grandpa would approve of the changes."

He agreed. "Shay, do you… Do you ever think about really taking on that challenge someday?"

"What challenge?"

"Opening your very own place? With your knowledge and experience, you could open a five-star luxury resort of your own anywhere in the world."

Shay frowned. Sure, she used to talk about building her own place from the ground up, but that was before Grandpa Gus had left her the inn. And she really did feel like she had managed to make it hers. Was he insinuating that she shouldn't be satisfied with what she'd accomplished? Because she'd inherited it? Or because she didn't earn a zillion dollars a year like he did?

She could hear the emotion in her voice but she couldn't seem to stop it. "I feel like this is my place, Jonah. Sometimes dreams come true in ways that aren't exactly how you imagined them—but they come true nonetheless."

His eyes went wide, like he suddenly realized what he may have implied. "No, I know. I didn't mean that it wasn't..."

She waited for him to clarify, not wanting to jeopardize the tenuous peace they'd just reached.

"All I meant to ask is—has it been everything you thought it would be? Owning your own place?"

Shay thought about that; she'd poured her heart and soul and every penny she had—and some that she didn't—into this inn. She'd had to—the Faraway Inn was her life. She was incredibly grateful for her family and her few close and solid friends. Not that she didn't sometimes long for a little more depth to her personal life, but she didn't want to discuss that, not with him.

"I've enjoyed every minute of it." There was enough tightness in her tone that she didn't even sound convincing to herself. She braced herself for him to pounce on the lie.

"Come on, Shay—every minute?"

His expression made her uncomfortable,

fidgety. He'd always been able to do that—hound her for the truth with a simple look.

She glanced down to where she was clutching one hand in the other, her fingertips turning red like a nervous third-grader's before the spelling bee. She unwound her fingers and smoothed her hands over her hips.

"I guess if you insist on splitting hairs, Jonah, then no, not every single minute, but overall it's been more than worth it. However, there are things—"

"What things?"

His tone seemed to demand an answer. She wondered how different her life would have been if Grandpa Gus hadn't died, and if he never would have willed her the inn. Because then she would have been able to move to Connecticut with Jonah while he attended law school. But, she told herself, the outcome would have ultimately been the same because Shay had gotten pregnant that summer. She hadn't realized it herself until Jonah was already gone, but she had made plans to tell him.

Even though the timing was all wrong and even though they'd been broken up, Shay had been happy about the pregnancy—ecstatic about becoming a mother. A miscarriage had left her devastated and she'd had to share the news that they were having a baby at the same time she'd told him that they weren't.

Then later, when she'd discovered that there would never be another pregnancy for her, there wasn't enough of a relationship left between them for her to want to share that news with him. She consoled herself with the notion that it was better that Jonah had ultimately been spared the same fate. Shay had gradually accepted hers, but didn't think she'd ever really get over it; choosing instead to devote herself to the inn and to her family.

Shay forced herself to put on a teasing smile. She hoped Jonah couldn't see the pain in her eyes. "Things I don't want to talk about. Why are you interrogating me again? I thought we were going to try and get along."

He chuckled, but there seemed to be a tinge of sadness in his expression. "Sorry, could that be considered an occupational hazard?"

Shay opted for a subject change. "Speaking of your occupation—rumor has it you've been helping Caleb with some of his cases."

Jonah nodded, his lips forming a smile that trembled with laughter. "I have. And I thought my job in Chicago was a challenge."

Shay grinned. "I also heard that you might be handling Gary and Ingrid's divorce."

His brows dipped down into a scowl. "What? No...not exactly."

Gary and Ingrid's solid marriage was the stuff of legend, until a few weeks ago when somehow things had turned sharply south. There were rumors that Gary had given Lucille Croft a ride on his four-wheeler. Such behavior could be construed as a courting gesture in Rankins. And Shay knew how much Ingrid disliked Lucille—she'd tried to steal Gary away from her back in high school in a similar incident involving Gary's motorcycle. Lucille's car had "broken down" and Gary had come upon the "stranded" Lucille and given her a ride. As it turned out, Lucille had set the whole thing up.

Lucille's plan had gone awry when Gary had swung by Ingrid's house. Gary had pulled in with a smug Lucille clinging to his back like a spider monkey. Ingrid's father ran the garage in town and Ingrid knew everything about cars, so Gary, in an unfortunate case of mancluelessness, asked Ingrid if she would, after he dropped Lucille off at her house, go back and take a look at the car with him.

Ingrid had agreed, but the couple had nearly broken up over the whole business. After a cursory inspection, Ingrid had asked Gary why he hadn't checked out the car before allowing Lucille to treat him and his motorcycle like a jungle gym? Any moron could see that Lucille had disconnected a battery cable. Allegedly Gary had fallen prey to Lucille's desperate machinations once again.

Shay had been on Ingrid's side then and she tended to suspect, if the rumors were true, that she would be this time as well. Men could be so oblivious sometimes.

"So they're not getting divorced?"

"Attorney-client privilege prevents me from commenting further."

"Jonah, you know I would never—"

He silenced her with a wink. "I'm kidding. I know how close-mouthed you are, Shay. We are talking. They are talking. Working some things out. They are coming back in to the office and I'm hopeful. Of all the couples in Rankins that I most want to see make it—Gary and Ingrid are at the top of the list."

Shay gazed at him warily.

"Why are you looking at me like that? They've always been great together and now they have three children. Plus, I have very fond memories of their wedding reception. That whole day was pretty much perfect."

Something hitched almost painfully in her chest. "What?"

"Shay, why do you always seem so shocked when I bring up a happy memory from our relationship? Am I not allowed to talk about the good times we had? We were friends forever, until we started dating and then we were together for five years. That's a lot of memories for me—all my best ones in fact."

His voice was gentle now. "And you can't just wish them away because of what happened… after."

She stared at him, thinking… She did do that. Why did she do that? Because the memories hurt, that's why. But she realized that she needed to get a handle on that pain if she was ever going to truly get over him.

So she dredged up a smile and said, "Remember how those stupid heels I wore were killing my feet? You finally plucked them off my feet and threw them into the bay because you wanted to dance? At first I felt weird but then other women started taking their shoes off, too. But then you had to carry me all the way to your house where we'd left your pickup." She laughed at the memory and it felt good—genuine.

Jonah winced. "I remember, my *back* remembers. You're not exactly a feather, Shay.

And I never should have let you have that second piece of cake."

"Jonah." She scowled playfully.

"I'm kidding, and you know it." He lifted his hands in a gesture of surrender and the sound of his laughter nearly stopped her heart. "I could carry you to Anchorage and back. Seriously, Gary and Ingrid's reception was hands down one of the best nights of my entire life. That whole day was."

"Mine, too," she said, but barely heard the words come out of her mouth because they seemed to have such precious little air to propel them.

"Can we talk about some things, Shay? About what happened with us? About what went wrong?"

"Come on, Doc. It's a solid plan."

Doc rocked back on his heels and then forward onto his toes. "Nothing about this scheme of yours is solid, Caleb. Look at them over there, right now. They seem to be fighting."

Caleb grinned and leaned against the polished stone wall in the lobby of the Faraway Inn, flecks of mica and quartz sparkled among the assortment of stones. The wall was one of Shay's new additions to the inn and probably his favorite—that or those gorgeous carved beams in the dining room. Normally he'd take a minute or two to admire the stones and the craftsmanship, but not now. His focus was on the couple standing near the hostess station—waiting for him and Doc.

"I know. I was thinking the same thing. Isn't it great? Nothing like a good argument with a woman to get the blood flowing."

"That's not—"

"I'm right about that, Doc, and you can't deny it."

Doc's face evolved into a silly grin and Caleb knew his friend was thinking about his late wife, Ruth. Bickering had been their love language.

Caleb took another peek at his grandson and Shay. Jonah stood closer than a man normally would to a woman and Shay had this way of tipping her head when he was talking, like he was the most interesting person in the world. Although right now she looked mad enough to spit and Jonah was gesturing with his hands like he did when he was trying to really hammer a point home.

Shay adjusted her stance and glared up at Jonah, reminding Caleb of some kind of fierce female gladiator from ancient times. Jonah threw his hands up in surrender.

Caleb chuckled. "Do you see that, Doc? That girl is nearly as feisty as Gus was and twice as smart. There's a spark between those two that has never been extinguished. And we need to fan that spark back into a flame if these two stubborn youngsters are going to have any chance at a happy future. They're both miserable and neither one of them knows why—or refuses to admit why."

"You'd better be sure about this, Caleb. And I wish you'd quit saying 'we' like I've been in on this from the start."

"I am—and you have been."

"Well, she looks like she's about ready to set him on fire so I guess you may be right about that spark at least to some degree."

"A spark is a precious gift and you can't make one where one doesn't exist."

"Boy, do I know that."

Caleb could sense he was winning him over so he tried to ensure Doc's commitment. Was it fair to play the Ruth card? Maybe not, but Caleb needed all the help he could get.

"Imagine how your life would have turned out, Doc, if I hadn't meddled where you and Ruth were concerned."

Doc grinned, a fresh look of nostalgia transforming his troubled brow. Caleb had set Doc and Ruth up on their first date.

"That's true enough."

"Darn straight, now let's go over there and do this."

Doc nodded. "Fine. I've come this far. Shay probably wouldn't believe that I haven't been in on this the whole time anyway."

"I hate to point it out—once again—but you have, in fact, been in on it the whole time."

"Not… Reluctantly!" Doc sputtered. "And I never agreed to anything this extreme."

"Said the accomplice right before the judge sentenced him to twenty to life," Caleb rebutted and then added a satisfied chuckle.

JONAH WATCHED SHAY'S expression as she contemplated his request.

Then her face broke into that heart-stopping smile and for a split second Jonah remembered what it was like to feel that all was right in the world.

But the smile wasn't for him he quickly realized as Doc and Gramps joined them.

Shay asked, "What kind of trouble have you two gentlemen been getting into?"

Doc grinned.

Gramps replied, "We're still hoping to get into some."

Doc nodded toward Caleb. "You know me, kiddo—I wouldn't get into any trouble at all, ever, if it weren't for this good-for-nothing hack I can't seem to shake."

"Bah," Gramps sputtered. "You'd sit in your recliner all day reading medical journals if it wasn't for me."

Doc shrugged like this was a possibility and they all laughed.

"Remember how we were talking the other day about going fishing, Jonah?"

"Of course, Gramps. Did you two plan something?"

"We did. You, me, Shay, Doc—we're heading up the Opal. Like old times."

"What?" Jonah and Shay said at the same time.

Gramps brought his hands up and slapped them together once, hard. "Isn't this great news? I bought a three-day trip with Bering's outfit at the Rotary fundraiser months ago. Called Bering—he had a cancellation, so I booked it!"

"The Opal River? Gramps, are you sure you're up to that?"

"I'm not dead yet, Jonah."

Jonah rubbed a hand across the back of his

neck. "I wish you would stop talking about dying."

"Why? We've all gotta go at some point." Caleb chuckled and then looked eagerly at Shay. "Any chance you could take the time off, Shay? I'd, uh, I'd sure like a couple days of not worrying about this whole…thing, you know? Before my appointment and the heart doctor tells me something crazy like I can never fish again. With Agnes's passing and all I just have this craving to do all the living I can."

Jonah rolled his eyes. "Gramps, he's not going to tell you that you can never fish again. Why would he do that? Fishing is not exactly high-impact cardio."

"Doctors do a lot of weird stuff, Jonah. Trust me on this one." He angled his head and flipped a thumb toward Doc.

Doc shot Caleb a scowl. "Do you want me to start with the attorney jokes?"

"Oh, no!" Caleb exclaimed. "No one wants to hear one of your corny—"

"I haven't heard one for a while," Shay interrupted eagerly.

Caleb groaned.

Doc perked up. "How does an attorney sleep at night?"

Shay shook her head, already grinning. "I don't know."

"First he lies on one side—then he lies on the other." Doc bent at the waist and laughed hard at his own joke, his belly shaking like a trimmer, but every bit a jolly version of Santa.

Jonah and Shay laughed while Caleb tried to smother a chuckle, which earned more laughter.

Caleb admitted, "That's actually a pretty funny one, Doc, did you make that up?"

Shay was grinning from one incorrigible would-be comic to the other, and Jonah doubted she'd be able to resist Caleb's boyish eagerness or his emotional plea. Not to mention Doc's seemingly endless supply of attorney jokes. Jonah glanced around at the cheerful, enthusiastic group and wondered how in the world he was going to manage this.

Right now, two of the worst things he could dream up were happening to the two most important people in his life. Gramps was ill and Shay's livelihood was being threatened by a stranger claiming to be her cousin and he couldn't even tell her. How was he supposed to go fishing for three days and act like everything was fine?

Although, he did want to clear the air between them: he wanted to talk about their broken engagement, the miscarriage, the decisions they had both made… Maybe this trip would at least allow him the opportunity to do some of that.

SHAY DID A mental calculation. This trip up the Opal River would mean three days away from the inn. Now that they had more hands in the restaurant, Hannah could handle the business if she were to agree. The new employees were working out well and Adele had been a godsend. She and Hannah had seemed to really hit it off and she'd been taking on significant tasks at the restaurant without Shay even having to ask. She'd even streamlined the order pickup procedure for the servers and somehow managed to not anger Javier in the process.

Shay hadn't taken a day off in so long she couldn't even remember, and she hadn't been away in forever. Sure, she took hours here and there—the occasional breakfast or lunch date, or a gathering at her parents' house, but to be away from the inn in the midst of the busy season and out of touch for more than twenty-four hours? She couldn't recall that ever happening.

To see Caleb this excited about something made the invitation so tempting. His enthusiasm gave her hope and quelled her anxiety, and that was what she needed right now—what they all probably needed. Even though the idea of being there with Jonah made her heart hurt with a particularly sharp pain; the Opal River was a special place for them. But maybe this could be part of her healing process, too. She just hoped Tag didn't somehow get wind of the excursion before they left.

"When is this trip?" she asked.

"A week from this coming Sunday."

Shay looked at her phone and clicked on her calendar; no high-maintenance guests coming in those days that she knew about, no major events happening at the inn or the restaurant, and apart from Story Fair there was nothing immediately pressing in her personal life either. Not that there ever really was.

The timing seemed almost too perfect. A part of her wanted to jump in and say yes for Caleb's sake, but the cautious, ever-present, put-the-inn-first businesswoman in her knew she needed to think it over before she committed, talk to Hannah, and maybe have a private conversation with Doc to assure herself that the physical exertion wouldn't be too much for Caleb.

"It sounds like a blast. Let me see what I can do with my schedule."

Caleb was grinning like a kid who'd just been told that a trip to the toy store may be on the horizon. Doc seemed rather pleased about the idea as well. And Jonah…? Jonah she couldn't quite read.

CHAPTER NINE

SHAY FELT THE REALITY sink in that this would be the first year Agnes wasn't front and center at Rankins' Story Fair—chatting and mingling with the kids, directing volunteers, and just generally ensuring that all was running smoothly. Shay knew that Agnes would want her to carry on, so she put on a brave face, adjusted her elaborately coiffed blond wig, and stepped into the crowd.

It wasn't difficult to muster a true smile when she heard the giggles and excited voices of so many children participating in games, crafts, puppet shows and other story-themed activities while trying to decide which books to choose.

There were tables and tables full of books, and every child who attended up to the age of eighteen could choose a free one. Additional books could be purchased at a highly discounted rate.

Shay worked her way through the crowd,

greeting kids and parents alike. She spotted Janie dressed as her fairy godmother across the room. She lifted a white-gloved hand and executed her best royal wave. They were working the Cinderella-story booth together.

She had several minutes before her first volunteer shift began so she headed in the direction of the concessions, where her mom was in charge. She almost ran into her new waitress. Adele wore a brocade gown and a long veil pulled upward so the tulle stretched over her head and streamed down her back almost to the floor. She held a cup of a steaming, spicy-smelling liquid in each hand.

"Adele? Hi, what are you doing here?" Shay didn't remember seeing her name on the volunteer list. Besides, the schedule had been filled weeks ago, before Adele had even arrived in Rankins.

"Oh, Shay, hi. I came with Hannah. She's working the booth over there with the knights and dragons." Adele tipped her head to the left.

Shay spotted Hannah in the preschool castle, dancing in her blue-and-green-scaled dragon costume. Hannah took the hands of a miniature princess in a sparkling silver-and-blue dress and twirled her around. The little girl giggled wildly.

"Your mom is at the concession area and Hannah and I stopped by there to say hello. She seemed stressed because someone called in sick, so I volunteered to fill in. She found me this costume and now I'm on my way to deliver this, um, grog and then head over to the young adult section."

"That's awesome, Adele. Thank you for helping out."

Adele smiled and Shay was struck with the thought that some of the heaviness surrounding her seemed to have lifted over the last couple weeks.

"Hannah told me you started this whole thing—Story Fair?"

Shay looked around cheerfully. "Yes, eight years ago with a friend of mine, Agnes Garner. She recently passed away, so this year is kind of tough."

"I'm so sorry for your loss. But this is an amazing legacy for her—for both of you. It's just…incredible."

Shay liked that thought. "Thank you, Adele. I can't tell you how much that means to me to hear that right now. But the support from the community and volunteers like you is amazing, too. Books can change lives, and there's nothing like a room full of happy kids to put life in perspective, right? To make us realize and appreciate what's really important?"

Adele stared back at her blankly.

"Adele, are you okay?"

"Oh, yeah. I was just thinking."

Shay reached out and placed a hand on one of her puffy sleeves. "If you ever need to talk about anything my door is always open. And I don't care how busy it appears that I am. I can always make time."

"Thanks, Shay. I might…I will actually… take you up on that one of these days. You are so lucky. Your family is the best."

Shay waved a hand carelessly through the air. "Just wait till you get to know us a little better. We've got plenty of our own crazy."

Adele chuckled. "I don't know about that. All I know is that you gave me a job and Hannah helped me find a place to live. Your brother, Tag, fixed my car yesterday and your mom just invited me over for dinner… I mean…"

"Ah, yes, that's something you should know if you're going to be hanging around the James family, Adele. We like to gather and eat—a lot. It's one of the ways we show affection and the main reason I don't have the body of a supermodel." Shay joked and patted her hips.

Adele smiled but Shay thought she saw sadness there, too. She wondered again what this woman had been through in her young life.

"Where are you headed with that—what did you call it?"

"Your mom called it grog, but I hope there's no alcohol in it. I've seen kids drinking it. I'm dropping it off for your dad and brother who are in the puppet booth."

Shay laughed and reached out to relieve her of one of the cups. "No, no alcohol. I think it's just spiced cider, but don't tell Mom I said that. She *really* gets into the spirit of the theme. Come on, I'll walk with you."

They began heading toward the opposite side of the room.

Adele said, "Seriously…I don't know how I'll every repay you all."

Shay shrugged, carefully trying to navigate through the crowd. "I'm glad I have the means to help and honestly, Adele, you've been a treasure to have in the restaurant. Please don't let Tess at the Cozy Caribou lure you away."

"You don't have anything to worry about there—I love the Faraway Inn and I love my job, but I wasn't talking about that. You guys all seem so kind and so…honest."

Shay grinned. "Well, lucky for all of us in this world, kindness isn't something you have to repay. You just pass it on, right? At least I think that's the way it should work."

They arrived at the puppet venue and dropped off the drinks for her dad and Tag. They all visited for a few minutes and then Shay pointed at a group of tiara-wearing pre-teens giggling around a table covered with books.

"That's your spot, Adele. And there's a crowd of five- and six-year-olds waiting to decorate their glass slippers—which are actually made of plastic but we won't tell them that. So we'd better get going."

Adele nodded happily. "I'm looking forward to it."

"Maybe you and I and Hannah can hook up later for a mug of that grog?"

JONAH COULDN'T GET Gary and Ingrid Watte out of his mind. The issue between them seemed so silly, like a simple misunderstanding that should resolve itself. And yet, he knew that sometimes these were the kinds of circumstances that could spiral out of control, stir up other issues, and ultimately end a relationship. One hurt led to another and another until it was too late to salvage.

These thoughts were what prompted him to accept their barbecue invitation. It had been one of those "Hey, you should come over because we're grilling on Friday" kinds of invitations. He knew he wouldn't be expected, yet he also knew he would be welcome.

He liked that about Rankins, he realized, that the company and the camaraderie were more important than the event itself, unlike the business dinners and fundraisers he regularly attended back in Chicago.

He swung by the store and picked up a half-case of a popular Alaskan micro-brew and two family-sized bags of chips.

"Jonah!" Gary met him out in the yard, holding a giant set of tongs and wearing an apron that read, Me Grill. You Eat. "So glad you could make it. How do you like your burger? Crack me open one of those Grizzly Quake brews."

Jonah did as requested, chatted for a few minutes, then carried the chips inside. He greeted several people he knew from high school with a promise to do some catching up after he delivered the snacks he'd brought. He found Ingrid in the kitchen, visited briefly, and then placed the chips on the table with a few other bags. He grabbed a handful of chips and turned to make his way outside where people seemed to be gathering.

A tiny blonde girl with pretty blue-green eyes and a bright pink T-shirt stood blocking his path. She appeared to be eyeing him intently.

"Hi, I'm Izzy."

Jonah brushed his fingers on his jeans and stuck out a hand. "Nice to meet you, Izzy. I'm Jonah." She looked surprised by the gesture but wrapped her delicate little fingers around his and gave his hand a firm shake.

Then she giggled and Jonah felt his heart begin to melt.

"Are you friends with my mom and dad?"

"I don't know—who are your mom and dad?"

"Ingrid and Gary Watte. My brother's name is Jake and our baby sister is Erin."

"Well, then, yes, I am. I went to school with your mom and dad."

"That must have been a *looong* time ago."

"It was." Jonah responded solemnly, resisting the urge to laugh.

She nodded like he'd passed an important test. Then she gestured out the window where a bunch of kids were playing a game of bean bag toss in the yard. "Do you know how to play that game?"

Jonah nodded. "I do, indeed. It's been a while, however, so I may be a little rusty."

"That's okay," she said splaying out all ten fingers in an attempt to reassure him. "It doesn't matter if you're not good because you're big."

Jonah tried not to smile as she imparted this puzzling bit of logic. He nodded, hoping for clarification.

"The other kids said I couldn't play because I was too little and I don't have a partner. But no one will be my partner because I'm little and I can't throw the bean bags very far. But if you will be on my team then I know they'll let me play."

Jonah grinned. He'd heard high-priced attorneys with arguments much less compelling. "Well, Miss Izzy, what do you say we go challenge the winner of the next game?"

She executed a little leap of excitement and her face erupted into a smile of pure joy. And Jonah couldn't remember the last time he'd made another person so happy—or felt that way himself.

A FEW NIGHTS LATER Shay walked into the Rankins High School gymnasium with Janie's two oldest boys, Gareth and Reagan. Their

heads collectively snapped around in amaze-
ment—all three of them silently absorbing the
incredible scene.

Emily had transformed the gym into a movie
theater.

An enormous white screen hung suspended
from the ceiling at one end of the room. Shay
recognized the music streaming clear and crisp
from the speakers as the theme song from the
fantasy blockbuster that would be kicking off
the first of Rankins' "Summer Movie Mad-
ness" series.

A crowd was gathered around the snack bar
at the far end of the gym and the hot buttery
smell of fresh popcorn filled the air. They took
a slight step up and Shay immediately looked
down as the floor beneath them began squish-
ing softly with every step. There was a layer
of green canvas covering the padding so she
couldn't be sure what the material was, but
it certainly made the idea of lounging on the
gym floor for the evening quite a bit more ap-
pealing.

Blankets already lay like patchwork across
the gym floor. Several rows of portable movie-
theater-style seats, complete with cup holders,
had also been set up along one edge of the gym

for those patrons who might not relish an evening of camping out on the floor, padding or no.

Excitement seemed to fill the air and Shay knew Emily would be thrilled with the turnout for her latest venture to raise money for a community center and pool.

Emily rushed over to greet them. "Hey! I'm so glad you guys made it."

"Em, this is spectacular. I don't know how you can still surprise me after all this time, but…wow." Shay had first met Emily when she had been working for Cam-Field Oil & Mineral. She had come to Rankins with the intention of developing its oil resources—and the town along with them. Emily's campaign to win the town favor was the stuff of legend. Thankfully, she'd fallen in love with Shay's cousin Bering and the town of Rankins right along with him.

A few minutes later Shay was lounging on the fleece blanket she'd brought, while Emily gave Gareth and Reagan the deluxe tour. She closed her eyes, grateful for a moment of peace, when a familiar voice pierced her contentment.

"Pretty cool, huh? This is not something I ever expected to do in Rankins—go to the movies."

Her pulse quickened and she lay there wondering how just the sound of his voice could cause her body to react like this. Shay opened her eyes and pushed up to rest on her elbows.

"Jonah, what are you doing here?"

He gestured at the kids flanking him, both of whom were grinning from ear to ear. "We're here for the movie."

The Watte kids? Jonah was babysitting? Her spirits sank at the reminder of Gary and Ingrid's possible split.

She sat up and greeted the kids with a bright smile, determined not to let them see her concern.

"Iz, if you're going to be driving at your age your parents need to talk to you about picking up hitchhikers." She pointed a thumb at Jonah. "It's not safe and this guy looks shady. He could be out to steal your popcorn. Heck, he could steal all of our popcorn."

"Shay," Izzy drawled with a giggle, "this is our babysitter Jonah."

Shay put on a skeptical face and made a show of surveying Jonah up and down. "Well, if you say so, but I'm not sharing my popcorn with him."

"You should see him play bean-bag toss, Shay. We were the champs!"

"Bean-bag toss? Really?"

"A barbecue at Gary and Ingrid's," Jonah explained.

Shay and Jonah used to be virtually unbeatable as partners at the bean-bag-toss game. They exchanged smiles, but before Shay could comment, Gareth and Reagan returned full of excitement at the technology Emily had managed to secure for the evening's show—some kind of fancy projector and a state-of-the-art sound system.

Shay handed Gareth some money. "You guys want to head over to the snack bar and get us set up? Don't be shy with the butter on the popcorn."

"Jake and Izzy, you guys want to come?" Gareth asked.

They looked at Jonah for permission and he was already reaching for his wallet. He handed Jake some bills.

"Do you want us to bring you anything, Jonah?" Jake asked.

He quirked a brow at Shay. "Licorice?"

"Um…sure," she said.

She couldn't quite meet his eyes, choosing instead to stay focused on the kids. "You guys, stay together, okay?" She had to say the words even though she knew they would be perfectly safe in this theater wonderland that Emily had somehow managed to create.

Jonah lowered himself onto the blanket beside her. His voice was soft. "I never look at a piece of licorice without thinking about you. Still your favorite candy?"

"Still my favorite candy," she answered flatly, trying to ignore the flutter in her chest. She didn't want him remembering her favorite candy. Arrogant, selfish, materialistic Jonah she could handle. She could even manage bitter and sarcastic Jonah. Kind and thoughtful Jonah was too much like Old Jonah, and Old Jonah, she reminded herself, was dangerous.

He leaned back on an elbow.

"Interesting…both of us here with borrowed children."

Shay's eyes darted to his and her heart began to pound. Such a seemingly casual statement— did he mean it to sound that way or was he leading up to something? She wasn't going to fish around and find out because she didn't want to instigate a discussion about their past.

"What prompted this?" She bobbed her head toward the kids.

He let out a chuckle. "Actually, I volunteered. I was at Gary and Ingrid's and they were trying to figure out how they were going to be in two places at once. Gary got called in to work and someone needed to stay home with the baby, who has an ear infection. Ingrid was the obvious choice there. And hey, I love this movie."

"I can't picture you going to the movies in Chicago."

One side of his mouth lifted as he asked, "What do you picture me doing in Chicago?"

"Interrogating people, driving around in your expensive car, playing golf, counting stacks of money…"

The other side joined it in a smile. "I get paid to do that stuff—except for the driving. Although, sometimes I get paid for that, too. But I need something to do with my spare time."

"I don't picture you having much of that."

"That's kind of true. I don't. I wouldn't mind having a little more, especially for stuff like this."

His eyes met hers and Shay's pulse kicked up again. She kept her gaze focused across the gym, refusing to get caught up in that superhero stare of his.

"And I have to confess that there is not much that little Miss Izzy could ask of me that I would deny."

Shay grinned. "She's something else, isn't she?"

Jonah glanced around to make sure no one was listening. "She certainly is. They are such great kids. I can't stand to think about what a divorce would do…"

His discretion didn't surprise her but his concern did. Jonah babysitting and worrying about what a divorce would do to these three children he'd only recently met?

She watched a muscle twitch in his jaw. "That's great, Jonah." She forced out the words and knew she sounded awkward. "It's really nice of you—it's just…"

"I know," he said tightly. "Surprising, right? Shay, I don't think I'm as bad as you think I am."

"I've never said you were bad, Jonah."

"I know, just an arrogant, selfish, materialistic, self-centered, money-obsessed attorney whose priorities are all screwed up."

Shay's cheeks reddened. His quote was uncomfortably accurate. She wasn't proud of the way she'd lost her temper during their conversation two years ago.

"Jonah, I shouldn't have—"

"And just for the record, while I do love my car, I don't love it more than I love Gramps."

Had she also said that? Yes, she had. Wow… that was mean.

"Okay, for *that* I owe you an extra apology," Shay said. "It was out of line. I was angry."

"We both were, Shay."

She could feel his blue eyes studying her. There was something different about how he was looking at her now—softer, kinder, less animosity—and there was some heat there, too. What was going on?

"You may have been right about some of the things you said… Gary and Ingrid, this whole thing with Gramps, Agnes's death, and Hannah actually said some things while we were playing bingo. It's all got me thinking."

"About what?"

"About what's really important in life, I guess. Family, relationships…" He swallowed and tipped his chin up for a few seconds, but then his eyes shifted back to her face.

Don't say it, she pleaded with him silently. *Please, don't say it.*

"Children," he added in a quiet voice, pinning her with his stare.

She stared at him as tears clouded her eyes. She didn't speak. She couldn't speak. Her heart was in her throat and it felt as raw and painful and as damaged as if the miscarriage had happened yesterday and not ten years ago.

She stared at the white screen, waiting for

a picture, not wanting to talk about the child they'd almost had—not wanting to talk at all, but unable to stop herself from making the comparison between that stark blank screen and her childless life—her childless future.

"Shay, I think we need to talk about what happened."

Just the thought of having that conversation terrified her. She didn't want to talk about it because she didn't want Jonah to know everything.

"Well, that's not going to happen tonight, Jonah. The kids are on the way back." It was difficult to smile and hold back tears at the same time. "Apparently bad timing is our thing."

The look of concern and sympathy on Jonah's face nearly did her in. She could only imagine what he would say if he found out she was unable to ever have children.

Shay dredged up a more genuine smile as the kids settled in, munching on popcorn and candy. She managed to talk and joke and make the kids laugh, but she felt relieved when the lights finally dimmed. She lay back on the blanket and stared up at the dark ceiling trying to find some snippet of that peace she'd been hoping this night would bring. But peace seemed futile with Jonah lounging beside her. She couldn't help but wonder if true peace between her and Jonah was even possible.

CHAPTER TEN

EARLY IN THE MORNING on the day of Agnes Garner's memorial a blanket of fog crept in from the ocean and shrouded the town of Rankins in a dull gray mist. This was fine with Shay because the sun made her happy and she was in no mood for happy this day. And to make an already difficult day even more trying, she had agreed to attend the service with Caleb and Jonah.

She'd stopped by Caleb's house the night before to drop off a casserole, relieved when she'd learned that Jonah was out for a run. She'd happily, guiltily made up an excuse not to stick around.

Caleb had walked her to the door. "So, we'll pick you up tomorrow morning at nine. Service doesn't start till ten, but I want to get to the church in time to get a seat. There's gonna be a full house."

Shay had found herself agreeing, and although she couldn't remember previously making plans to attend with Caleb, it wouldn't be an odd thing for her to do under normal circumstances. Clearly the stress was getting to her, and the circumstances didn't matter because here she was, walking into the Rankins First Baptist Church with Caleb and Jonah.

Light filtered through the stained-glass windows set into the church's thick walls, turning the sanctuary into a kaleidoscope of color. They walked down the wide center aisle, a row of hand-crafted wooden pews on either side of them.

Some of Shay's family had already arrived; Tag and Hannah were seated next to their parents, Ben and Margaret, along with Bering and Janie's mom, Claire. Janie and the boys were getting settled in the pew behind them, so Shay, Jonah, and Caleb filed in next to her.

As Caleb predicted, by the time the hour rolled around for the service to start the church was overflowing. Shay braced herself as Pastor Brock began to speak. He was always eloquent, and because he'd known Agnes well, she knew the tribute would be especially heart-wrenching. He described Agnes's generous nature and seemingly endless contributions to the community and Shay could hear the sniffles and sobs from the crowd around her.

There was a moment of lightness when Pastor Brock told the story of how Agnes had single-handedly—well, at first it had been single-handed, but then she'd inspired nearly the entire community to get behind the attempt to capture and spay the feral cat population. The vet, Ned Dobbins, had ended up with cat scratch fever and police chief, Ricky Grade, had reeked of mink stench for days after he'd crawled under the roots of a large tree along the river's edge at Agnes's urging in search of a family of tiny brown kittens.

But even this story filled Shay with nearly unbearable sadness. She knew she had a problem. She knew her fear of death was irrational—like her fear of fire. She wished she could get a better grip on death—more acceptance of loss. Loss was inevitable, something she couldn't control, and she knew what Caleb had said the other day was true—they all had to go some time. But she didn't fear her own death—it was losing her loved ones that filled her with icy cold terror. Shay wasn't sure which was worse—the drawn out passing of a loved one or the sudden, tragic loss. Agnes had been ill for months so when she'd finally passed away it had generally been considered a blessing. Grandpa Gus had suffered a brain aneurysm and died almost instantly. The shock of his sudden death combined with the loss had been overwhelming.

There were so many things she'd wished she could have said to him, time that she had planned to spend. Shay had been able to say goodbye to Agnes, and Agnes had had some time to cherish those last days before she became too ill and slipped into a coma. But sometimes people didn't have enough time to prepare—like her grandpa, Jonah's parents, Janie's husband, Cal, who'd been killed in a logging accident while she was pregnant with the twins.

She inhaled deeply and studied the lovely program she'd been gripping tightly in her lap. The thick paper was colored in light shades of blue and mint green. She traced the photo of Agnes on the inside with her fingertip but couldn't bring herself to read the poem that Agnes's niece Chloe had written in her honor. Agnes hadn't been blessed with any children of her own, but had been close with her family. Like Shay.

Shay could only hope that when she died she had friends and family who loved her enough to miss her like this, too.

Her thoughts turned toward Caleb. The idea of losing him was agonizing. And Jonah… She couldn't help it—she wondered what he would do. She knew in her heart that he would have regrets about the time he hadn't spent with his grandfather. He'd lost his parents so tragically and at such a young age. Caleb was all he had left—and her of course.

Jonah would always have her; she realized that now as she sat in the church and mourned for Agnes and for all the cherished lives that had gone before her. She thought of their baby and knew this connection they shared could never be severed...

She couldn't stop herself from speculating about the tiny baby that she and Jonah might have had. Would their child have been a boy with his wavy black hair and mischievous smile or a girl with his striking blue eyes? Would it have had Jonah's intelligence and self-confidence or her compassion and quick temper?

She pressed her knuckles tightly against her mouth and stifled a sob. Why was she doing this to herself? She couldn't seem to stop thinking about what might have been. Was Jonah right that they needed to "talk" and tackle some of the issues between them? She pressed her feet to the floor, trying to dispel the urge she had to get up and bolt from the church. She needed to think about that…

She glanced up at Jonah and was shocked to see tears shimmering in his thick black lashes. His long fingers were spread out, lightly gripping the tops of his knees. She reached over and placed a hand over his, sensing that his thoughts had turned along the same line as hers. He threaded his fingers through hers and held on tight; Shay didn't even think of letting go.

And while her heart ached at this blatant display of Old Jonah, she was relieved, too. It was a side she was afraid he'd buried forever somewhere in that tall cold skyscraper in the city where he spent his life using the law to make money.

That was something she would never understand; how his career, his seemingly endless quest for wealth, could replace the basic human need for love, for family, and yes—for her.

After the service ended, they stood and Shay released his hand. She turned to exit the pew. Jonah stood close behind her and when his hand ran up her arm to the top of her shoulder a tremor sped through her. She turned to face him and he whispered her name and that's when she felt it…a familiar tingle in her chest—near her heart, reminding her once again of everything she had so loved about him.

Then the heat of his voice took over as he bent his head next to her ear and said softly, "I'm sorry, baby. I'm so sorry."

He wrapped his arms around her and held her tight. She thought her heart might shatter from the sweet and painful ache his embrace evoked. More sweet than painful, obviously, because she didn't make any move to let go. She just let him hold her while she cried into his chest, all over his expensive shirt and his lovely gray-and-purple tie.

After a while—probably too long—she snuffled out one last sob.

He gripped her shoulders and pulled away slightly so she could see his gorgeous blue eyes so filled with compassion and sorrow and...? She let the sight of him, the feel of his hand caressing her back comfort her—she let him comfort her—the way he used to do. He'd always been so good at that—making her believe that everything would be okay.

Finally, at the edge of her vision she saw people shuffling out of the church in that slow, heavy-footed way that they seemed only to do when leaving a church. But she wanted to stay in his arms forever...

Until he ruined it.

"Shay, we should talk about it."

She took a small step back, reeling from her emotions. "You might be right, Jonah, but I don't know if I want to…"

He looked encouraged by her semi-agreement and continued gently, "There are some things *I'd* like to say and I—"

Shay backed away and gestured around at the church and the remaining people. "Okay, but maybe not a good time right now, Jonah,"

He followed her gaze and seemed to realize where they were. "You're right, not now. Ugh, I really need to work on that timing thing, huh?"

Shay blew out a breath of relief and forced a smile.

"We are going to talk though," he said. The tone of his voice told her that to argue would be pointless; arguing was what he did for a living. "You know what I think?"

"What?" he returned hesitantly.

"I think we do need to go fishing."

He studied her face for a few seconds. His eyes remained tense and unwavering, but he went with the new topic.

"Yeah," he said, "I've actually been thinking that, too."

SHAY DESCENDED THE STAIRS two at a time down into the church basement toward the reception. She made a beeline through the crowd and relief flooded her at the sight of Janie, Emily and Laurel already seated at a round table in the corner. Was she fleeing from Jonah like a coward and seeking solace in the company of her friends? Yes, she was. And she was okay with that. She'd agreed to an eventual discussion at some later, unspecified time. That was the best she could do today.

Laurel stood as she approached and wrapped her arms around Shay for a long moment. She released her and said, "Shay, sweetie, we all know how much Agnes meant to you. Are you okay?"

Shay nodded. "Yep. Okay." Emily hugged her, too, then she sank down onto a chair and let out a sigh.

Emily reached over and squeezed her hand. Laurel handed her a tissue.

Shay exchanged a look with Janie, who was studying her with those intense, vigilant, best-friend-cousin eyes. Janie—the person who knew her better than anyone else in the world, except maybe for Tag, but Janie knew her differently. And maybe because she was a woman, and because she knew everything, and because she had suffered so much loss herself, Shay knew that Janie understood how painful this day was for her. And Shay knew that it was painful for her, too. She was thankful that she had these people—these incredible friends and family—in her life.

"Janie?"

"Yeah, sweetie?"

"Can I hold Finn?"

"Of course." Janie scooted forward and handed her the sleeping baby. Shay cuddled him close, inhaled his sweet baby scent and once again mourned her broken circle of life.

CHAPTER ELEVEN

SHAY SPENT THE remaining days leading up to the fishing trip telling herself she wasn't avoiding Jonah. She had a lot to prepare to be away from the inn for three days—and *with* him for that same amount of time. Thankfully, Hannah was on her best behavior and seemed to be absorbing all of her instructions.

"Okay, got it." Hannah tapped a finger on the list that Shay had printed out. She scribbled a note in the margin.

"Now, my turn—do you know when Mr. Konrad is checking out? He is such a pain in the..." She paused, clearly searching for an appropriate word. "Butt," she finally said. "Yesterday he told Penny that she was stupid because he asked where he could find some extra-large binder clips in town and she said she wasn't sure. She offered to call around for him, but he declined. He's such a jerk."

"He called her stupid?"

"I believe the words he used were 'I should

have known better than to ask advice from a simple hotel worker.'"

Shay shook her head in disgust. "I'll talk to Penny. I'm glad you brought him up though. Unfortunately, he's extended his stay through the week, so make sure every day that his special sheets are ready. And remind the maids that he doesn't like his room to be cleaned before ten and no later than noon."

Hannah made a face as she picked up a paper clip and twirled it in her fingers. "Why is he staying? The rest of the attorneys left ages ago. He doesn't even act like he enjoys it here—he complains about everything."

Shay reached over and patted Hannah's hand. "I've reached the conclusion over the years that some people just like to complain. But I believe he's staying because he fancies himself something of an amateur photographer. He wants to photograph some wildlife."

"What kind of wildlife photographer doesn't get out of bed before ten?"

Shay chuckled. "I know, and he keeps complaining that he hasn't seen anything. I gently suggested that he might want to get an earlier start, but he shooed me away. What else can I do?"

"Well, he'd better not cross me Shay, because I will take that camera of his and I will—"

"Ask him if there's anything you can do to make his stay more comfortable?" Shay smoothly finished her statement.

Hannah hesitated before they both let out a burst of laughter.

Then Hannah muttered, "What I have in mind would be anything but comfortable."

JONAH HAD MET with Gary and Ingrid three more times to discuss their "divorce," which had somehow turned into a series of amateur counseling sessions. He'd also joined the couple at their home for dinner on two additional occasions, where he'd fallen even deeper in love with their three kids.

That taste of their family dynamic had only fueled his belief that the couple belonged together.

"So," Gary said with Ingrid standing beside him, "we just stopped by to let you know we've made a decision."

Jonah found himself holding his breath. He'd done everything in his power to help the couple get over the "four-wheeler incident" as he'd taken to calling the unfortunate episode in his mind.

The event had happened pretty much as Shay

had heard. Gary and a group of friends had gone out riding four-wheelers. They'd come across Lucille and her friend who were also out for a ride. Lucille's four-wheeler had become stuck in the mud on the far side of a fast-running creek. Her friend was afraid she would also get stuck if she tried to retrieve Lucille. So Gary had given Lucille a ride across the creek on his new bulletproof-airless-tired wonder of an ATV.

No one seemed to know why Lucille had been wearing a dress.

"We're going to renew our wedding vows."

"Congratulations! You guys, this is so great." Jonah knew the smile on his face had to reflect both his happiness and his sincerity. He couldn't wait to see Shay's face when he relayed the news.

She'd been purposely staying out of his way and he'd been looking for an excuse to see her. The way she'd felt in his arms at the funeral, the sorrow he'd heard in her voice, had him believing that she needed someone. Not that he could ever be that someone but, maybe he could be that someone for a little while? At the very least, he could solve this matter with Adele Mason—*that* he could definitely do for her. He wanted to do that for her.

Plus, she'd agreed that they needed to talk…

"Jonah, thank you so much for everything. You know—if this law thing doesn't work out for you—you should consider marriage counseling."

He grinned. "Thank you, Ingrid. I'll keep that in mind. And remember—most of the time us guys really are just as dense as we seem."

Ingrid laughed as Gary pulled out his checkbook.

"Amen, to that. What do we owe you, Jonah?"

Jonah waved away the offer. "No way, Gary. Nothing. I won't take a dime even if you throw it at me. I billed you guys on Gramps's behalf for that initial consultation. The rest of this," he said, gesturing between them, "this is just… good stuff."

Gary started to argue. "Jonah, we can't possibly—"

"Please, seeing you guys back together is all the payment I need. And spending time with you two and your kids, I should be paying you."

Ingrid blushed.

Gary's chest puffed up like a male ptarmigan in the springtime. "You're good people, Jonah."

"Thanks, Gary. That means a lot. So are you both."

Jonah was overwhelmed with a kind of satisfaction he wasn't all that familiar with. He wasn't often called "good people" back in Chicago, in fact, never. And even though this wasn't exactly the kind of deed he had the opportunity to do in Chicago—this was definitely the kind that had him feeling like maybe he was more than an attorney.

The swoony-eyed couple shared a grin and some kind of nonverbal communication passed between them. They reached out and linked hands.

Ingrid spoke, "We, um, actually wanted to ask you something else, Jonah."

"Sure."

"Gary and I both think you're very articulate and so knowledgeable about life and relationships and—"

Jonah kept a straight face, but barely.

"—we'd love it if you would say a few words at the party. It's really going to be more of an anniversary celebration, no ceremony or anything, so maybe a short speech about love or something? We're going to do it at the end of summer on our anniversary."

Jonah was touched. "Absolutely. I'd be honored."

Hands were shaken and hugs were shared and a promise made to attend another barbecue the following week. After Gary and Ingrid left, Jonah sat grinning stupidly at Gramps's desk and tried to remember the last time he'd felt this good about his work. He was pretty sure the answer was never.

He watched out the window as the couple climbed into Gary's pickup and pulled away. There was almost nothing worse than knowing two people belonged together, but couldn't make a relationship work. He understood that better than anyone. Jonah suspected Gary and Ingrid would have found their way back eventually, but it felt good to think that he'd had even a small hand in their reconciliation.

Now all he could think about was telling Shay. He bolted up and jogged into the kitchen where Gramps was busy baking a batch of his oatmeal cookies. The smell of cinnamon stopped him in his tracks. He grabbed a cookie and ate it in two bites.

"These are excellent, Gramps. I'll be back in a little while, okay? I need to run an errand."

"Sure thing. Hey, can you stop at the store on your way home from the inn and pick up some milk?"

"Why would you...? Never mind. Yes, I'll get milk."

Jonah heard Gramps's chuckle as he grabbed three more cookies and hurried out the door.

JONAH PULLED OPEN the thick wooden door that led into the inn and looked around. The place was oddly quiet. There was no one at the front desk and he really didn't want to ring that crazy-loud bell and alert everyone that he was here.

Shay loved that bell. Her grandfather Gus had salvaged it after the fire had destroyed the original inn, taken the lives of his parents, and nearly killed him. The bell was one of a handful of objects recovered from the rubble.

A bout of nerves reminiscent of their college days surged within him as he walked toward Shay's office. Occasionally their busy schedules had kept them from seeing each other for a day or two and it had felt like torture to be away from her. But then finally, the time would come and he'd stop and buy her a flower or a package of licorice and show up at her apartment. That feeling of anticipation when he'd raise his hand to knock and know that in a matter of seconds her dimpled smile and sweet voice would be greeting him, telling him how much she'd missed him... Then she'd throw her arms around his neck and he'd kiss her senseless.

The door was open, but Hannah was seated behind the desk.

He tapped on the doorframe. "Hi, Hannah."

She glanced up, not seeming at all surprised to see him. "Hey, counselor. What's up?"

"Do you know where I can find Shay?"

"She's cleaning rooms. She should be finishing up right about now. The woman is a wonder. She can clean a room faster than I could ski the downhill course at Squaw Valley."

Jonah hesitated, not quite sure which way to go.

"Head along the hallway to the right." She pointed. "The supply room is at the end on the left. If she's not there, then she will be momentarily."

"Thanks, Hannah."

He turned to go, but then stopped. "Hannah?"

She looked up.

"You said something at bingo the other night that tells me you are already so much more than a skier. You are a very wise and thoughtful woman."

Hannah's face erupted with a surprised grin. "I am? Thanks, Jonah. That's so nice. Oh, and don't break my sister's heart again and I will let you live."

Shay was where she was expected to be, tucking tiny soaps and miniature bottles of shampoo into containers on the cart in front of her.

"Hey," he said.

She started and turned. "Jonah! Wow, you scared me."

"I'm sorry."—

"No, it's fine. Busy morning—one of our maids called in sick. But I'm just finishing up. What are you doing here?"

"I came by to tell you something."

She eyed him warily and her reaction felt like a little jab of pain to his heart. She still wasn't ready to talk. He was okay with that— for now—because he felt confident that deep down Shay wanted to resolve their issues as much as he did. His timing had to improve some time.

"It's good news."

She tipped her head, asking the question.

"Gary and Ingrid are back together."

Her guardedness fell away and her face lit with a smile. "Jonah, really?"

"Yep."

"This is wonderful news."

Her expression held a mixture of pride and approval, exactly the look he'd been after.

He returned her smile and felt a tug of affection flow through him at the pleasure shining in her eyes. He'd missed this. He missed her—this Shay, happy and smiling just for him. He slipped his hands in his back pockets to keep from touching her. Not only did he want to touch her, he wanted to kiss her until they were both senseless.

He leaned a shoulder against the doorframe. "Just thought you'd want to know."

"You're right—I do."

He searched his brain for something else to say to prolong the moment. He wasn't overly proud of his gratuitous self, but he asked anyway, "It is pretty great, right?"

"Jonah, it's very great."

He grinned some more. Was she feeling this, too? It took an unbelievable amount of self-control not to step toward her and take her in his arms. He just couldn't be sure that she would want that. Did he really want that? Yes, of course, he did, but he knew they needed to sort some stuff out first. He couldn't mess this up again.

Her lips were curling up at the corners, dimples flashing on her cheeks. "You came all the way up here to tell me this?"

"Yes, I did. That—and I'm craving some of

that fish with jam, as our friend Cricket keeps calling it. Would you like to join me for lunch, by any chance?"

A flash of anxiety crossed her face. "Uh…"

"No talking—I promise, no talking about anything that you don't want to talk about."

She beamed in relief. "Okay, then sure. I'm starving."

They cut through the yard, stopping for a few minutes to admire the koi, before continuing on into the dining area. As they passed the hostess station, Jonah was looking around, admiring the beauty of the inn, shameless in his contentment with how this day was turning out.

Then he spotted a figure serving a table in the middle of the room.

It couldn't be…

"Shay, who is that?" he managed to ask.

"Who?" Shay followed his gaze.

"Waiting on that table."

"Oh, that's Adele. She's the new waitress I was telling you about. She's fantastic. I don't know what I'd do without her right now. I don't think I'd be able to take this fishing trip, that's for sure."

Jonah fought valiantly for his usually reliable blank face, but failed obviously, because Shay asked, "What? Jonah, what is it?"

"Nothing," he replied after a few drawn-out seconds.

Shay was giving him an odd look, which he knew he deserved but Jonah couldn't think of any good reason why Adele Mason would seek a job at the Faraway Inn. He could however think of several nefarious ones.

She glanced at Adele Mason. "Does she look familiar to you, too? I swear she reminds me of someone."

He opened his mouth to respond but she said, "Come on, let's get a table. I'll introduce you."

Jonah trudged with her through the dining area. Shay made introductions and they sat at a table in front of the windows that showcased the incredible view, but Jonah couldn't even begin to enjoy the scenery.

Almost immediately Shay received a text. She apologized and excused herself saying she'd return in a few minutes. Jonah scanned the place for the "waitress," but Adele had apparently been waiting for the same opportunity because she was strolling toward the table, carrying a pitcher of water, two menus and an anxious smile.

He didn't waste any time. "Adele, what are you doing here?"

She placed the menus on the table. "Um,

working. I know it probably looks weird but it seemed like a good idea at the time and now I'm really—"

"How could this possibly seem like a good idea to you?" Adele had now put him in an even more awkward position than he'd already been in. It was bad enough that he couldn't reveal her identity to Shay, but now he had to pretend like he didn't know who she was in front of Shay?

Adele let out a nervous laugh. "Well, it's kind of funny actually… I didn't come here to get a job. I came here hoping to talk to Shay because she didn't return my phone calls. Then it just sort of happened."

"*What* happened?"

"Shay hiring me happened," she answered tentatively. .

Jonah put on his skeptical face. "How does getting hired for a job 'just happen'?"

"It's hard to explain. I…"

Jonah rubbed a frustrated hand over his jaw. "You know what? The circumstances don't matter. Can you not see how Shay—and the rest of the James family—might interpret this? Sneaking around and not revealing who you really are—or who you are claiming to be? Getting a job at the very place you are trying to get a piece of?"

"Claiming to be?" Adele looked shocked, like the notion had just occurred to her that her identity might be doubted.

Jonah didn't buy it. He shrugged. "I'm an attorney, Adele. It's in my nature to analyze every possibility. And if it's occurred to me, I can guarantee you it will occur to the Jameses."

"But I'm…I'm not some lowlife gold digger. And I'm not out to steal the inn from Shay. I only want…"

"You only want what? What are your intentions? And why haven't you revealed them or told anyone else who you claim to be?"

Adele gaped at him, started to respond, but clamped her mouth shut instead. She turned on her heel and strode away, leaving Jonah with an unfilled water glass and a simmering pot full of anger. He actually found himself hoping that she was simply interested in a big payday. Money he could handle.

A few minutes later Shay slid into her seat. "I saw you talking to Adele. Isn't she great?"

"Mmm," he answered noncommittally. "What do you know about her?"

Shay smoothed some brown hair that had come loose from her ponytail as she checked the list of specials that Adele had left on the table. "Not much really. Oh, yum, Javier is frying razor clams today. The breading he uses is so good—light with subtle seasoning so it doesn't overpower the flavor of the clams. That's what I'm having." She looked at Jonah again and grinned. "I hired her on the spot—no résumé or reference checks or anything. She said she had experience so I took a chance. It has totally paid off. She's the best waitress I've ever seen."

Jonah widened his eyes in disbelief. "Shay, why in the world would you do that?" He could hear the disapproval in his tone, but ignored it.

She blinked a couple times in surprise. Her brows dipped down between her eyes and Jonah wanted to reassure her. He didn't want to spoil this moment, but he was also dismayed by this tricky situation she had inadvertently wedged herself into.

While Adele Mason was learning everything she could about Shay, her family and the Faraway Inn, an unsuspecting Shay had opened her arms and heart wide open and invited her in.

Jonah hoped she took pains to keep her financial records secure. He'd noticed her laptop left open on her desk and he wondered how often she changed her passwords. "What do you mean?"

He couldn't say what he was really thinking

for fear of breaching the attorney-client privilege. He sighed in exasperation. "She could be a serial killer, Shay. This is Alaska—you've lived here your entire life. You should know better."

She let out a burst of surprised laughter. "A serial killer? Come on, Jonah, let's be real here. I do believe she has a story, but that's her business to share or not."

Jonah was so close to blurting out the truth. Too close. The only thing preventing him was the knowledge that he was Shay's best chance at thwarting whatever scheme it was that Adele Mason had hatched.

"I asked her if she was running from the law."

He let sarcasm absorb some of his angst. "Oh, perfect. Good job. That's great, because serial killers are notoriously honest as well as homicidal."

She tipped her head back and laughed.

Jonah was struck all over again by her beauty, which he knew had as much to do with her soul as it did her physical attributes. She just embodied kindness and such selfless, unabashed generosity. Too much generosity probably—why did she feel like she needed to take care of everyone? Who took care of her? He suspected no one had in a very long time, not since they'd broken up. Did he want that job again? Right now he thought he might.

She shook out her red-cloth napkin and placed it on her lap. "It's kind of sweet, that you're worried about me like this."

Jonah felt a jolt of emotion surge through him at the expression on her face. She was proud of him for helping Gary and Ingrid and now she was feeling all soft because she thought he was worried about her safety. Which he was, but keeping her safe from a serial killer might be easier than this legal undertaking brewing with Adele Mason.

She reached over and put her hand over his. "Jonah, look at what you just did for Gary and Ingrid. And for Will Traeger? Everyone knows he never would have won that case against the town. You saved him thousands of dollars— dollars that would have gone into your pocket.

"And what you're doing for your gramps? I do realize how difficult it must be for you to take this time away from your job—and your car." Her grin was full of teasing good will, and utterly adorable. "I know how important your career is to you. And even worse—you're stuck here in Rankins indefinitely, which I know you hate more than anything. I really admire what you've done—what you're doing. I'm proud of you, Jonah.

"Sometimes you simply know when something's the right thing to do. You can feel it. That's exactly how it was for me with Adele. I just…knew."

Jonah mumbled an agreement because all he could think about was the feel of Shay's warm skin on his, combined with the dazzling smile on her face and the fact that *she* was trying to reassure *him* that everything was going to be okay. He wanted to laugh and cry and kiss her all at the same time.

CHAPTER TWELVE

JONAH STUFFED THE rest of his gear into his tattered blue canvas backpack and asked himself how it could be possible that ten years had gone by since he'd taken the time to enjoy one of the things he most loved to do on this earth. Still, he wished he could be more excited about this trip.

It was four in the morning and he'd spent most of his restless night alternating his worry about Gramps, trying not to think about his own work in Chicago, while simultaneously fretting about Adele Mason's intentions.

And Shay.

Always, in the midst, or at the very center of all of these thoughts and concerns was Shay, and these feelings he had for her—feelings he'd always been able to somehow skirt around in Chicago. But now...

He wasn't in Chicago. Not even close.

"Gramps?" he called out. "Are you ready?"

Gramps trotted out of the bedroom with his

pack strapped on his back. He began bouncing on his toes and twisting his torso from side to side, testing the weight and fit.

"I can't tell you how ready I am, son. Bering said the fish have been biting like crazy."

Caleb had dropped Francis off the night before at Mary Beth's house so Jonah guessed they were ready to go. As ready as he could be for three days of…Shay.

"We're picking up Doc and Shay on the way, so we should probably get going. You know how prickly Bering gets if he's kept waiting."

"How do you have the energy to pace like that at four-thirty in the morning? You're going to be doing plenty of hiking in the next couple days, you might want to rest up." Hannah took a loud sip of her coffee. "Mmm, that's good."

Shay kept pacing. "Don't forget to pick up mom's cholesterol meds today. She took her last pill yesterday."

"I'm on it."

"Okay, and don't forget that Marcie doesn't like the chicken food, only the beef or salmon." Marcie was curled on Hannah's legs like a calico lap blanket. Two more cats were sprawled on the sofa near her.

"Yup." Hannah reached over to pet Roscoe.

"Shay, please don't worry. I've got it under control—meds, cats, koi, the inn, the restaurant—all of it."

"I know. Thank you, Hannah. I totally trust you, and…"

"You're freaked out about spending time with Jonah. That's what this is all about, right?"

"Yes and no."

"No, because…?"

"Things have gotten a little better between us…"

"Well, that's good. So, yes, because…?"

"He wants to talk. And I've agreed—sort of. I keep putting him off though because it won't really solve anything. Ergo, maybe we should just maintain the status quo."

"Yeah, that sounds superhealthy," Hannah said drily. "Keeping the past buried and all those emotions and issues tucked away where they belong. Good idea. That won't eat away at you at all."

Shay abruptly stopped pacing. A snort of panicked laughter came out her nose. "It is ridiculous." She smoothed both hands over her ponytailed hair. "I need to face this, don't I?"

Hannah met her eyes and responded with a simple, "Yes, Shay, you do."

Caleb's Land Rover pulled in the driveway, so

she thanked Hannah and hugged her good-bye, and went out to meet her ragtag fishing crew. A quick greeting, then Jonah stowed her pack as she climbed into the front seat. Caleb and Doc were already ensconced in the backseat like a couple of eager school kids on their way to a field trip, which made Shay smile. They were cheerful and kept up an entertaining stream of their usual chatter-bicker, a welcome reminder for Shay of why she was bouncing down the road away from civilization as she knew it and toward a three-day wilderness getaway with Jonah.

Jonah seemed quiet and thoughtful—like she felt.

When they arrived at the launching ground for James Guide and Outfitter Service, Shay let out a groan. Tag was standing next to the boat talking to Bering. She should have known better than to think she could get out of town with Jonah without Tag hearing about it.

As Caleb and Doc climbed from the vehicle, Jonah reached out a hand to halt her departure. "Why is your brother here?" His whispered tone was filled with a level of annoyance that matched her own.

"I have no idea, Jonah. That's not true—

I think we both have an idea. Get my stuff, please? I'll go talk to him."

She got out and marched toward Tag and Bering, while Jonah, Caleb and Doc gathered packs and gear.

"Mornin', Shay," Bering said cheerfully, without quite meeting her eyes.

"Good morning, Bering." She smiled too-sweetly at her cousin and then riveted her glare on Tag.

Her voice came out like a too-loud, bingo-type whisper; she hoped Caleb and Doc couldn't hear. "What are you doing here?"

"I'm, uh…I'm coming along to help Bering with some stuff."

"What stuff?" she demanded.

She nearly laughed at the look they exchanged—it hadn't changed much since they'd been caught reading her diary twenty years ago.

Bering answered, "Oh, uh, I've got a broken window in one of the cabins and Tag is going to help me fix it."

"Oh, puh-lease—you could have thought of something better than that. You didn't even bother to come up with a story, did you?" Shay looked at her traitorous cousin and then back at her meddling brother and wondered if these two would ever quit trying to protect her.

Tag gave up the charade, leaned over and said with a voice even more crisp than the morning air, "I will not let you take off into the wilderness with him—again. I made that mistake once, Shay, and it ended in disaster. Do you hear me? I won't. Do it. Again."

His eyes were almost as piercing as Jonah's and Shay could see the tightness in his jaw. She'd heard the determination in his voice.

But still, she had to try. "Tag, that was more than ten years ago. I'm a thirty-two-year-old woman who doesn't need my big brother to protect me anymore. And I wouldn't exactly call it a disaster, and this time we're not alone in case you haven't noticed."

"It doesn't matter," he said stubbornly and Shay knew that she would not win this argument with her big brother. "I made a promise to myself—and to you—ten years ago, and I'm keeping it."

She thought about negotiating like she'd done when they were younger, but it was too late; Jonah, Caleb and Doc were already approaching with their packs and gear.

SHAY DID LOVE to fish.

If there was anything that could snap her out of a funk, it was fishing. Even if the feeling didn't last, she was grateful for the respite. She couldn't think of another activity that equaled such a perfect mixture of relaxation and excitement. And when the fish were biting, like they had been today, there wasn't much in life that she enjoyed more.

The day's catch included king salmon, dolly vardon, grayling, whitefish and rainbow trout. After landing the largest trout, she opted for a break, to sit back and take in the scenery. The air was still cool but the sun was bright in the nearly cloudless sky.

She'd seen this gorge many times, but still marveled at how the river had managed to cut a path so dramatically through the mountains. The channel was narrower here, which caused the current to run faster. A hundred-foot-high wall of rock rose straight up out of the river on one side. Birds flitted in and out of the holes and ledges weathered into its face.

Shay adjusted her sunglasses and watched Caleb fight yet another monster on the end of his line. A flash of silver broke the water's surface and then disappeared again. He let out a whoop. She smiled. He and Doc were both clearly having a ball.

This made it all worthwhile she reminded herself—leaving the inn, camping with five men—one of whom she'd once been engaged to, and her over-protective brother who, silly as it was, blamed himself for Shay getting pregnant in the first place.

Tag had covered for her and Jonah. It was that simple; the reason for his guilt and this hyper-protective stunt. It had been a little later in the year, but with weather every bit as glorious, bright and sunny yet still plenty of morning coolness, when she and Jonah had taken off for a short camping trip.

They were celebrating. And they had so much to celebrate: they were engaged, they'd earned their undergraduate degrees—hers in business administration and his in pre-law. They'd come home to enjoy one last Alaskan summer—or what they'd believed would be their last summer at home for a long time before they eloped and moved to Connecticut together.

They'd both made excuses to their families about where they were really going for those three days. Jonah had told Gramps he was off to Glacier City to visit with a friend, and Shay had told her parents that she and Tag were flying to Anchorage to visit cousins and do some shopping.

She and Jonah had borrowed a boat from

Bering and disappeared up the Opal River for three nights. Tag had even flown to Anchorage alone to make their story believable. Shay wasn't sure there was anything that could have kept them apart at that point—camping unaccompanied in the wilderness or not.

By late afternoon on the present trip, they were approaching their stop, and Shay was beginning to worry about Caleb and the hike to the cabins. If he did have a heart problem, would the hike be too strenuous for him? What if he had a heart attack? At least they had Doc, and Tag was a paramedic. That was the first good reason she'd thought of for her brother coming along.

A short time later, Shay felt herself beginning to relax again. Caleb didn't seem to be struggling at all as they traveled along the trail. After a while Bering stopped so they could take a rest and drink some water.

Shay pulled her camera out of her pack and snapped a couple photos of Caleb and Doc. Then she walked a ways off the trail to check out the view. The light was stunning and perfect for some photographs.

"Bering," she called out. "I'm going to go along farther and take a few photos for our websites. Out on that bluff up there around the bend."

Bering raised a hand in acknowledgment. "Sounds good—it's been a while since you've been up here, Shay. I don't need to remind you that it's bear country, do I?"

Shay patted her side where the short-barreled .44 Ruger Blackhawk was secured in a shoulder holster under her zip-up sweatshirt. She gave him a thumbs-up.

"I'll go with her," Jonah volunteered.

Tag stood up and glowered. "No, I'll go."

Shay stalked off up the trail, not bothering to wait for either one of them.

TAG STARED JONAH down and then followed his sister.

Jonah took his exasperation out on Bering. "It's been ten years. Don't you think Tag could ease up a little? I mean I understand to a point, and I've always been patient about his anger with me. I get it—I'd be angry, too."

Bering adjusted his cap and looked over to where Caleb and Doc were seated on some rocks a good distance away talking and munching on trail mix.

"I'm not…sure."

"What?" Jonah asked.

Bering looked over Jonah's shoulder for a few seconds before he answered. "What's going on with you and Shay? Are you guys…"

Jonah started shaking his head. "No—nothing—I mean other than our combined interest in Gramps. And I guess we've kind of been working things out as much as we can. Shay refuses to talk about the past and I'm trying… but no, nothing like that, Bering. I would never make that mistake again—even though I don't believe that anything that happened between Shay and I was a mistake."

Bering nodded slowly. "I think Tag is worried that you'll break her heart again."

Why, Jonah wondered, in this tragic tale was it always he who had done all the breaking of hearts? Shay had had a choice in the matter, too, and she'd chosen the inn. She'd chosen her career just as much as Jonah had.

"I understand, but if things had happened differently, we'd be married right now with a few kids—probably eight or ten if Shay had had her choice."

Bering focused on the ground. He'd picked up a stick and began tapping it on the rock beside him. Jonah could tell he was figuring out what to say. Surely he couldn't agree with Tag?

"Tag's behavior is over the top, Bering. It's

comical, in fact." He let out a frustrated laugh and added, "No wonder she never dates."

Bering turned his face up toward the sky and muttered something. Then he sighed and looked in Jonah's direction. "Jonah, for pity's sake, man, Tag's protective big-brother thing is not the reason Shay doesn't date."

The tone of his voice, the tension in his body, told Jonah there was definitely something he was missing. But before he could ask for any more information, which he felt sure wouldn't be forthcoming anyway, Bering stood up, hurled the stick he'd been holding and strode away.

CALEB AND DOC watched Shay head up the trail with Tag following close behind.

"Is Tag going to ruin this whole thing, you think?" Caleb asked Doc as he munched on some tasty mix of almonds, dark chocolate and other unidentifiable nuggets that Doc had packed for them.

"I don't know, maybe." Doc glanced over to where Jonah and Bering were seated. "That boy is plum ticked at Jonah. You gotta give him credit for staying power though, right? Ten years is a long time to stay mad at someone."

"Well, he's got a reason."

"You're not supposed to know about that reason, remember?"

"I'm not an idiot, Doc."

"I'm beginning to think this scheme is idiotic."

"You've mentioned that already, you know? More than once in fact and it's been duly noted. So let's stay focused. Do you think I should say I don't feel well and then ask Tag to take me back to town?"

"No, I do not. You say that, and then we'll all be going back to town and I'm having a good time. Fishing was great today." Doc removed his camouflage bucket hat, smoothed a hand through his puff of unruly white hair, and then readjusted the hat on his head.

"Sure was," Caleb said with a grin. "I'm looking forward to seeing what we can catch tomorrow. I love fly fishing in these streams. I sure would like to hook another big grayling or two."

"No one would believe the size of that one you caught this morning if Shay didn't have that camera of hers. She sure is handy with that thing."

"Doc…I might have an idea."

Doc sighed wearily. "Now why doesn't that surprise me?"

THEY SOON CAUGHT up to Shay and Tag who were standing several feet off the trail near the edge of a cliff. Jonah could see why Shay had wanted to take some photos. The valley opened down below and the Opal River widened and flowed through a flat expanse of grass and vegetation. The trees were wearing too many shades of green to count and the river shimmered in the middle like the gem that shared its name. In the background, rocky snowcapped peaks reached up into the sky.

Jonah was relieved that neither Shay nor Tag appeared upset. Shay wore a smile as she looked down at her camera. Tag was munching on a candy bar.

"There's a nice bull moose in velvet down there, on this side of the river," Tag informed them in between bites.

Gramps and Doc moved in closer for a look. Tag pointed the moose out to them and handed Doc a pair of binoculars. They oohed and ahhed and talked about moose hunting for a while.

Gramps asked if Shay could take a photo of the whole group. She loved the idea, so she set the camera on a rock and set the self-timer. She hurried over to join the group and then they laughingly repeated the process. Caleb offered to take one of Shay and Bering with the view of the valley in the background.

Then Gramps spotted a bear.

No one happened to see the animal and Jonah could only pretend to act interested. Soon they were back on the trail.

THE DAY'S HIKE ultimately ended when they reached a small open meadow where two cozy-looking cabins awaited them. Bering had pushed on ahead earlier to prepare camp and the smoky scent of a campfire filled the air.

Jonah paused and forced himself to take a minute to appreciate the stunning setting. Summer days were so beautiful. A buzzing sound in his ear reminded him that they were also insect-filled. He reapplied some bug spray and went to stow his pack in the cabin he would be sharing with Gramps and Doc.

Then he headed toward the fire where the rest of the group was already gathered. Jonah could see what he assumed were potatoes already foil-wrapped and nestled among the coals. A pot of something simmering along with the heavenly scent of bacon teased his senses. Fresh fish had been cleaned, filleted and readied for frying. His stomach growled and he realized he was famished. He'd skipped lunch; he'd been distracted all afternoon by his conversation with Bering. Beyond his comment about Shay not dating, lurked a bigger question that for some reason Jonah had never considered—why hadn't Shay found someone else?

CHAPTER THIRTEEN

THE NEXT MORNING Shay pulled her hair back and quickly got ready for the day. She only needed her daypack as they would be fly-fishing up one of the tributaries that ran into the Opal River, eventually reaching a sub-alpine lake. They would be hiking back to the cabins in the evening to spend another night.

Shay looked forward to hiking and photographing the rough and spell-bindingly beautiful terrain almost as much as the fishing. There was something awe-inspiring about being this close to the jagged mountain peaks. There were wildflowers in the midst of their too-brief blooms that she only had the opportunity to see here on the slopes of these mountains.

When she emerged from her room, she wasn't surprised to find that both Bering and Tag were already up and out of the cabin she was sharing with them. She stepped outside and the heavenly scent of fresh-brewed coffee floating over from next door told her right where the guys would be.

She noticed Jonah sitting outside in a chair by the cold remains of last night's fire. He waved and something propelled her toward him.

He sipped from a steaming cup, and when she walked up he held it aloft in offering. A part of her wanted to decline. Sharing a cup—that felt like such an intimate gesture, yet another part of her said that to decline would seem petty. Plus, it was coffee.

"Hot," he said, when she reached out to take the cup. "I forget how good camp coffee is— and hot."

"Thank you." She lowered herself into the camp chair beside him.

"Did you sleep okay?"

"Surprisingly, yes. I thought I would be up worrying about the inn, but I slept great. How about you?"

"Worrying about the inn?"

"Yeah, you know, thinking about the myriad of things that could go wrong in three days. Three days can be a long time."

One side of his mouth tugged up, but it was only natural, she supposed, that he found her anxiety amusing. She highly doubted he'd ever had a law emergency that required him to use a sewer snake in the middle of the night to unclog an overflowing drain—or make a 911 call because a group of drunken rowdies wouldn't settle down.

"What's the worst you came up with?"

"The worst is *always* that it burns down. You know about that fear. I don't think we need a psychologist to tell us where that one comes from."

Jonah's eyes lit with alarm. "Those fire nightmares still crop up?"

Shay nodded, even as she felt this bit of concern tapping on the hard shell around her heart. "Occasionally, but now I also worry about things that are more likely to occur, like plumbing problems or the computer system crashing."

Caleb and Doc came out of the cabin, daypacks strapped on, fishing poles in their hands. As they approached, their argument about the best fly to use to catch grayling could be heard loud and clear. Caleb looked happy and healthy and in that moment Shay found it difficult to believe that anything could be wrong with him at all. Please don't let anything be wrong with him.

She headed back to her cabin to get her daypack and her camera, but the camera was nowhere to be found. She rifled through the contents of her pack to no avail. She reemerged and walked toward the group intending to ask if anyone had seen it.

Bering was busy outlining the day's plan when she joined them. "Tag and I are going to take off for the upper cabin and get that window fixed. Hopefully bears haven't been in there, but regardless, it should only take us a few hours. We'll cut down the bluff and meet you guys at the lake. I'll put one of the emergency radios in Doc's pack to be on the safe side."

They agreed and Bering and Tag set out. Shay knew Bering would never take off like this if he was guiding tourists, but as she, Caleb, Doc and Jonah—though it had been a while for him—were all experienced hikers and familiar with the territory and the dangers, it seemed a logical plan. Everyone had a canister of bear spray, while she and Doc, as well as Bering and Tag, were also carrying sidearms. Shay picked up her pack to strap it on when she remembered her camera.

"Oh, hey, has anyone seen my camera? I can't find it."

"Ouch," Caleb cried.

"Sorry, Caleb," Doc said. "I didn't mean to smack you with that. You certainly didn't deserve that, did you?"

Caleb rubbed his arm and scowled at Doc. "Well, Shay, you had it yesterday when we were taking that group photo, remember?"

"Yep." Shay nodded and tried to think. "That was the last time I remember seeing it, now that I think about it."

"Did you pick it up after Caleb was done fooling around with it?" Doc asked with his glare focused on Caleb.

"I don't...know." Shay remembered Caleb snapping a few photos.

"Uh-oh," Caleb said. "In all my bear excitement, I set it right on top of that rock next to the trail. The one you propped it on to take the group photos?"

The last thing she recalled was Caleb spotting the bear. She didn't remember picking up her camera after that.

"Well, silly me," she said. "I guess I'm hiking back down the trail a ways. I'll catch up with you guys."

"Not by yourself you're not," Caleb said. "I'll go with you."

"No, Caleb," Shay protested. "I'll be fine. You go fishing. I'll only be a little ways behind you all."

"I'll go with her," Jonah said.

"Great idea!" Caleb cried enthusiastically.

"No, Jonah, that's not necessary. Go fishing with your gramps."

"No—you're not going by yourself. I'm going with you."

"No, I can—"

Jonah sighed. "Please don't argue, Shay, because it will be weird if I have to try and follow you like some stalker."

"Perfect," Caleb spouted happily. "So, we'll be safe—you'll be safe. We'll see you in a couple hours. Come on Doc, let's hit the trail. The longer we wait the more slippery those fish get."

As she and Jonah began their treck back to the bear sighting, Shay tried to relax and focus on the scenery—the limited-edition wildflowers and the soft green of the trees—but it was impossible with Jonah breathing down her neck and making her skin tingle. She estimated they were about halfway there when the first question came.

"Shay, why haven't you ever gotten married?"

"I planned to once," she quipped, hoping without any real hope to keep things light. "It didn't work out."

"You know what I mean—after us. Why didn't you find someone after we broke up?"

Here we go, she thought, the topic she'd been expecting and dreading at the same time. Yet in that moment she suddenly realized how emotionally tired she was of holding on to it.

"Because I can't have children, Jonah."

Shay had to stop and turn around when Jonah reached out and caught her by the elbow. She took a bit of satisfaction in the fact that for once his face seemed to wear more emotion than he probably intended—a mixture of shock and confusion.

"What? Of course you can—we almost had one."

"We made one, yes. But that was the easy part. The difficult part, for me, was holding on to it."

Jonah's expression revealed he didn't comprehend what she was saying. Understanding, then concern and sorrow followed, showing all over his face and Shay felt a sob forming within her. Tears began to well in her eyes and she blinked rapidly, forcing them away. Why couldn't she get over this?

"After the miscarriage I saw a doctor—a specialist. He said I would probably never be able to carry a baby to full term."

"Probably?"

"Most likely," she clarified. "But it doesn't

matter because I could never take that risk again."

"But, Shay—"

"Don't you see, Jonah? It was my fault our baby died. There's something wrong with me, and I could never knowingly do that again to a man who loved me—or risk the life of an innocent baby that I helped to create."

JONAH FELT HIS head spinning. The sensation worsened as the significance of Shay's words sunk in. Shay not having children seemed too cruel and impossible to believe, like some kind of beautiful flower not ever being able to bloom.

"Why didn't you tell me?"

Her voice held a note of sorrow. "When would I have told you, Jonah? We had broken up, remember? You were away at law school. Then you moved to Chicago. I've seen you a handful of times in ten years and our only real conversation was a disaster."

Jonah raised his face toward the sky. He peered upwards for a moment before lowering his gaze back to hers. This was going to hurt but he had to say it.

He kept his tone as gentle as he could manage. "Maybe if I would have known you were pregnant at the time, Shay, instead of finding out later the way I did, things would have been different. Maybe they would be different between us now. Have you ever thought of that? That you were wrong in not telling me that you were pregnant until the baby was already gone?"

She didn't answer. Only stared. Like a statue—a beautiful, lovely, wounded statue.

It hurt to look at her, so he tore his eyes away and muttered, "I never should have listened to your stupid brother when he told me I couldn't see you…" He looked at her again. "When had you planned to tell me?"

Shay's voice sounded strong, but Jonah's heart ached to see the tears streaming down her face. "When you came home for Thanksgiving—I was going to tell you then because I hoped it would be too late for you to withdraw for the semester. You had just started at Yale, Jonah. That was your dream. I didn't want you to come back home just because I was pregnant."

Jonah fought hard to keep his composure. Finally, he looked up and absorbed her pain-filled expression like a blow. "I see."

She blew out a loud breath. "I'm glad—that

you understand, Jonah, because it felt like the right thing to do—"

She seemed so relieved by the out she'd perceived that he was giving her that he nearly shouted with frustration. What she'd done hadn't been fair to him. Yes, he'd screwed up, but so had she.

"No, no," he said. "That's not what I mean. I'm still angry. You should have told me sooner, Shay. It was my baby, too. And as selfless as that decision felt to you at the time—you were being selfish, too. You don't get to decide how someone else might feel or think or react and then make decisions for them. You always think you know what's best for everyone else…"

Jonah felt himself choking up at the stricken look on her face, but he forced himself to finish the thought.

"That's what you did, Shay. You made a decision for me instead of allowing me to make it myself."

SHAY LISTENED AND took the hit and was too tired of fighting the tears. They felt hot though and stung her skin, so she wiped at them with a frustrated hand.

Jonah was right; he'd had every right to know. And she had done that—made that decision for him. Why *should* he make this easy on her? She'd never done that for him. In fact, she'd been so blinded by her own pain that she'd never really stopped to consider how he might feel. How many times over the years had she called him selfish? She prided herself on being accepting and not judging others, but that's exactly what she'd done. She'd judged the man she loved more than any other person in the world—and she'd judged him the harshest.

"You're right, Jonah. I'm sorry. I should have told you about the baby when I was pregnant, not after I had lost it, but you had so much on your plate. We both did. I was grieving over Grandpa and I had just inherited the inn. I was reeling from the idea of running my own business and terrified about having a baby without you, and absolutely heartbroken over our break-up, but still, it was wrong of me to keep it from you."

Jonah stared at her.

"I'm a control freak. I know that about myself and that it's not pretty. I don't know why I try to control everything."

Shay wished she could read his mind. His exquisite blue eyes were wide and serious and filled with something that looked like pain and…pity? She didn't want him to pity her.

Which is partly why she'd never told him—
why she'd only told so few that she couldn't
carry a baby to full term. She didn't want pity
and she didn't want her failing as a woman to
be a topic of conversation. Only a handful of
people knew—Janie, Tag, Bering, the requisite medical professionals, and Hannah—whom
she'd only recently told in light of Hannah's
own struggles.

Then, like a shooting star, something he'd
said flared brightly through her brain. "Tag said
you couldn't see me?"

"Yes, but looking at things from his perspective I would probably have done the same
thing. And Shay—if I would have been stronger, if things hadn't already been so messed
up between us—I would have just shoved your
brother out of the way and barged through the
door. I was scared and I didn't know what you
would do—"

"Door? What door?"

"The hospital door."

"The hospital…?"

"I went to the hospital, Shay. I flew home
after you called me and told me you'd lost the
baby. I called Janie. You didn't know?"

Something cracked open inside of her—the
tightly sealed container where she'd kept so

many emotions secreted away all these years. She felt forgiveness begin to bloom; Jonah *had* come to see her?

She'd always had this vision of him laughing and talking with his law-school friends without a care in the world, walking the campus paths of Yale, too busy to think about her or what she was going through—or to mourn the tiny life they'd created out of so much love and then lost. She'd imagined him filled with relief that he wasn't saddled with her and an accidental family back in the small town he despised.

"I didn't know," she whispered.

"I came back to Rankins, missed a couple weeks of class—thought I was going to flunk out, tried *not* to call you every day, moped around and felt utterly helpless. I called Janie instead to see how you were."

"I can't believe you were there," she repeated. The idea that he had been in Rankins—that close to her for all of those days that had turned into weeks, trying to muster the energy to go on without him and without their baby—her last link to this man she'd loved with all of her soul. Thinking of that time, even now, was almost more than she could bear. He could have held her and comforted her and made everything so much better.

"I was."

Shay's chest felt so tight she could hardly breathe, barely speak. "Janie told me you called, but she never said you were in town."

"She probably didn't know—I never told her. I didn't tell anyone. I didn't want to see anyone except you. Gramps knew of course, but he kept it to himself at my request."

Shay let out a strained chuckle through her tears. "That was quite a feat to pull off in Rankins."

Jonah smiled and his face was a mix of pain and affection. "Tag also told me that you said you hated me."

"Did he?" Shay asked. She looked at Jonah and placed a hand to her forehead for a few seconds. "That might be true. I was so confused I probably did. Those hormones are brutal. I hated everything there for a while—myself included. If I hadn't had to pick myself up to run the inn I don't know what I would have done."

Jonah shrugged the pack off of his shoulders and lowered it to the ground. He stepped toward her and took her in his strong arms. And she let him. Again. She turned her head to rest her cheek on his broad chest and she cried. Again. She cried for the impossible circumstances that had resulted in their breakup, the excruciating pain of losing their baby, and for the cruel fact that she'd never be able to have another. The thought slipped out that if she could only have Jonah it would make that last one so much easier to bear. She instantly felt guilty because she knew she could never do that to him, deny him a family.

Jonah kissed the top of her head and whispered into her hair, "When I think about how things were between us during the years we were together—how happy we were, and I compare that to then? And to now? I don't get how we managed to make such a mess of things."

Shay lifted her head and stared up at him. "I didn't hate you, Jonah. I've never hated you."

"I know," he said and his eyes were all soft and smoky. And then his gaze traveled down toward her lips, and suddenly his mouth was lowering toward hers. A thousand thoughts, wants, needs, protestations, started to tumble around in her brain, but they all dissolved the second his lips touched hers. His kiss was sweet and gentle and created a painful stab of longing within her. She wished it didn't have to end, because like all those years ago, and then the other day at Agnes's funeral, being in his arms made it seem that everything would turn out okay.

He pulled away, but held her face for a few long moments. "That," he finally said and kissed her again quickly, "feels like progress."

"WHICH FLY YOU gonna start with—a little hairy caddis?" Caleb had asked as they started walking along the trail.

"I was thinking a prince nymph."

"Ha, good—you use that and I'll use an elk-hair caddis and we'll see who has better luck."

"Deal," Doc said.

And then, when they'd been on the trail a while with no chance of being overheard, Caleb waited for the inevitable question.

It didn't take long. "Caleb, you purposely left that expensive camera of hers on that rock, didn't you?"

"Desperate times, Doc. Desperate times…"

Doc emitted a heavy sigh. "There wasn't even a bear down there, was there?"

"Well…probably."

"You didn't see a bear though, did you?"

"When?"

"Caleb!"

"Darn it, Doc," Caleb said with a chuckle. "Do I need an attorney here?"

THE INEVITABLE CONFRONTATION went down much more smoothly than Shay had anticipated it would.

Shay and Jonah had caught up to Caleb and Doc, who were hooking one fish after the other and then arguing about everything from who caught the most to who caught the biggest. Then they all trooped to the lake where Bering and Tag were waiting for them as planned.

Tag pounced on the first opportunity to talk to her alone. She stood at the edge of the lake after rinsing her hands of fish scales in the ice-cold water.

"So, I heard you guys had to hike back down to find your camera?"

She nodded. "Yep."

"Everything okay?"

"Tag, you never told me Jonah came to the hospital."

"I didn't?" He looked truly confused and Shay knew he was telling the truth.

"No, and you also told him I hated him."

"Well, that you did say."

"I was hormonal, Tag. I hated everything."

"So…you don't hate him?"

"No. And you should probably lighten up— maybe even apologize. There were some misunderstandings."

Tag frowned and said, "I won't let him break your heart again."

Shay wished there was a way he could keep that promise. "You don't have to worry about that, okay? We aren't getting back together. He's returning to Chicago. I'm staying here." She didn't clarify that she could never be with Jonah, knowing she couldn't give him the children she knew he wanted.

Tag reached over and took her wrist and squeezed gently. "I love you, you know that, right?"

She grinned and responded the same way that she had hundreds of times over the years to that very same statement. "Me, too. Always have, always will."

They exchanged a smile and then she asked, "Tag, was the window really broken?"

"Yes, but that isn't why I came on this trip."

She felt a stab of love for her overprotective oaf of a brother. "You really are the best brother in the world."

"I am," he said soberly. "I only wish you were a better sister."

She punched him hard on the shoulder.

"Ouch," he said, rubbing the spot as he walked over and picked up his fishing rod.

Bering kept a couple canoes at the lake. He

rowed Gramps and Doc out in one, while Tag and Jonah went out in another, presumably exchanging a series of one-word sentences and grunts that would pass as apologies and explanations. Shay opted to stay on shore and fish around the lake, where she did more thinking than she did fishing.

She realized that Jonah was right—they had made progress, a lot of it really, when she thought about it. And even though the kiss had been a mistake—a case of getting carried away in an emotional moment—she realized that they had managed to slay the biggest monster that had prevented them both from reaching a place of true forgiveness.

Something profound had changed inside her as well because Jonah had, after all, come home.

CHAPTER FOURTEEN

"SHAY, BEFORE YOU get too upset, let me explain."

"Hannah," she said carefully, "are there or are there not goldfish in five of our guest's bathtubs?"

"No…"

Shay had turned her phone on as Jonah drove past the inn and pulled up in front of her house, which was a mere hundred yards away from the inn's front door. She'd discovered three texts from Hannah asking her to come straight to the inn when she returned from the fishing trip. She'd had Jonah turn around and drop her at the inn. Hannah was working at the front desk, so she'd stowed her pack behind the counter and waited until the guest Hannah was helping departed.

So, here she was, three days without a shower, still in her hiking clothes and undoubtedly oozing an aromatic combination of fish, dirt, bug spray and sweat while learning a valuable lesson; three days away from the inn could, in fact, result in consequences as bad as she'd feared—and apparently even some that she could never have dreamt up.

"Then why—"

"Shay, we call them koi—remember?"

"Hannah!"

"Yes! Yes, there are koi in some of the guest rooms, but I don't want you to worry—everything is fine."

"Fine?" In all of her worrying and wild speculation she had never anticipated this one. Fire, earthquake, flood (unlikely, she knew, but she'd still considered it), but not guests sharing their rooms with live fish. She prayed no one had called the health department. She should have known better than to leave.

"Shay, don't worry. The koi are all fine. We didn't lose a single one. We had to work really fast. Thank goodness Adele grabbed some of those big bins from the kitchen that we store vegetables in."

Shay made a mental note to place an order for new vegetable bins—and to thank Adele for her quick thinking.

"Anyway, I called Mr. Takagi and he told me I did the right thing. He left a portable aerator in case of an emergency, which we are moving from tub to tub, so the koi are getting plenty of oxygen. And thankfully, Mrs. Milner will be ready for the fish to be delivered tomorrow. We don't want to stress them out any more than they already have been. Tomorrow—isn't that great? I'm excited for them all to have a permanent home."

"That is…great."

"I know. Mrs. Milner's pond is spectacular."

"But, Hannah, where are the guests that are supposed to be in those rooms now?"

"Oh, right. Two of the people don't mind sharing their bathrooms with the koi until we can get them out, two of the couples are at Abigail's Bed & Breakfast, and one guy hasn't shown up yet."

"Now please explain how this happened."

"Before I do that I need to tell you the bad news."

If Hannah was inferring that the fact that there were valuable ornamental fish being housed in the inn's bathtubs as "good news," she didn't think she even wanted to hear the rest.

"What?"

"Well, you know Mr. Weird-Sheets?"

"Mr. Konrad?"

"Yeah, the jerk-face might be suing us."

"Suing us? Hannah, you didn't—"

"No, I didn't do anything to him, Shay. Bear with me—it all ties in. But I feel I need to preface this story by pointing out something that you obviously already know—we have warnings posted all over the place about getting too close to the wildlife. There's even one on the paper that guests sign when they check in. This whole unfortunate incident was totally his fault. We should sue *him* for the pain and stress he's caused us and the koi."

Wildlife? Shay couldn't even conjure up a visual of what Hannah could possibly be referring to. She gestured impatiently for her to continue.

"So, Mr. Konrad was out at the pond looking at the koi and photographing them. Probably that's the only *wildlife* he's seen at this point—the jerk—"

"Skip the director's commentary for now."

"Okay. Clara came in with her calf."

"No."

"Yep, probably looking for a cool drink for her and the baby—that calf is so funny..." She nodded once as if to get herself back on track. "Anyway, Mr. Konrad gets all excited and decides to take some photos of her and the calf—close-up photos. You can see where this is going, right? I can tell by the look on your face that you can. He got too close to the baby and Clara charged. He tried to run, but the pond was in the way. Toppled right into it, Clara went in after him—or the front half of her did anyway—stomping feet and thrashing."

"Is he in the hospital?" Shay had visions of the trampled man lying in intensive care with tubes criss-crossing his broken and mangled body.

"No, no, he's fine. A little banged up and a lot ticked off. He asked who our attorney was and I told him Jonah because you said he's been handling things for Caleb. I hope that's okay."

"Of course."

Hannah went on, "Thankfully, Vince was able to get Clara to back off. With all the thrashing and kicking and probably Clara's sharp hooves—I'm not sure—but the pond liner was leaking fast. We had to get them out of there. We acted as quick as we could, and we didn't lose a single koi."

Shay looked at Hannah and then around the inn, which was busy—good busy. People were milling around, smiling and looking happy. An elderly couple Shay had checked in a few days before greeted her as they walked by. And suddenly Shay had an epiphany: the inn was still standing.

It was in one piece. It hadn't burned down or blown up or any of the myriad of disasters she'd feared. Was everything perfect? No. But was it ever, really? No. There was always something that didn't go quite right or that needed her attention. Most of these people probably didn't even know that there were ornamental Japanese fish being stored in some of the guest rooms.

And she'd survived, too. She'd survived three days with Jonah. And most importantly—she'd survived talking about the past—about the miscarriage, and for the first time in a long time she felt…better about it all.

Shay looked at Hannah and felt the smile bloom across her face. Laughter welled up within her as she thought about Mr. Weird-Sheets going toe to hoof with Clara. She wondered what a fall into a pondful of koi and a fight with an angry moose would do to a person's vertigo.

She pulled her sister into her arms and hugged her tight for a few long seconds and let the laughter roll.

Hannah backed away and peered at her in astonishment.

"Shay, are you okay?"

"I am better than okay. Hannah. Great job. I am so, so proud of you—all of you. I don't see how I could have handled things any better myself."

"Really?" Hannah's face was a mixture of relief and happiness.

"Absolutely. Really, Hannah—great job. I love you."

She grinned at Shay and then let loose her own bout of laughter. "Thanks. I love you, too, Shay."

Something caught her eye on the counter in front of Hannah, an expensive-looking, unfamiliar cell phone with a bright blue case.

"Did you get a new phone?"

"Um, not exactly," Hannah said, and then changed the subject. "How was your trip?"

JONAH RETURNED TO find that a letter from Adele's attorney in Utah had arrived. He read the contents, disappointed at the lack of information contained within. It simply stated that Adele Mason was establishing her claim as the only living descendent of Eli David James. She would be willing to take a DNA test to prove her heritage. There was also a paragraph of legalese informing Jonah that he remained "legally bound" by the confidentiality agreement between he and Ms. Mason.

Shay's ring tone alerted him to her call.

A smile formed on his lips. He was missing her already even as he dreaded her impending confrontation with Adele Mason.

"Hi," she said. "I know you're probably very busy."

"I would think you'd be the busy one."

"It has been a little crazy, but Hannah did a great job while I was gone. I'm calling because I may have a legal problem."

Jonah felt a surge of nerves. *Already?* he thought. And then, *Bring it on.*

"This is the strangest thing, Jonah. It's probably difficult to believe in this day and age but I've never been sued before."

Sued? He hadn't expected this level of aggression from Adele before she'd even revealed herself. She really was a good actress. But why did Shay sound so calm? Was she in shock?

"I don't know if anything will come of it, but the guy threatened to take legal action. And he's an attorney."

"Who's an attorney?" Jonah asked slowly.

"Oh, I'm sorry—Mr. Konrad—the guy who fell into the koi pond."

Jonah felt relief settle inside of him, but he didn't know why—she would find out soon enough, or he would tell her. "Maybe you'd better start at the beginning."

She belted out a laugh and did.

By the end of the story Jonah was laughing, too.

"Ugh, that'll teach me for taking off for three days, right? But it was worth it. I had a fun time, Jonah. And I'm so glad we were able to clear some things up between us."

"I feel the same." In spite of the information sitting on the desk in front of him and awaiting her, he wanted to see her now. Would it be weird to ask her out in the midst of all of this chaos? Ethically in a case like this, it wouldn't be a problem as they could prove a prior relationship status but…

"Caleb and Doc had fun, too—don't you think?"

"Gramps hasn't stopped talking about it."

"That makes it all worthwhile as far as I'm concerned—even this stupid lawsuit. Besides, I don't think I could have stopped the incident from happening if I'd been here."

"I don't think so either, and you've got a great attitude about it. Something like this could knock a normal person to their knees."

"Normally I would be more upset, but in light of everything else in my life it doesn't seem like that big of a deal. And I don't feel like much is going to come from the suit, I mean, these kinds of people are usually just out for money, right?"

"Usually." Jonah silently hoped Adele was one of these people, too.

"There's no way I can— Oh, hold on a sec, Jonah, I've got another call."

He waited a minute until Shay came back on the line.

"I've barely been home long enough to shower and change, and work is already calling," she explained. "And now, I need to go because someone is at my door."

"No problem. There's nothing we can do tonight anyway. Let's see if he files anything. You said Hannah gave him my name, right?"

"Yes. Thank you. I feel so lucky to have retained such stellar legal counsel."

"You're welcome. But Shay, can I ask your advice about something before you go?"

"Shoot. You know you can talk to me about anything."

"Okay. Do you think it would be a conflict of interest if I asked a client out on a date?"

She paused for so long that Jonah was worried something had happened to the telephone connection.

"Shay?" he asked.

"Jonah, are you…talking about me?"

"Who else would I be talking about?"

"Oh," she said, and he could hear as she exhaled a breath of relief along with a nervous giggle. "In that case then—um…"

"Shay, I just want to spend some time with you, that's all."

"Okay, Jonah, sure."

"Great," he said, and he could hear the relief in his own voice now. Jonah glanced at the calendar. Caleb was playing poker with Doc and some of their buddies tomorrow evening. "Tomorrow night?"

"I'll look forward to it."

JANIE HAD KNOCKED on her front door while Shay was still on the phone with Jonah. She opened the door and waved her in as she finished up the call. Janie made herself comfortable on the sofa as the cats began to swarm. Shay hung up and then settled in between cats on the soft cushions.

"I'm gathering things went well on the fishing trip?"

"Yes, pretty well."

"Tag didn't do anything stupid?"

"It was touch-and-go there for a while."

They shared a chuckle. "I was half-expecting them both to come back with black eyes or something."

"I think most of it was cleared up." Shay quickly explained the actions and misunderstandings by each of them.

"Wow," Janie said when she was through and had asked a few questions of her own.

"I know. Do you think it would be crazy for me to go out with him?"

Janie smiled her wise and gentle smile, and flipped a wave of her long red hair over her shoulder. "Not as long as you both know what you're getting into from the start."

"Nothing can come of it, I know that—but it just feels good to be with him, in spite of, or maybe partly because of everything we've been through... And I told him everything, Janie. So he's aware nothing could ever come of a relationship with me."

Janie focused on the cat now curled in her lap. She stroked its smooth gray fur for a moment and then looked at Shay. "Shay, has it ever occurred to you that there are men out there who wouldn't care that you can't have children? That Jonah might not care?"

"No, they might say they don't want kids, but

they actually do. Besides, I know Jonah wants kids—we used to talk about it all the time."

"All young, happy couples talk about having kids. Listen Shay, please don't take this the wrong way. You're my cousin, my best friend, and I love you—"

"I love you, too," she said quickly, knowing that Janie was about to say something she probably wouldn't like.

"You can have a fulfilled life without having children."

"Said the woman with four perfect boys."

"Oh, they are far from perfect. I love them with all of my heart and soul, but I look at you sometimes and imagine what it might be like to have your life—to not have kids."

"What? Why?"

"It's just that I had Gareth and Reagan when I was so young, I never really had a chance to be a woman without children. To have the freedom to go where I want and do what I want—to travel to England—or even to the grocery store, whenever I felt like it. To stay up all night and then sleep in…to, to…*not* fix dinner because I'm not hungry or to fix chicken pesto because I am. And to watch whatever I want on TV—something that doesn't involve a team and a ball, or a dinosaur or a robot."

"I'm not... I don't do any of those things, except maybe the not fixing dinner. I rarely watch TV."

Janie's face took on a wry expression. "But you could—that's my point. For so long you've been so focused on what you can't do that you've never taken the time to really enjoy the things that you can. And again, you need to consider the fact there might be someone out there—Jonah even—who wants that, too."

EARLY THE NEXT morning Jonah was sitting at Gramps's desk trying to concentrate on a case, but mostly he was staring out the window and analyzing the wisdom of his impulsive decision to ask Shay to dinner.

He leapt out of his seat when he heard the thud—partly because it surprised him and partly because Francis jumped to her feet with a woof loud enough to burst an eardrum. She charged through the office and into the house, barking maniacally the whole way.

At first, even though it was early, Jonah thought someone must be at the door. Francis wasn't the best watchdog, used to the comings and goings at the office—welcoming people, in fact. So if she was barking like this, likely it meant that she was excited because someone she knew had arrived.

That notion was short-lived as Francis tore through the house straight to Gramps's bedroom. She whined and barked as she jumped repeatedly and pawed at the door.

"Francis, off," Jonah said, trying to get her to move away. But the dog was relentless, her nails clicking away like she fully intended to dig the door down.

"Gramps?" he called out.

And then he heard another sound, like a muffled shout.

He knocked on the door. "Gramps?" He definitely heard a voice. Jonah's pulse accelerated along with his knocking. "Gramps?" He tried the door. Locked. With Francis going crazy and his worry taking an exponential turn, Jonah threw his shoulder against the door, but it didn't budge. Stupid, he immediately realized, it was solid oak.

His mind flashed back to locking himself out of his own bedroom as a child and how easily he could get back in—the interior doors all had simple privacy locks. He sprinted back to the office and found a small screwdriver that Gramps used to fix his reading glasses. He ran to the door and slipped the tool into the knob.

He freed the lock and quickly opened the door. Francis bounded inside and Jonah followed.

"Gramps?" he yelled.

"Yup, it's me, son."

His eyes darted around the room as he tried to take in what he saw—or didn't see.

"Where are you?"

Francis was whining at the open window, paws up on the sill, tail wagging wildly like the rudder on a storm-tossed ship.

"Out here," came the reply.

He hurried over and looked out. Gramps was on the ground, leaning against the side of the house with his hands wrapped around one leg just below the knee.

"Gramps, what are you doing down there?"

"Breaking my leg, I think. You'd better call Tag and Doc. Looks like I'm gonna need a ride to the hospital."

Jonah pulled his cell phone from his pocket and called 911. He headed toward the front door, Francis hot on his heels. He opened it and Francis zipped through like some kind of fuzzy greyhound fresh out of the gate. Jonah dialed Shay as he jogged around the side of the house, quickly filling her in on what had transpired. She agreed to meet them at the hospital.

Jonah stopped and knelt next to Gramps

where Francis already pranced by his side, her nose busily sniffing his ear.

"Gramps, what happened? How in the world did you fall out of the window?"

"Well, I, uh, I didn't fall out…exactly. I actually fell in…sort of." He let out a pain-filled chuckle. Only Gramps could manage to find humor with a broken leg.

"You fell in?"

"I fell out—climbing back *in* the window."

"Climbing back in? What do you mean? Why in the world would you be climbing out the window in the first place?" The acidlike burn of worry nearly made him ill as thoughts of Alzheimer's and dementia and stories of the wanderings these cruel diseases wrought flashed through his brain.

Please no, he begged, as the realization overtook him that he wanted more time—needed more time—with this wonderful, thoughtful man. Shay was right. He hadn't been the grandson that Gramps deserved—not even close.

"I forgot my wallet."

"Your wallet? Gramps, what are you talking about? Why did you crawl out the window in the first place? Were you sleepwalking?"

Gramps grimaced with pain. "No, son, I wasn't sleepwalking. I wasn't even asleep. In fact, I haven't been napping at all since you came home from Chicago. I've been crawling out the window so you would think I was napping."

"Gramps, that's crazy. What are you—"

"I'll explain later. I am in a fair amount of pain here."

Jonah assessed his grandfather warily as something occurred to him; something so impossible he couldn't even believe he was considering it.

"Gramps, there's nothing wrong with you, is there?"

"As a matter of fact there is, Jonah. In case you didn't hear me the first time—I think I've broken my leg."

CHAPTER FIFTEEN

TALK ABOUT A hospital bed confession, Jonah thought, as he and Shay stared down at Gramps from opposite sides of the bed. Thankfully, Gramps was going to be okay—that is, he would be if Jonah didn't kill him first for the deception he'd admitted to perpetrating. His ankle was broken in two places and he was sporting a bright green plaster cast from just below the knee down, but other than that he was perfectly well.

No heart problem, no dementia, no difficulties at all—except, he was about to face Shay's wrath. Jonah looked forward to that.

"So, Caleb, you're not really sick," Shay began.

"Nope, he's not," Jonah interrupted.

She frowned in his direction, and then looked back at Gramps.

"Let me get this straight—you made this entire thing up to try to get me and Jonah back together?"

Jonah chimed in again. "There's absolutely

nothing else wrong with him, right Gramps? Go ahead and tell her."

"You could sound a little less disappointed there, dearest Grandson. I *do* have a broken ankle." Gramps added a wince and glowered at Jonah. "Which hurts like the dickens, thanks for asking."

Then he smiled at Shay with his charming, innocent-grandpa best. "And yes to the other question, sweetheart. And it worked, didn't it?"

He narrowed his eyes at Jonah and added, "You should be thanking me."

Jonah grimaced. "Thanking you? And you don't get to be cranky with me here, Gramps. I put my life in Chicago on hold so you could play matchmaker. What you did is…outrageous and…and shameful. Shay and I have both been worried about you to the point of losing sleep. Shay has sacrificed valuable time away from the inn to run errands and cook for you. I've been working on your cases, while my own career in Chicago is suffering. All of this and more—while you've been climbing out the window to go fishing with Doc and…sneak around with Mary Beth. We're the ones who've—"

Jonah stopped mid-rant. He'd caught the expression on Shay's face

Jonah could imagine what she was thinking;

torn between wanting to hug Caleb because he wasn't dying from some incurable disease, comfort him because his broken ankle had to hurt, and strangle him for the worry he'd caused them both. That's certainly what he was thinking.

"Caleb, Jonah and I are not back together," she stated flatly.

"Maybe not yet, but you're heading there. Got a hot date tonight from what I've heard."

Jonah stared down at his shoes. A few weeks ago just hearing about this underhanded stunt would have sent him flying back to Chicago with barely a second thought. But now, in a strange way, he understood what Gramps had been trying to accomplish. He was actually having a difficult time mustering up the requisite amount of anger the situation probably merited. He was acting outraged because he felt like Gramps deserved it, but in fact he was too filled with relief for much of any other emotion to squeeze its way in. He was appreciative of the time he'd been spending with Gramps in spite of the circumstances.

And, he had to admit, he was kind of grateful to Gramps for the healing he and Shay had begun to achieve in their relationship. That fishing trip never would have happened if Gramps hadn't cooked up this scheme.

However, it was also the trip they had taken at his request because they thought he might be dying. Jonah felt his irritation spike again, and he was glad.

"No," Shay answered, a little too forcefully for Jonah's taste. "We're not getting back together."

Maybe he and Shay weren't getting back together, but the state of things had definitely improved between them. And he was looking forward to their "hot date." Especially, now that it occurred to him, they wouldn't have this worry about Gramps casting a pall over the time they were able to spend together.

Shay pointed at Doc who was seated in a chair in the far corner and who, it seemed to Jonah, was trying his best to remain as inconspicuous as possible by keeping uncharacteristically quiet.

"And you," she said sternly. "You should be ashamed of yourself, too. Isn't this against your Hippocratic Oath or whatever? Didn't you take a pledge to do no harm?"

Doc, on the other hand, at least looked contrite.

"It doesn't violate it directly, but… But Shay,

honey, from the bottom of my heart, I am so sorry. I never meant to hurt you. I promise I didn't even want to go along with this goofy plan in the first place. You know Caleb—he coerced me."

Caleb made a loud snorting noise. "Coward," he said.

She scowled at Gramps. "Caleb, do you have any idea how worried we've been about you? No, you couldn't possibly have, because you never would have done this if you'd had even the tiniest inkling." She held up her fingers so there was barely any space between them. "I was this close to going to the doctor and asking for some sleeping pills or anti-anxiety medication or something. And I…"

Shay was doing a pretty good job of scolding them both, but Jonah thought Gramps was also doing an excellent job of looking feeble and pathetic as he twisted the crisp white hospital sheet in his hands. Jonah saw right through his act and was far from ready to cut him any slack.

"I am so sorry about all of that, Shay," Caleb responded solemnly.

Shay wanted to be mad, Jonah could tell. But, like him, he suspected the relief was taking precedence. He could see her visibly relaxing as she came to the same realization that he had; Caleb wasn't dying—at least not in the immediate future like they'd feared. And he wasn't suffering from dementia or senility or diabetes or…or gout or any of the myriad of ailments they'd speculated about. Deceitfulness—yes, but that was probably incurable.

"Shay, my sweet girl, can you ever forgive me?"

"Eventually… Maybe." She was trying to sound stern, Jonah could tell, but she was losing it. He needed to get her out of here before she collapsed in a puddle of tears and forgiveness and assured Gramps that everything was fine and all was forgiven. Jonah thought he deserved to suffer at least a little.

"Ha!" Gramps said and grinned. "Good enough for me."

Jonah walked back toward the bed and Gramps grumpily asked him, "I suppose you'll be heading to Chicago now?"

"No, Gramps, I won't. I can't, thanks to you. I can't go back until that cast comes off."

Gramps didn't even try to stifle a grin. "Doc said that'll be at least a month—maybe six weeks."

Jonah nodded and said in a matter-of-fact tone, "I heard him. Someone has to take care of you. So I guess you got your way there, didn't you, you devious and sneaky old codger? I'll be around for a while yet."

"Are you going to be mad and surly the whole six weeks? 'Cause if that's the case I'll find someone else to—"

"Maybe," Jonah replied. "It wouldn't be out of line if I was, and you know it. You'll be lucky if I forgive you in six weeks. Right now, Shay and I are going to go get a cup of coffee and maybe some breakfast. Enjoy your hospital food."

Gramps eagerly rubbed his palms together. "I will. I'm starving. I hope they have that salmon-cheese soufflé thing." Rankins Hospital was known for its delicious hospital fare.

"Oh, I wouldn't count on that. As I didn't want to take any chances with that potential heart problem of yours, I told the nurse to bring you something from the heart-healthy menu. I think you'll be getting unsweetened oatmeal and a fruit platter."

"Now, that's a low blow, Jonah. You didn't have to—"

"I'll be back later."

Jonah reached down and enfolded Shay's hand in his. She didn't pull away and he felt his growing affection for her and his intense relief mingling in a very nice way as they walked hand in hand through the hospital. They exited through the sliding-glass door and by silent consensus headed toward the Cozy Caribou.

They settled into a booth across from each other. They both ordered the fisherman's special—two eggs, sausage, hash browns and a biscuit with a dollop of gravy, and black coffee. Their beverages were promptly delivered and they sat in silence as they tried to absorb exactly what had just unfolded.

"YOU'VE STEPPED IN it now, haven't you—you numbskull? No, you've tripped and fallen in it and the worst part is—you've dragged me down right into this big pile of stink with you."

"For the love of Pete, Doc—can't you see this for the breakthrough that it is?"

Doc narrowed his eyes and repeated skeptically, "Breakthrough?"

"I swear, sometimes I wonder how you managed to fumble your way through medical school. They have a date—did you miss that?"

"Boy, you are touchy, aren't you? You might need some more pain meds."

Caleb tried to hold back a grin. "Yeah, well, a broken ankle hurts more than you might think. But my doctor probably wouldn't even know that I'd broken my ankle if I hadn't told him."

Doc chuckled and hit the call button to alert the nurse's station.

"All right, I'll give you this one. I can see where the date might be progress. But what can possibly become of it, Caleb? Shay still has the inn and Jonah still has his fancy law firm in Chicago."

Caleb nodded thoughtfully. "I have an idea about that, too."

"Oh, no. No more schemes. Leave me out of it. I won't lie to Shay again. Did you see the look on her face? My already cracked heart nearly broke right in two."

"That's a little dramatic even for you, but I know what you mean—she gets to me, too. That's why I'm going to resort to something I should have done for my Jonah a long time ago."

"What's that?" Doc frowned. "Why am I even asking? Somehow I feel like I'm going to be dragged into this, anyway."

"Don't worry, Doc. You're out of it at this point—unless Jonah comes to you for confirmation on some facts. What I'm talking about is some good old-fashioned tough love."

"You're going to tell him the truth about his father, aren't you?"

"What do you think of that? It might be the nudge he needs."

"It might be—but it might also send him back to Chicago faster than you can say lateral malleolus fracture."

"I can't say that anyway. Is that what I've got?"

"Yep, you're lucky you don't need surgery."

"According to who? You've been secretly dreaming of taking a scalpel to me for years."

Doc chuckled as the nurse came in with a syringe. She handed it to Doc. "Maybe a shot of this will shut that devious brain of yours down for a while, huh?"

"As long as it drowns out your yapping too, that's fine with me."

"You're going to need some stronger drugs than this to turn off my angelic voice in your head. Everyone needs a conscience, and fortunately for you, I'm yours."

Caleb snorted with amusement. "Seriously though, Doc, what do you think of my telling Jonah about his dad? I always hoped he could hold on to the image he has of Burke as this perfect man—perfect father, perfect role model."

"There's no such thing as a perfect man, Caleb, and you know it. I understand why you've never told him the truth. It's a tough thing to lose your parents at such a tender age. But as far as role models go—I think you're the best thing a grandson, or a son, like Jonah could hope for. I don't know what went wrong with Burke. But I've always thought that maybe you should let Jonah decide for himself which one of you deserves his adulation. There's no contest—and there shouldn't be. You're the truth—the real deal. But this image that Jonah has of Burke is not. Not to mention the fact that you're alive and Burke is dead."

Caleb felt his eyes growing a little misty. "You're the best friend a man could ever ask for, Doc—do you know that?"

"Gee whiz—are those meds making your head soft already?" But Doc smiled as he reached over and squeezed Caleb's hand.

JONAH WINCED. "CAN you believe those two?"

Shay wrapped the fingers of one hand around her steaming mug of coffee. She was staring down at the table, playing with a sugar packet, which she would never use in her coffee. Slowly she looked up at Jonah and then slapped her free hand over her now-grinning mouth. A snort of laughter spilled forth despite her effort to contain it.

Then they both burst out laughing. And the more she thought about it, the funnier it became.

After a few minutes Shay dabbed at her wet eyes with a napkin. "We have to give your gramps points for creativity. Do you think there was even anything wrong with the washing machine?"

"Nothing that he didn't cause. Remember how he stuck his head back there after you took it all apart and put it together again? Probably reconnected whatever he'd disconnected earlier."

"And my camera…"

They spent the next few minutes rehashing the intricate details of Caleb's scheme and speculating about the lengths he'd gone to and what was real and which parts had been contrived. Then they tried to formulate a plan for not revealing their own already-granted forgiveness too quickly.

After breakfast Jonah walked Shay to her car, still parked in the hospital's lot.

Instead of opening the door, he leaned a hip against it and looked at her. "Do you still want to go out tonight?"

Shay felt her pulse speed to a gallop. They'd just had breakfast together so why would his reference to a date make her all tingly with anticipation?

"What about your gramps? Shouldn't you stay home and take care of him? You told him you would, in spite of everything. Do you want me to come over there instead?"

Jonah grinned. "Nope. No way. He'll still be in the hospital. They want him to stay overnight to keep an eye on the swelling, and Doc can sit with him while we go out. It's the least he can do for his part in this whole scheme. I think we deserve our own celebration here, don't you?"

Shay returned the grin. "Okay, what are we going to do?"

Jonah reached out a hand and took a hold of her fingertips. He tugged until she had to step closer to him. And closer still, until they were practically chest to chest. Then he slipped a hand around the back of her neck, bent his head and kissed her.

They'd kissed a million times when they'd been together, but she couldn't remember it ever feeling quite like this. This lovely, heart-wrenching sensation that her world may finally be righting and that she was finding her balance.

"Some of that, I hope," he answered with a

whisper. He leaned his forehead against hers as they both took a moment to catch their breath.

SHAY KIND OF floated through the rest of the day, taking care of every detail that needed her attention, and even some that didn't. She tackled a good portion of her backlist of non-urgent concerns as well. She told herself her good mood had as much to do with Caleb's confession as it did with her impending date with his grandson.

Hannah poked her head into her office late in the afternoon. "Hey, how are you holding up?"

"Pretty good. How are the koi?"

Hannah had supervised their transport from bathtubs to pond. She came in and plopped down in the chair across from Shay's desk. "Good. Everyone seems to be settling in very well. Those are some lucky fish, but I'm going to miss them."

"Seriously?" Shay asked.

"Yes, I'm serious. They already recognize me. They learn to recognize individuals, you know?"

"No, I didn't know. That's actually really cool."

"Speaking of what's not cool—any word on Weird Sheets' lawsuit?"

"Not yet, but probably soon. I know he's back in the lower forty-eight because an attorney called here asking some questions. But, I haven't had a chance to tell you about Caleb."

"Oh, no, Shay—what about him? Isn't his appointment with the heart specialist coming up in a couple days?"

"It was, but it seems that he won't be going to that appointment at all." Shay sat back and filled her in on the details.

"Whoa," Hannah said when Shay finished telling her. "All of that to get you and Jonah back together?"

"That's what he claims, but I think it was as much to get Jonah back to town as it was to get us back together."

"Huh." Hannah drummed her fingers on the arm of her chair for a few seconds. "Clever."

"Very."

"And it seems to be working?"

Shay shook her head. "No, we're not getting back together."

Hannah's face revealed her skepticism.

"We're not, Hannah. There's too much…"

"So, how are things between you guys now?"

"Better. Good. We're going out tonight."

"Like a date?"

"Sure, I guess." She grinned as she thought

about Caleb's "hot date" terminology. And if that kiss this morning was any indication, he may not be too far off the mark. Of course, Shay would never let it go further than that. "It's just to have some fun and hang out without all this worrying about Caleb we've been doing."

"But you're not getting back together?"

"It's just a date, Hannah."

Hannah's lips tugged up into a grin. She slapped the top of Shay's desk with an open palm and stood. "Okay, I've gotta go. I need to make a phone call."

CHAPTER SIXTEEN

"WHERE ARE WE GOING?" Shay asked that evening as Jonah opened the door so she could climb into Caleb's Land Rover.

"I thought we'd have dinner at this really interesting place I heard about. It's supposed to be very private, with a gorgeous atmosphere, an innovative menu and excellent service."

"Oh, no, Jonah—we're not going to the inn, are we?"

"My goodness, Shay—we do feel good about ourselves, don't we?"

She laughed and fastened her seat belt. "No, it's not that. It's just that it's really difficult for me to be at the inn and not work."

"Do you really think I'd take you on a date to your own restaurant?"

"So, if we're not going to the inn, that leaves the Caribou, right? And if we show up there together everyone will think we're dating."

"Well, we can't have that, can we?"

"You know what I mean."

"Unfortunately, I do," he said. "But please relax—we're not going to either of those places—or the café or the Donut Den."

"Oh, okay." Shay didn't want to mention that the long drive to Glacier City and back wouldn't get them home until the middle of the night, so she decided to stay quiet. She could do middle of the night for dinner with Jonah at this point.

But then Jonah turned onto the winding drive that led to Mrs. Milner's house. Edith Milner lived in a custom-made log home that she and her late husband had built nearly thirty years ago. Mrs. Milner had recently added on the atrium with the koi pond Hannah kept raving about.

Jonah stopped the car and flashed her an enigmatic smile. He got out and opened her door, tucking her hand in his as they walked toward the house and then up the wide stone steps of the front porch. Large pots overflowing with colorful flowers stood on either side of the massive and ornate double-hung doors.

One of the doors swung open, revealing a smiling Hannah. "Good evening," she said brightly.

"Hannah? What is going on?"

"Right this way." Hannah swept her arm

through the doorway like a butler from by-
gone days.

"Hannah, what are you up to? Where is Mrs.
Milner?"

"She's in Italy. I'm taking care of her house
and the koi while she's gone—starting tonight,
as it happens."

"Italy? You're a little old to be having parties
while the grownups are away, don't you think?"

Hannah laughed. "Don't worry. She knows
all about this and she approves. But we'll talk
about that later. You're supposed to be on a date,
so come on."

Shay had been here before many times. Mrs.
Milner loved to host parties and fundraising affairs at this five-thousand-square-foot marvel
of craftsmanship that she called home. They
strolled through a short breezeway and then
Shay let out a gasp. The large rectangular-shaped
room appeared to be made entirely of thick glass
with wrought-iron trim. Potted plants and flowers abounded, basking in the muted light.

Tiles covered the floor with an intricate Art
Nouveau design in shades of countless pastel
colors. A sculpture rose up out of the center of
a gurgling fountain. They walked over to find
the koi swimming gracefully around lily pads,
plants and rocks that decorated the pool.

"Hannah, you were right—how could a fish not be happy in a home like this?"

"This is incredible," Jonah added.

Hannah folded her hands in front of her. "I know. Mrs. Milner is an awesome person— she is literally a genius. She has patents on pump mechanisms for fountains and aquariums." Hannah gestured at the pond. "Everyone thinks her money came from her husband, but it didn't—she earned it. I mean, Mr. Milner did well with their investments, too, but most of this came from her hard work."

Shay relished hearing the passion in Hannah's voice—learning, appreciating, enjoying things that weren't snow-covered.

"You two can have a seat over here." Hannah pointed toward a pair of matching chairs and a small round table by the pond. A single candle in a blue glass plate flickered in the middle of the table.

"By the way, this all came about because Mrs. Milner told me she wanted to do something to thank you for being so accommodating to Mr. Takagi, and for housing her koi. Jonah was trying to decide where to take you for a date—someplace private, and I thought of this. I hope you like it, Shay. I wanted to thank you for everything you've done for me, too."

"Hannah, you didn't have to go to so much trouble. You're my sister—I'd do anything for you. And you're the one who took care of the koi. Mrs. Milner should be thanking you."

Hannah grinned. "I know that, Shay. That's why I wanted to do something for you—you do stuff for everyone. And don't worry—she has. Now, sit down and have a glass of wine. I'll bring out your salads in a few minutes."

Shay suddenly felt awkward. What were they doing? This was too romantic—too intimate. Jonah probably hadn't realized what Hannah had planned. Her gaze flicked around nervously until she noticed that Jonah was watching her. She settled her eyes on him.

He grinned in that lopsided, playful way that Old Jonah used to. Her heart executed an official flutter, and that was when she knew she was in trouble.

Jonah took her elbow and guided her to the table. He pulled out her chair and she sat, wondering what he might be up to as he lingered behind her. Then he brushed the hair away from her neck, bent and kissed the spot he revealed. Just like that—one quick kiss and she was left with a warm feeling throughout her entire body.

He sat and took a corkscrew to the bottle of

wine that had been chilling in a bucket. She watched him and felt a mix of disconcerting emotions taking hold of her again—equal parts of fondness, attraction and panic. Then she was struck with a thought—why hadn't *he* ever gotten married? He was smart and funny, rich and successful—good-looking. Yes, he could be extremely, annoyingly confident at times.

He was also materialistic and self-centered; although to be fair he did have the means to be. As a single guy what else did he have to spend his money on? And he was extremely generous with his money where his gramps was concerned and to various charitable causes according to Caleb.

Over the years Shay had silently criticized him for buying Caleb stuff; he was always ordering things and having them sent to his house—oversize television, laptop, e-reader, ice-maker, bicycle, fishing poles...

She could probably name a hundred things like that that he'd done for Caleb over the years. And she'd been particularly harsh about the washer and dryer he'd wanted to buy. Why was she so cynical about him being generous with his money? She'd always viewed these actions as a substitute for his time, but she supposed they could also be seen as gestures of his affection. Lots of wealthy people weren't generous with their time or their money and some of the poorest people she knew were the most giving. Greed knew no socioeconomic bounds—and neither did generosity.

He handed her a glass of wine and she took a sip.

"This is really nice, Jonah. Thank you. I can't remember the last time I felt so relaxed." Sort of, she added silently, or she would be if he wouldn't stare at her with those blazing blue eyes of his.

"I wanted to do something special for you. And, like Hannah, I wanted to thank you."

"Thank me? For what?"

"For taking such good care of Gramps all these years. Hannah is right—you're always taking care of everyone else."

"That's what I do," she said lightly, dismissing the compliment. "It's not that big of a deal."

Jonah raised a brow in doubtful consideration.

She made a conciliatory face. "Okay, but, I love your gramps—like he's my own. And he's really good to me, my whole family."

"I know," he said quietly. "But, who takes care of you?"

"Tag, I guess and—"

"I'm not talking about looking out for you. I know you have Tag and Bering for that." He added an exaggerated eye-snap and she grinned. "I'm talking about the personal stuff."

Her chest tightened. "What kind of personal stuff?"

"Like bringing you coffee in the morning, setting the DVR so you don't miss your favorite show, or…buying you licorice when you go to the movies?"

"Jonah, stop—that kind of relationship is not possible for me."

"Why?"

"You know why."

"Shay, just because—"

"Why don't you tell me who does that stuff for you, then? Why haven't you ever gotten married? Who's bringing you coffee, Jonah? And buying you chocolate peanut-butter cups?"

"Peanut-butter cups?" He smiled a slow, sly smile full of affection and heat and suddenly Shay wished she'd never asked.

"I remember stuff, too, you know," she shot back and had no idea why her tone was defensive.

"That's good," he said and the timbre of his voice seemed to flow through her like a current. "I like to remember us, Shay. That brings me to your first question, the answer to which is simple—you. I've never married anyone else because of you. In my heart I committed myself to you that weekend we went up the Opal River. I asked you to be my wife. I had a… All we needed was the ceremony, which is all that is as far as I'm concerned—a ceremony."

Shay was stunned. What was he saying? That he'd never been with another woman? That seemed unrealistic, although she'd never even considered being with another man. Although part of that was because she knew she couldn't have children…wasn't it?

"Jonah, um…"

"I know you're not comfortable talking about us, but I do want you to know where I stand."

"What do you mean—where you stand?"

"I…I have feelings for you, Shay. I always have, and I'm pretty sure I always will. And I think maybe if we spent more time together we could get to an even better place."

Shay stared at him dumbly, not knowing whether she wanted to smile or cry. His words made her feel impossibly happy, but that was the thing—that word—*impossible*. Sadness soaked in along with that word, diluting the happiness, because the fact remained that he never had given her a ceremony—or even a ring.

Instead, a bitter reality had come crashing down on them.

They were two different people who wanted different things. Shay felt a welling of despair. She didn't want to spoil the moment, but she was too practical not to address the issue head-on.

"But things are just as impossible for us now as they've always been. So why say it, Jonah?"

"Because it's how I feel and because I believe we could work something out."

"Work something out. How?"

He shrugged. "I don't know. But for now I propose that we spend the rest of the summer together, see how we feel, and let things sort themselves out."

A niggle of irritation mingled with her already uncomfortable mix of emotions. Relax and chill—like a couple of college kids. It would never work. "Jonah, I don't think…" She couldn't bring herself to say what she was thinking. "You've given me a lot to take in here."

"I get that." He reached over and slipped his hand into hers and Shay nearly crumbled right there.

"Don't overthink it."

Shay wasn't sure what to tell him. Was it possible that he still loved her? Did they even know each other anymore? Her life had been so static compared to his. Not much had changed for her in ten years while he'd been out conquering the legal world, acquiring one "success" after another, making piles of money and living the high life.

And his lifestyle had changed him. Hadn't it? She'd thought so. For years she'd believed so, but when she thought about his generosity toward Caleb in this new and different light she wasn't so sure. Then there was his surprisingly cheerful attitude about her sticking him with bingo duty, the lawsuit with Will Traeger, movie night with the Watte kids—not to mention Gary and Ingrid. Oh, what he'd done for Gary and Ingrid alone was worth taking a chance, wasn't it?

"Give me a chance, Shay," he added, apparently reading her mind. "Give us a chance."

She met his eyes and the pleased expression on his face told her he could see her agreement. But as she was ready to say the words aloud Hannah came running into the atrium.

"Shay! Crap, I'm so sorry. But Dad is on the phone."

"Is it Mom?"

"No, Shay. And this is so unbelievable that

I can't believe I'm even saying it, but apparently there is a woman at Mom and Dad's house right now who insists she is Uncle Eli's daughter. Dad says this might mean that a part of the inn is hers or something... Shay, how could that be?"

Shay took the phone, pressed it to her ear, and felt her entire world begin to tip over.

CONCERN BUZZED THROUGH Jonah as he watched Shay's face turn white. He squeezed her hand.

"Dad, don't do anything. We'll be right there." She lowered the phone.

"Shay, I'm sure—"

"Apparently she has some documents. We need to get over there."

Jonah's brain shifted into attorney mode. "I'll drive you."

"You don't need to get involved in our family problems."

"Shay, I want to. Besides, I have a feeling this could easily escalate into a legal matter." Something kept him from mentioning that he already knew this to be true.

She stood, then leaned over and blew at the candle. The fire flickered and resisted her attempt. She tried again, but it only seemed to fan the flame.

Jonah placed an arm around her shoulders and then reached over with his free hand and snuffed the wick between his fingers. Now, if only he could just as easily deal with the fire that Adele had started...

BY THE TIME SHAY, Hannah, and Jonah arrived at her parents' house, the rest of her siblings were already gathered. The youngest three, triplets—Seth, Iris and Hazel were all still in college and had only recently returned home after spending part of their summer break in Europe.

Their parents, Ben and Margaret, were seated on the plush gray sectional that had been delivered the week before. Her parents had been doing some remodeling and the house still smelled of new furniture and construction. Tag sat next to their mom. Seth and Iris were seated on the other branch of the sofa, with Hazel perched on the arm next to Seth.

And Adele? Why was Adele here?

Adele was sitting on the damask-covered antique wingback chair that no one ever sat in because it was so uncomfortable. Their mom refused to get rid of the chair because it had belonged to her grandmother.

"Shay," her mother cried when she and the others walked in. "Thank goodness you're here."

"What's going on?" Shay looked around for the dangerous usurper. "Who is this woman? Where is she?"

All eyes turned toward the uncomfortable chair.

"Adele?"

Adele was sitting up straight, one leg crossed over the other, hands folded demurely in her lap. "Hello, Shay. Hannah."

"Yes," Margaret said. "Adele believes she is Uncle Eli's daughter."

"Dad?"

The look of utter shock on her father's face, Shay decided, meant he definitely thought this claim might be genuine.

Adele began speaking, "This is not going well so far…I need to explain. My mother's name is—was—Stella Mason. She passed away six months ago. She only told me about my father a short time before she died. I never knew my father. I grew up believing that I didn't have any family, except my maternal grandparents. They're both gone now, too."

"You poor thing," Margaret said.

Shay looked at her mom, astounded by the

depth of her mother's compassion in this bizarre, surreal moment.

"Are we supposed to accept this—just because this woman says so?" Seth chimed in.

Hannah was upset—Shay could see it. And she was sure everyone could hear it when she started to talk. "This is really awkward, Adele. Shay hired you at the restaurant. I thought we were friends. Why didn't you say something sooner? And I don't understand how any of this means you are somehow entitled to a share of the inn."

All eyes turned toward Adele again.

Adele looked at Jonah. "Would you excuse us for a minute, Mr. Cedar?"

"No, I will not, Ms. Mason. As Shay's attorney of record and knowing what you're about to reveal I will not do that."

Shay turned toward Jonah as a cold feeling of dread rolled through her. How could Jonah possibly know about this? "Jonah?"

"Shay, listen—"

But Shay shifted her attention toward Adele as she began speaking again.

"Hannah, I didn't say anything initially because I didn't know how you would all react. I was going to, but then after talking to Jonah I wasn't sure if you would believe me. Though now that I've gotten to know some of you—particularly you and Shay, I knew I couldn't let any more time pass solely because of my fears.

"My mother revealed to me before she passed away that Eli James was my father. I didn't think much about it at the time because my mom was dying and that's all I was concerned with. However, once a few months went by I started doing some research and obviously it led me here."

"But Uncle Eli?" Shay's sister Iris said. "I still don't see the connection between Adele being his daughter and Shay's inn."

Adele took a deep breath and continued. "There's a chance that through my father I might partially own the land that the inn is built on."

There was only a beat of silence and then chaos erupted. Everyone started talking at once and asking questions. Hannah was bombarding Shay with commentary, her mom was crying and her dad sat frozen and silent. Tag was peppering Jonah with questions and the triplets were talking amongst themselves.

Shay stared at Jonah because the idea of losing the inn wouldn't compute. Was it this simple? Could her entire life be taken from her faster than she might even process the information?

For some reason all Shay could think about was the fact that Jonah had somehow known about this and not told her. Jonah steered her down the hall and into her old bedroom. Her parents used it as a guest room now, but some of Shay's stuff was still there.

She glanced at the shelf on the wall where her basketball trophies sat—Most Valuable Player two years in a row. If only life could remain as carefree and simple as it had been back then. Things certainly weren't simple anymore.

And now she might have to hand her inn, or some share of it, over to this woman—this... this stranger that she'd hired at the restaurant but knew virtually nothing about? And whose fault was that, a little voice chimed from the back of her mind. She recalled Jonah's chiding that day, after he'd found out that she'd hired Adele. That thought brought forth another: he'd known. Already at that time—he'd known about Adele's true identity.

How long had he known?

"Shay—look at me."

She did. "You knew I could lose the Faraway and you didn't tell me?"

"I couldn't tell you. It would have been a breach of client confidentiality."

Her voice went up several decibels. "She's your *client*?"

"No, she made an appointment to see Gramps and that was when we thought he was ill. Adele's attorney in Utah referred her here—to Gramps. She came into the office assuming Gramps would help. I was there instead. She told me who she is, or who she claims to be, but as soon as I realized what she was up to, I told her that we—I—could not represent her. But everything we discussed that day would fall within the attorney-client privilege. It would have been unethical for me to have told you anything."

"Unethical? I can't—" She bit off the rest of that sentence. But it wasn't easy because she wanted to tell him that she thought keeping this information from her was unethical. That the way he'd always chosen his career over her was unethical. But she knew that saying the words would be pointless. Jonah was an attorney first and foremost and this proved absolutely where his loyalties dwelled. *Stupid.* She'd been stupid and careless to even consider opening her heart to him again.

"Yes—unethical. Meaning I could be disbarred. Shay, please—I can see you shutting down. Inside—you're turning away from me. Don't do this—please. Not this time. We need to communicate, remember? If this ordeal with Gramps taught us anything—it's that. My experience with Gary and Ingrid taught me that, too."

Shay didn't really hear him and she couldn't seem to find any words. She just felt so cold and her head was swimming. The sensation reminded her a little of how she'd felt for all those weeks after she'd lost the baby and tried to accept that there would never be another.

He stepped toward her and took her hands. "Shay, you're shaking." He started to wrap his arms around her but she stepped away.

"No. Don't touch me anymore, Jonah." By sheer force of will she somehow managed to move back. She had to get away from him. She wasn't going to fall for the Old Jonah routine again. She had to accept that he no longer existed.

"I know you're upset about this, but Shay, it's going to be fine, I promise. I will help you, okay?"

She nodded and willed the tears not to fall. She wanted to be strong even as she craved the feeling of Jonah's arms around her. She imagined this frustrating push and pull, this want and not-want sensation must be similar to that of a drug addict without their fix. And just as unhealthy she told herself. But the yearning was so strong that she reached her hands out and placed them on the dresser to keep herself from seeking the comfort of his embrace. She couldn't let him touch her and make her believe everything would be okay.

Everything was most definitely not okay.

She didn't want to need him. She didn't need him, she told herself. Except for his legal expertise—the one thing she knew he was capable of giving freely and the one thing she could accept without getting her heart broken—again.

"I need to talk to my family. I need to figure this out." She turned and walked out of the room.

CHAPTER SEVENTEEN

ADELE WAS GONE. Shay's family was still gathered in the living room. Her mom and dad were now talking quietly. The triplets were asking questions of Hannah and trying to catch up on what was already known about Adele.

Tag told Shay he'd called Bering, Janie and their mom, Claire, and that they were on their way over. They arrived quickly with Laurel— she'd been visiting Janie so she'd driven both her and Aunt Claire over. Shay invited her to stay, and Bering and Emily showed up a few minutes later.

Tag asked, "Jonah, is this possible? I mean, I understand that Great Uncle Eli could have had a child, but the part about Adele owning a part of the inn? There has to be something we can do."

Jonah stood in front of the family and explained. "Ms. Mason came to see me—she actually came to see Gramps, but talked to me instead. So I've had time to do some research.

"As most of you probably know, Gus, Eli and Lyman's parents, Isaac and Viola, built a home where the Faraway Inn stands and ran it as a boardinghouse for years, along with Gus and Eli's help. After that original structure burned to the ground and Isaac and Viola perished in the fire, the property passed to all three of the brothers equally.

"Eli soon moved to the lower forty-eight to enter into business there with his brother Lyman in Colorado."

More nodding and anxious anticipation from the Jameses. "Gus eventually rebuilt the boarding house as the Faraway Inn, but the main point here is that the structure was built on Isaac and Viola's homesteaded property, which at one time belonged to all three of the brothers.

"Gus purchased Lyman's third of the property, and is shown in court documents. However, I have been unable to find any evidence or documentation showing that a purchase was ever concluded between Gus and Eli. As far as I have been able to ascertain, Eli's interest in this property has never been adequately or legally addressed."

Jonah took a second to gather his thoughts. "Long story short, this means that if Adele Mason is Eli's daughter, she may rightfully have a claim to as much as one-third of the property the inn is situated on.

"There are other legal issues here that I am still researching, but we now know there is a probable direct heir to Eli, unknown at the time of his death, so the courts will eventually decide how this will all shake out…unless a settlement can be reached instead."

"But Shay has been paying the taxes on the property and the inn since Grandpa died," Hannah pointed out.

"Yes, she has," Jonah agreed. "Unfortunately, that doesn't mean anything with regards to property ownership. The only way property can legally change hands is through a deed."

"The inn was built with Gus and Ellen's money and hard work. And Shay has poured so much into the building and grounds since she inherited it," Margaret added.

Jonah replied, "That's true and according to my estate specialist colleague those improvements should not be considered part of the settlement. We can only trust the court will take all of this into account—if it gets that far. But the fact remains that for the purposes of ownership you can't separate a structure from the property it sits on. If Adele's claim is true—if she is in fact Eli's daughter—she is probably entitled to something. At this point, we don't know what that something is—or even what she will be asking for."

"Poor thing," Margaret said quietly. Every head turned in her direction.

"Mom!" Hannah exclaimed. "Quit saying that."

"Well, really, Hannah, think about it. Imagine not having any family in the world and then finding out you may in fact have some? How do you tell them? She was obviously terrified that she wouldn't be accepted. That's sad and I feel sorry for her. As far as I'm concerned if she's a James, then she's family. I don't think she's probably had a lot of love in her life."

"Mom, how could you possibly assume something like that?" Hannah asked.

"Why else would she think that we wouldn't want to get to know her?"

"Margaret," their dad, Ben, said. "Biology doesn't necessarily make someone family in every sense of the word. Her behavior has been questionable. We welcomed her into our home and I don't care if she was scared—it was deceitful to befriend Hannah and Shay and not disclose who she really is. *If* she really is Uncle Eli's daughter." The family continued discussing the issue and Jonah couldn't help but think that Shay had inherited her mother's compassion, the same compassion that had allowed her to hire Adele at the inn without checking into her background.

Jonah didn't comment, although he definitely agreed with Ben. But his place at this point was to offer up the legalities, not express his personal opinion about Adele James—at least not to the entire family.

SHAY DID HER best to carry on like everything was okay. She had to; she had guests to take care of, rooms needed cleaning, bills needed to be paid. She was also increasingly aware of how much time she'd spent in the past worrying about the inn—worrying about things that she shouldn't have wasted so much of her energy on. Because here she was, all of a sudden, with real and serious problems, including a lawsuit brought by Mr. Konrad.

Jonah had received an intent to sue letter, targeting both Shay and the inn—the inn which might not even belong solely to her. It might be funny except that it wasn't.

She found herself in the unwelcome position of needing Jonah, but not wanting to need him. She had to extricate herself from the personal entanglement she'd foolishly begun, even as she had to rely on him for the legal problems she was suddenly mired in.

And, she realized as she walked down the street toward the hardware store to pick up a new toilet kit, because toilets also needed fixing, that she needed to eat. She ducked into the Caribou to grab a sandwich to go.

She paid for her food and browsed through the *Bargain Blitz* while she waited for her order. Shay circled an ad for a hot tub, the same model that she had at the inn, which could be a good way to secure replacement parts. A lump of emotion clogged her throat as she acknowledged that those hot tubs might no longer belong to her—the hot tubs that she and Tag had painstakingly installed.

Shay accepted the white paper sack containing her order and turned to go, and that's when she saw, on the far side of the restaurant's crowded interior, Laurel seated at a booth with Adele Mason.

An unwelcome feeling of apprehension claimed her as her brain registered the sight. The two women were hunched over the table as if their conversation was extremely riveting— and private. Laurel knew everything about this situation with Adele—she'd been there when Jonah had informed the family.

She wouldn't be doing a story on this, would she? Without consulting her? Shay had to admit the circumstances would make a great story; "long lost relative returns to claim share of family's heritage." Shay nearly cringed at the buzz this would undoubtedly cause in town.

Laurel was as passionate about reporting as Jonah was about the law, but the difference was that like Shay, nothing was more important to Laurel than her friends and her sister Piper—the only family that she did have. Laurel had always been devoted to the James family—she probably knew more about the family than Shay did. Grandpa Gus had been the one to help Laurel become emancipated at the age of sixteen so she could acquire custody of Piper after their mother abandoned them. So what was Laurel doing with Adele?

She exited out the door and the blast of bright sunshine chafed at her already-frayed nerves. She told herself she was being paranoid—it was disloyal to even contemplate whether Laurel might betray her.

Still she wondered how much worse things could possibly get.

AND THAT WAS a question she should have known better than to ask because things can always get worse. Jonah was waiting in her office when she returned to the inn with her newly purchased toilet kit and her uneaten, now unappetizing sandwich.

Shay knew what he wanted to talk about and she knew what she needed to say, but closing the book on her and Jonah would cause more pain that she wasn't quite ready to bear.

"Jonah, I don't have the time for this."

"That seems to be the story of my life where we're concerned, doesn't it?"

"Jonah, there is no 'we' and I really am very busy."

"I realize things are crazy for you right now, but I think there is a *we*, and what I said on our date the other night is true. I meant every word. I know you're angry with me for not telling you about Adele. But now that you've had some time to think things over, I hope you can understand why I couldn't tell you."

Shay clenched her teeth together in frustration. Why was it that he always implied that their arguments were the result of her being too emotional or irrational? Like her *reaction* was the problem rather than the fact that his priorities were all wrong.

"Jonah, I have been thinking—"

"Good, because my feelings haven't changed."

Shay looked into his face and was sure that this had never happened; she could see what Jonah was thinking but wished she couldn't. His blue eyes seemed to be searching her face for some kind of encouragement, some sign that she returned his feelings. But she couldn't give him anything.

"Mine have."

And just like that the curtain dropped, replaced by a stony expression.

"What are you saying?"

"Jonah, you chose the law over me ten years ago and you did it again with Adele. You believe you were doing the right thing—the ethical thing—by keeping this from me. No doubt it was the *legal* thing to do. But I don't even care about that so much as…the fact that it made me see how different we truly are.

"I used to believe that it was money that you were after, and I still think that's a huge part of how you measure success. But I was getting around to accepting that about you because you are a very generous person, Jonah. I can see that now. You have a wonderful heart. But it seems to me that we live life with such a completely opposite focus."

Jonah closed his eyes for a few seconds, and then he looked directly at her. The absence of emotion on his face made her feel far worse than his original disappointment.

"Shay, I'm not sure what to tell you. There is so much about what you said that I want to dispute, but there's some truth there, too…"

Shay waited for him to continue.

"My career is important to me—that's true. But I believe this inn is just as important to you as the law is to me. I know you don't want to hear this, but we both made choices all those years ago, Shay. I had reasons for the decisions I made, just like you did.

"I feel about the Faraway Inn the same as you do about the law. I believe *this* place is what kept us apart—not only *my* career, and yet I'm…"

He stood up.

"You're what?" Shay asked. Each beat of her heart seemed to amplify her sadness and regret. Why did it always hurt so much to do what was right where Jonah was concerned?

Jonah moved toward the door. "Nothing— never mind. I have an appointment, but we'll get these legal matters taken care of, okay? I'll be in touch."

JONAH CHECKED THE time again and worried as to where Hannah was. Konrad would be arriving soon for a settlement conference. Jonah still didn't know what this "evidence" consisted of that Hannah said might help their side of the case.

Hannah burst through the door holding up a cell phone with a bright blue cover. "Sorry it took me so long. I had to recharge it. I've watched it too many times."

"You have video?"

"Yes, just a sec and we can watch it on the monitor." She plugged something into his computer and then stood back. "I like to call this Man versus Moose," she said with a grin as the screen came alive, showing Mr. Konrad snapping photos by the koi pond.

"Let me turn up the volume because the kid filming and his friend provide some commentary. It's hilarious." She reached over and adjusted the sound.

A voice began narrating. "Here we have an old guy tourist stalking the wily, wild goldfish."

Jonah assumed it was the voice of a teenager, but he was doing a superb imitation of those wildlife shows where they talk in an exaggeratedly low tone so as not to scare the wildlife that they'd undoubtedly filmed the day before.

"They are koi," Hannah whispered. "Why can't people get that right?"

"Will he get the shot? Or will the crafty fish dodge the lens once again? Oh, there's an orange and white one—they are notoriously camera shy, those fish. They've only been caught on film eighteen-million times in the last month alone. Hold still little fishy…"

The commentary went on, but the video blurred as another voice murmured an expletive and then said, "Holy crap, dude—moose."

"Whoa! Awesome." The picture focused on a large cow moose and her gangly calf as they strolled toward the pond.

Konrad was no longer in the picture.

"Wow. That baby moose is cute."

"Mom has super long legs—like as tall as you, dude."

"Funny. Oh…hey, what is that tourist guy doing?"

Konrad was back in the scene now and snapping away like some kind of wannabe wildlife paparazzi, but without the agility—or the common sense.

Jonah winced as the videographer panned out and Clara came into full view on the screen; hair standing up on the back of her neck, ears laid flat. Konrad kept moving closer to the calf.

"Uh-oh," Jonah said, riveted by the naiveté of the man on the screen, clearly risking his life. Jonah was also surprised by Clara's level of tolerance at this point. He'd once been with Bering, Tag and Cricket when they'd come upon a cow moose with twins in the middle of the road. The protective mother had rammed Bering's pickup when he'd tried to drive around her—twice.

The teenagers were snickering and Konrad kept getting closer. Clara warned him with a foot stomp and a snort. Konrad moved so that he was now between Clara and the pond. The film suddenly zeroed in on the sign next to the pond, warning about keeping a safe distance from wildlife.

"Brilliant," Jonah breathed.

Hannah snickered. "I know, right? This kid has a future as a journalist."

"Whoa, she's getting ticked," the second teenager said. "She's like blowing snot out of her nose."

"Yeah. Emmett, do you think we should warn him?"

The second teen called out, "Hey, mister?

You might want to back off a little. She's getting really upset and—"

Then both boys started shouting. The picture jumped and blurred slightly as Clara charged, but remained on the scene. The image was refocused quickly.

Jonah couldn't help himself—he had to laugh because Konrad reminded him of a cartoon character as he whipped his head over one shoulder and took off at full speed. But on about the third stride he hit the edge of the trough and face-planted into the koi pond.

The boys were yelling for help, the video kept running, Konrad was flailing, and Clara went in after him, hooves stomping, head butting.

Suddenly a young man came into the picture banging on a pot with a spoon.

"That's Vince," Hannah said. "Clara knows that sound because Javier does that when he feeds her vegetables from the kitchen."

Clara's head came up, ears perked, and she backed out of the pond. She shook like some kind of giant, scraggly dog, then turned and jogged away with her baby glued to her side.

Konrad now stood sputtering, shaking and drenched in water nearly up to his waist. His head whipped back and forth as if searching for evidence of his attacker. Then he reached down and snatched something out of the water.

He stared at his camera and the second teen said with an ill-concealed snigger, "Dude, do you think it's waterproof?"

"Wicked! Man—that guy's so lucky he's not like dead right now."

"Isn't that the truth," Hannah remarked, as she reached over and stopped the video. "Have you ever seen a bigger blockhead in your life? I thought you attorneys were supposed to be smart."

Jonah asked in his best lawyerly tone, "Do you realize what you've done here?"

Hannah's eyes went wide. "What do you mean? Am I in trouble? I haven't showed anyone yet—not even Shay."

Then he grinned. "Hannah, your quick thinking undoubtedly saved your sister thousands of dollars."

Hannah blew out a breath of relief. "Phew. Good."

"How did you get this? How did you even know about it?"

"Vince," Hannah answered. "He saw the boys outside, thought they might be witnesses. I asked around until I found them, learned they'd recorded it, and then bought the phone from the kid. Paid way too much for it, too."

The bell chimed and Jonah looked at the clock. Konrad was right on time—and in for the surprise of his life.

CHAPTER EIGHTEEN

SHAY THOUGHT JONAH looked comfortable here in Caleb's office, lording over this legal microcosm he'd created, however temporary it may be. The notion gave her an extra boost of confidence about the conversation they'd had only the day before about their relationship—or lack thereof.

This was where Jonah thrived—where he belonged—and no matter how disappointing, she needed to concentrate on that because right now she needed him. Well, not him, but his legal expertise. He might not be able to separate the two, but she could.

"Jonah, I want to thank you again. Hannah told me about the meeting with Mr. Konrad. You left out a few details." She couldn't help but smile as she recalled Hannah's humorous rendition of events.

"I can honestly say that I enjoyed this one, Shay. You should have seen the look on his face when I mentioned YouTube."

"I am so grateful. This really had me scared—even as silly as it was."

"Unfortunately these kinds of frivolous lawsuits are prevalent. They can end up costing a lot of money."

"Speaking of that—how much do I owe you?"

"Shay, please—I would never take money from you."

"But Jonah, I know how valuable your time is."

"Shay, no. I wanted to take care of this for you. I can be just as stubborn as you sometimes so don't argue with me about it. Besides, Hannah is the real hero here anyway."

Shay stared at him, absurdly pleased by his words. Not because she didn't have to pay him, but because of the reason he'd given—even though he had called her stubborn.

"Now, if only this situation with Adele could be solved as simply."

"How do things look at this point?"

Jonah held a pen in one hand and tapped it against the palm of the other. "I think she wants money, too."

"What makes you say that?"

"A couple conversations that I've had with her."

Shay tensed at the painful reminder that Jonah had known about this for days before telling her. He'd known before the fishing trip, before he'd kissed her, before their date where she'd nearly slipped under his spell again.

"So, what do we do? Offer her money and hope she goes away?"

"Maybe."

"One little problem there, I don't have any money, Jonah. I've poured every penny I have into the inn—the remodel and the restaurant."

"Don't worry about that. There are always ways to get money, Shay."

She gave him a wry look. "Really? Are you going to loan me your golden goose? Because I'm not asking my family for help with this."

"Yes, I will, Shay, if it comes to that. I will do whatever it takes. First things first—we have to find out if she's related. She's agreed to a DNA test through her attorney."

"I'm not sure that's necessary. She looks just like us. The first day I saw her I thought her appearance was familiar, and now I know why. Have you seen her eyes? They're mine and Hannah's. The rest of her looks exactly like Uncle Eli."

"That doesn't mean anything necessarily. People can be very clever, Shay—con artists,

I mean. You haven't seen the things I have. She could have picked you out of a million people."

"You think Adele is a con artist?"

Jonah's face told her he believed it was a possibility. "I certainly don't trust her. I've had a private investigator looking into her background. She has a juvenile record—shoplifting, burglary."

"Burglary?" And after all of her and Hannah's joking about Kyla.

"I'm hoping to use it as leverage."

"What do you mean, like blackmail?"

"Influence," Jonah corrected smoothly. "Maybe it will help coax her toward a reasonable settlement out of court."

Shay stared at Jonah, his blue eyes were hard and cold, and she realized that she had never really seen Attorney Jonah in action. Hannah said he'd been brilliant with Mr. Konrad and Shay didn't doubt it. He'd always been the smartest, most articulate person she knew. Of course she was aware that he had this ruthless side—how else could he be such a successful attorney? She'd spent years criticizing it—him—for these traits in her mind. Okay, and sometimes out loud, too. Was it hypocritical of her now to be grateful for these qualities?

Shay was confused and unsure as to what

was the right thing to do. Yes, she believed that Grandpa Gus had meant for her to have the inn. Her dad was right—Adele hadn't been a part of the family in the ways that really mattered, but did that mean that she didn't deserve anything? Because her mom was also right—it wasn't Adele's fault that she hadn't been raised as a part of the family, or much of any family apparently, if what she'd revealed to Hannah about her upbringing was true.

"I don't see how her having a record helps me." Shay wasn't convinced it was relevant or fair.

"It's worth a try."

"I should talk to her." She couldn't see any other way around it—she had to find out what Adele wanted. If there was a solution that could circumvent these kinds of dealings, then Shay wanted to find it.

"No," Jonah answered firmly. "As your attorney I forbid it."

She definitely didn't like his attorney tone. "Can you do that? Forbid me from doing things because you're my lawyer?"

"Well…no, but I can discourage you highly. It is not a good idea for you to speak to Adele. From a legal standpoint—"

"Jonah, is it possible for you to separate yourself from your job here? To consider the family angle?"

Shay thought she saw a hint of disapproval on his face, but he was even more difficult to read than normal, now that he had shifted into this mode.

"Why would you want me to, Shay? We're talking about someone threatening your business—your livelihood. This is your family's history, your grandfather's legacy. Your life."

Shay couldn't help but think about their recent conversation; she was struck with the realization of what Jonah was really fighting for here—he was fighting for her, for the inn.

Would she fight this hard for him to keep his law degree if the situation were reversed? She'd spent so much of her life hating that degree, his profession—his obsession. And all this time he'd apparently felt the same about the inn, but here he was trying to save it for her. The depth of his empathy shook her and made her wonder about her own.

"I know that Jonah, but do things always have to be settled through legal means? Can't people ever just talk and work things out?"

"Shay, for someone as intelligent and as business savvy as you are that attitude is really naïve. Frankly, it's what gets people into unnec-

essary legal trouble all the time. Unscrupulous
people thrive on soft-hearted people like you.
Adele is probably banking on your sympathy.
The best way is *always* the legal way."

She didn't believe that—not really. And she
didn't think he really believed it either. He'd
proven it himself with some of the cases he'd
handled for Caleb. Did he not see that?

"What about Gary and Ingrid? You seemed
to handle that just fine without a big legal
mess."

"Shay, we're not talking about some old
friends of ours from high school who are considering divorce. This is serious. This involves
the inn. This involves a lot of money."

There it was again—money.

"Divorce is serious, too, Jonah. Way more
serious than money to me. In fact, there are a
lot of things in life more important to me than
money."

He huffed out a frustrated breath. "Shay,
look—I don't need another lecture about my
priorities. I know what I'm doing here. This is
what I do. Let me handle it."

"But—"

His look softened and his voice was almost a
plea. "Please, Shay. Trust me on this. For once

in your life, can you let someone—maybe even *me*—take care of you?"

SHAY SAT IN her office and tried to sort through some bills, but a replay of her meeting with Jonah kept interfering. Bottom line—she didn't trust him.

She trusted his intentions, but she didn't trust his reverence for the law and she didn't trust his priorities. Yes, her life—the inn, was at stake here, but what if there was another way to settle this? The part that he didn't seem to be taking into account was that if Adele was family, and Shay believed she was, then she would always be family. Didn't that mean something?

It did to Shay. And she knew it did to her parents. Even if her dad was skeptical of Adele, family was everything to him. It certainly had been to Grandpa Gus, as well. Were they the ones who were wrong and Jonah right? No, because Caleb didn't have these mixed up priorities either...

Suddenly she looked up to find Hannah standing in front of her.

"Shay, Adele is here. She's asking to see you. I didn't know what to tell her."

"Thanks, Hannah. I'll talk to her." Shay

stood and walked out to the reception desk to find Adele waiting.

She started talking before Shay had a chance to speak. "I have a shift in the restaurant tonight, but I don't know if I still have a job?"

"Adele, you still have a job here if you want one."

Adele's eyes met hers. She shut them for a few seconds and then opened them again with a whoosh of her breath. "Shay…could we sit down and talk for a few minutes?"

This could be her opportunity, but Jonah's words of warning flashed through her brain. Did she trust him enough to listen to his advice or did she trust herself and take this on like she was so used to doing?

It was far outside her comfort zone to let other people fight her battles for her. On the contrary, she was used to fighting other people's battles as well as her own.

JONAH THOUGHT HE had developed a good understanding of why people with pets lived longer than those without them. Walking Francis felt cathartic, and with Gramps laid up the responsibility had fallen entirely to him.

He wiped Francis's paws with a cloth that Gramps kept by the door for that very purpose.

He slipped his shoes off and started down the hallway only to find Gramps balancing on his crutches.

"Gramps? What are you doing up?"

"I'm not an invalid. It's just a broken ankle."

Jonah rushed to his side. "I know but Doc said it was best to stay off of it for the first couple weeks. What do you need? I can get it for you."

"Shay called, looking for you. She told me all about Eli's daughter and the inn. Jonah, why didn't you tell me all this was going on?"

"I guess because at first I thought you might be ill and I didn't want to cause you any further stress. Then you broke your ankle. I wasn't trying to keep it from you—just trying to save you the trouble. What did Shay say?"

"Apparently the young woman showed up at the inn for her shift at the restaurant. She asked to speak to Shay and Shay was uncertain about what to do. She said you told her not to talk to her?"

"I did." Jonah felt his heart kick up its pace. "What did you tell her?"

"I told her that she should probably follow her attorney's advice for now."

"That's good. This is a difficult situation,

Gramps. I could use your help if you're up for it. Do you have any thoughts?"

"Well, I'm not teetering around on these two sticks to enter a tap dancing competition. I'm headed to the office for a reason. I need to look at a file."

"A buyout might be the answer," Jonah offered as he helped Gramps get settled in the office, propping his broken ankle on a chair. "This woman is probably desperate for money. And I've got some information about her that might help, uh…sway her into accepting it."

"What makes you think so? That money is what she's after?"

"What else could it be? I can't think of any other reason she would have proceeded in the manner that she has. Can you?"

Gramps looked thoughtful. "I can. But if you're right, then it won't be cheap. And I doubt Shay has—"

Jonah tucked a pillow under Gramps's cast. "I have it. And I don't care about the money, Gramps."

Gramps flashed him a pride-filled grin. "Open that bottom cabinet drawer there on the right and hand me the file marked 'Gus' and then you'd better get to the inn. I'm afraid that Shay, as stubborn as that girl can be, isn't going to heed her esteemed attorneys' advice."

CALEB WATCHED JONAH'S face transform with alarm. He quickly located the thick file he'd asked for and then handed it over.

"Gramps, you're right. I need to get up to the inn. I swear she is the most exasperating woman. Will you be all right here?"

"Doc is on his way over. He can help me out."

"Okay, I'll keep you informed. And answer the phone in case I have any questions?"

"You got it." Caleb grinned as Jonah darted out the door. Francis climbed to her feet and watched him go. She let out a whine when the door shut behind him. Caleb chuckled and scratched her ears. She turned a couple circles and flopped back down with a disappointed wheeze.

"He makes a fine member of this pack, too, Francis. If only we could get him to see it, huh? You've been doing your part though, my girl, and I love you for it."

Caleb opened the file and rifled through the papers until he found what he was looking for. He pondered the situation for a moment and then reached over to where his crutches were leaning against the desk. He grabbed them and stood, wincing with pain until he got his balance. Then he turned toward the shelf full of legal tomes that took up most of one wall. He reached up to the top shelf and pulled down the three slim green volumes containing his son's journals.

SHAY STOOD BEHIND the front desk while a battle waged inside her head. Did she follow her intuition and have this conversation with Adele or did she listen to her team of attorneys advising her not to?

She'd asked Adele to give her a few minutes. Then she'd gone to her office and called Jonah. He hadn't answered his cell so she'd tried Caleb. Jonah hadn't been there either, but after filling Caleb in on the situation, he had gone along with Jonah's advice.

The door to the inn swung open and Laurel rushed inside.

"Laurel, what's going on? I've been calling you. Where have you been?"

"Hi, Shay. Sorry about that. I've been swamped with some research. Where's Adele?"

"Adele? She's getting ready for her shift. What's going on, Laurel? I saw you in the restaurant with her."

Laurel nodded like the revelation wasn't unexpected—or important. "There are some things Adele would like to discuss with you and I've agreed to help her."

"You—what? You're helping her?"

"It's not what you think, Shay. I know how you must be feeling."

"Laurel, I sincerely doubt that."

"Shay, we've been friends forever. I owe so much to your family. Do you really believe I would be disloyal to you?"

"No, but—"

Shay saw Adele walking toward them.

"Think of this as investigative journalism, okay? There are some things I've discovered and we want to share them with you. Adele, I'm sorry I'm late. I was waiting for—"

Laurel stopped talking as Jonah came charging through the door.

"Shay, what are you doing? Gramps said you called. You are not going to talk to that woman without me present." He cast an accusatory glare at Adele.

"Laurel wants to have a discussion with me and Adele. Apparently she has some information."

Jonah started shaking his head. "Nope, no way. Absolutely not."

Laurel fisted her hands and planted them on her hips. "Why not?"

"This needs to be settled through legal means. I am Shay's attorney and I—"

"Why?" Laurel interrupted.

"Why what?"

"Why does this need to be settled through legal means?"

Jonah scoffed. "Because that's how you settle complicated legal matters like this, Laurel. You're a reporter—you should know this. And if you're trying to coerce my client into speaking without counsel present—"

Laurel put out a hand. "Stop, right there, Jonah. Coerce? Me, coerce Shay? I don't know a person on this planet that could coerce Shay into anything. And since when did you adopt this condescending tone? You can dial down the lawyer act, Jonah, we've known each other since we were kids. I remember when you licked the glue off the bottle during art class back in grade school."

Adele snuffled out a surprised snort of laughter.

Jonah glared. "What is this about, Laurel?"

"Let's sit down and talk about it. Shay, can we use your conference room?"

"Absolutely," Shay said. Without looking to

Jonah for confirmation, she turned and led the others to the room across the hall from her office. She opened the door and they all filed inside. Laurel and Adele sat on one side of the table—Shay and Jonah on the other.

Jonah oozed impatience and superiority as he demanded, "Get on with it. And for the record I'd like to say that as Shay's legal counsel I am against this meeting."

Laurel lifted her hands, palms up, and shrugged. "Look around you, Jonah. There is no *record*."

Shay shot Jonah an inquiring look, but he was staring daggers at Laurel.

Laurel didn't appear to be intimidated in the least. She reached up and pulled a pencil out of her dark silky bun.

"Shay, are you okay with this?"

"Yes, of course, Laurel. I trust you."

Laurel pointed her pencil at Jonah along with a scathing look. "That good enough for you, counselor?"

"I'm warning you, Laurel. I will stop Shay from saying anything that could complicate this case for her."

"Whatever, Jonah. That's fine. But you're going to be surprised when I tell you that there is no case. We want to share some information and review a few things."

Jonah set his intimidating attorney stare on Adele, but Shay doubted that it was having the effect that it might have had before Laurel's glue-licking comment.

Laurel brought her palms together and tilted them so her fingertips were pointed at Jonah. "I'll start. When I heard about Adele's claim I decided to look into the matter myself."

"Why?" Jonah asked.

"I'm a reporter, curious by nature. Shay is one of my dearest friends. As you're well aware, the Jameses are the closest thing to family that Piper and I have. And I thought it might be useful if I learned as much as I could in an effort to help—which included both talking to and learning about Adele."

"I've learned plenty about her myself." Jonah's voice was cold, and thick with sarcasm.

"Let me guess, you're referring to her juvenile record? Which I'd be willing to bet you were hoping to use as some kind of leverage?"

Jonah didn't give anything away but Shay felt her already over-strung nerves tighten further. She knew very well that information had been Jonah's ace in the hole, even though she hadn't wanted him to use it. She prayed that Laurel knew what she was doing.

Laurel continued, "That information is not going to help you, Jonah. Adele was fifteen years old and in the wrong place at the wrong time with a boyfriend who was a two-bit criminal. She was young and stupid, and then she was misrepresented by an over-worked public defender. She pled to a misdemeanor when she shouldn't have. But it doesn't matter because nobody cares."

"Get to the point, Laurel," Jonah returned firmly.

Laurel turned toward Shay.

"Here's the important stuff. Shay, I talked to your Uncle Lyman. Adele's mom, Stella, was Lyman's secretary—that's how she met Eli. He confirmed the affair between them."

She looked at Adele. Laurel's expression conveyed a great deal of empathy. "He said your mom and Eli were in love. Stella was married at the time—unhappily by all accounts, but married nonetheless. Eli knew nothing about Stella's pregnancy because she quit her job and moved to Utah. We can only assume that your mom didn't want to break up her marriage, which is kind of sad because as you well know it ended anyway."

"That is such a touching and romantic tale of love, Laurel, but come on. This woman has been consulting attorneys, befriending Shay and her family, and apparently her friends, too, and just generally sneaking around."

Then he turned his piercing, dubious stare on Adele. "Why don't you cut to the chase and tell us what you want?"

Adele's lips had formed a grim line and it appeared as if she was trying not to cry. She shook her head and placed one hand over her mouth.

CHAPTER NINETEEN

AFTER A MOMENT, Adele managed to pull herself together. She splayed her hands on the table top in front of her.

"Honestly? I'm not sure now what I want. I came to Rankins to meet with an attorney named Caleb Cedar. My attorney in Utah is an acquaintance of Lyman James and he felt confident that Caleb could help ease me into a relationship with the James family, but *he* was there instead." She gestured at Jonah.

"My plan was to introduce myself to Caleb and Shay first, offer to take a DNA test—whatever it took to try and work something out. I called Shay a few times to set up a meeting but she never called me back."

Shay felt so guilty about that. And the idea that she could have avoided all of this by returning a simple phone call made her head spin. But just as quickly she realized that it didn't change the fact that Adele might still own a part of the Faraway Inn.

"I got impatient, so one day I went up to the inn to talk to Shay. I didn't intend to get a job."

She looked intently at Shay. "If you remember, Shay, you just assumed I was there to apply for a job, and then Hannah started interviewing me and you guys were so sweet, and I thought…it seemed like the perfect way to get to know you and Hannah. I planned on telling you both, but I was nervous…

"And then I went to see Jonah and he made me consider another angle—like what if you and your family didn't believe me? What if you thought I was attempting some kind of scam? I decided to wait until I could speak with Caleb or until I had some proof of who I am. Thanks to Laurel I finally have more than just my mom's word."

Her eyes were wide and sincere, and Shay felt herself being taken in by the honesty shooting from their unnervingly familiar amber-colored depths.

"I don't know why I didn't think about how it might look that I accepted the job without telling you who I was. I didn't even consider that aspect until Jonah pointed it out the day you had lunch together at the restaurant. Until then, I guess I thought I might seem cowardly… not dishonest."

Jonah looked defensive—and completely unconvinced.

Shay believed her. She knew Jonah would be disappointed, but she could understand Adele's fear. She knew all too well how difficult it was to think straight when you were scared.

"I'm really sorry, Shay. I can see now that I probably should have handled things differently."

Shay was ready to try and accept Adele as family. And if she was entitled to a part of the inn…well, then she'd have to trust that they could work something out. She'd certainly survived worse hardships than this.

Adele reached into her bag and removed an envelope and a tissue. She wiped her nose with the tissue and set the envelope on the table. "And as far as the property goes and the Faraway Inn? I know I'm not—"

LATER SHAY WOULD describe the following sequence of events like a scene from an old primetime network law drama. The door of the conference room slammed open, a voice yelled "Stop. Hold it right there." And then a wheel-chair bound Caleb sailed into the room followed by Doc.

"Caleb!" Shay cried.

"Gramps!" Jonah said at the same time.

Murmurs followed exclamations.

"I have it," Caleb said. "I knew I was right, but I didn't want to say anything until I had the proof."

"What proof?" asked Jonah.

Caleb rose carefully from the wheelchair and addressed Adele. "Allow me to introduce myself, Ms. James. My name is Caleb Cedar. I truly regret we were unable to become acquainted sooner. Maybe some of this could have been avoided."

Adele stood, moved forward and extended a hand, clearly taken in by Caleb's charm—and undoubtedly by the use of her rightful surname. "A pleasure to finally meet you, Mr. Cedar."

Then she introduced herself to Doc.

"Doc and I knew your father Eli very well, Ms. James. He was a wonderful man and I'm sorry you didn't get the chance to know him yourself before he passed."

Adele nodded happily, tears shimmering in her eyes. "Thank you, Mr. Cedar."

"Please—call me Caleb."

"Gramps?" Jonah interjected. "Do you want to have a seat and explain what's going on?"

Doc helped Caleb get settled in his wheelchair before scooting him up to the table. Then he claimed a spot, too.

Caleb spread out some papers. "I've brought documents—deeds, letters, conveyances and sales agreements... Here's the deed that shows Adele may indeed have a valid claim to a portion thereof..."

"We're already aware of that, Gramps."

Caleb looked sideways at Jonah and said patiently, "I'm not finished." His eyes scanned the rest of the group. "As some of you are aware, Gus was a close personal friend of mine. And I was also his attorney. I was Eli's attorney as well until he moved back to the lower forty-eight. Just after Eli moved to Colorado, Gus and Eli struck up a deal with regards to the property's value."

Caleb pushed a single sheet of paper into the center of the table. "He paid Eli for his share of the property and here's a copy of the check to prove it. It's partially my fault that a deed was never properly recorded. Now, of course I'm willing to testify to my knowledge—"

Adele interrupted smoothly. "That won't be necessary, Caleb." She removed some papers from the envelope that had been sitting in front of her and handed them to Caleb.

Every eye was fastened upon Adele.

"I had my attorney in Utah draft these documents transferring any claim I may have on the property or the inn to Shay."

Shay's heart was pounding wildly but she managed to ask, "What? Why…?"

"It was never meant to be mine. I know that now. Laurel talked to Lyman and learned that Gus paid my dad for his share of the property. That was all the proof I needed. I was never out to get anything that didn't rightfully belong to me. I've fallen in love with this family and I do not want to be the cause of any further anguish for any of you."

Shay stared at Adele; the tears filling Adele's eyes seemed to match her own. "Adele—"

"You're my family, Shay. You, Hannah, Tag, your parents, Bering, Janie… You guys *have* the family I've always dreamed of having and even if I've blown the chance to be a part of it I'm proud that this is what I come from."

"Adele, I'm confident I can speak on behalf of all the Jameses and say that you haven't blown anything at all."

"HEY, WHAT ARE you up to?" Caleb asked Jonah as he hobbled into his office. Jonah was seated at his desk, and Caleb wished he would hurry up and realize he was as comfortable there as he looked. But for now he was happy to have his darn itchy cast off and to have retired his crutches and the wheelchair that made him feel like an invalid. A few more weeks with this walking boot and he would be as good as new.

"Just reading Dad's journals."

Caleb thought Jonah's answer might be too good to be true. He'd been looking for a way to segue into this conversation. After removing Burke's journals from the shelf, he'd placed them on a stack of paperwork knowing Jonah would stumble across them. It had taken him long enough.

Jonah had seemed to enjoy his remaining summer in Rankins, fishing, hiking, reconnecting with old friends—even though Caleb knew he was missing Shay and battling with the choice of returning to his life in Chicago or coming home to stay. Jonah didn't voice his struggle outright, but Caleb knew.

"Uh-huh?" Caleb lowered himself onto a chair.

Jonah leaned back and sighed. "You know, it's been a long time since I've read Dad's journals. I think I was fourteen or fifteen when I last read them—*really* read through them. Not just skimming or looking at bits and pieces—or the parts he addressed to me directly."

"Little different perspective now?" Caleb asked, hoping the answer was yes. Maybe Jonah was figuring a few things out on his own—asking some questions that needed asking—and answered.

"Yes, definitely. Although I will admit that it was something Shay mentioned more than once that sparked this train of thought. She thinks I'm obsessed with money. Dad talks about wealth and success so much in these journals—intertwines them. I have spent my life believing that was an effective way to measure my success, but when I think about my job—it's the law I really love. I've been paid very well, and sure it's nice, but if I take money out of the equation I would still be happy doing this job even if I didn't make as much.

"But when this whole thing with Adele happened...

"Gramps, I might not be as good of an attorney as I think I am. Why did I automatically assume that she wanted money? Shay is right—I've been so programmed to think that's what everybody wants, but there *are* people out there who aren't motivated by money."

"That's true, thank goodness," Gramps said and then grinned. "Jonah, as attorneys we all have those moments when we realize that the strategy we've adopted is all wrong. Don't be too hard on yourself. Learn from those mistakes, apply them to the next case, and *that* makes you a better attorney."

Jonah shook his head. "It's just shaken me up I guess. I was so sure…"

Gramps offered an easy shrug. "You were too close. You let your feelings for Shay cloud your judgment. You wanted to fix this for her, make her happy—that's what we do for the people we love. There's nothing wrong with that, Jonah. It speaks to your character—to your love for Shay."

Caleb hoped he understood the subtle reference to his own deception in luring Jonah home. He still believed it had been the right thing to do. Even if Jonah decided to go back to Chicago, Caleb felt confident he would still appreciate these new-found discoveries about himself. But he didn't want him in Chicago—he wanted him here. He believed this was where Jonah would find true happiness.

"Gramps, you were right about your motivation for wanting me to come home. I do still love her."

"You two make up yet?"

"No, I'm afraid there's no making up this time, Gramps. She will never trust me. She thinks my career is too important to me—more important than the people in my life. She says I've always chosen the law over her." He let out a cynical chuckle. "And I suppose that last part is true as far as law school went. But what choice did I have? I mean Yale Law—what was I supposed to do?"

"I don't think she ever expected you to choose differently there, did she? I mean, she was all set to go with you when Gus up and died and gave her the inn. What choice did *she* have?"

Jonah nodded. "I know, but I've always felt like she could have opened a hotel anywhere. I couldn't go to law school anywhere."

He said it like Caleb should understand the significance of the prestige he'd been awarded. And he did. He'd attended Yale himself and could not possibly have been prouder when Jonah followed—except…

"But what about after Yale? You had a choice then. You knew you were welcome here."

Jonah smiled. "I know that, Gramps. And I've always loved knowing that, but I wanted to make my dad proud, to have my own success. His advice seemed so wise—about always making sure I had enough financially. I didn't see it as money buying happiness—I saw it as money buying security. I wanted to have the life Dad never had—the life he wanted. The life he wanted for me. But now, when I really think about it, I'm not sure I am motivated by money, Gramps. I think that would disappoint my dad."

Caleb felt a jab in the vicinity of his heart, worse than the jabs of pain from his healing ankle bones. He looked right at Jonah and realized they didn't call tough love "tough" for no reason. In fact he decided on the spot that it should be called "brutal" love.

"Son, speaking of your father—there was a little more to my motivation in getting you back here than pushing you and Shay together."

"What do you mean?"

"Have you ever wondered why your father didn't go out and have that life he was always chirping about?"

"He was stuck here in Rankins." Jonah's voice rang with certainty. He tapped on the journal lying open on the desk in front of him as if it were all the proof he needed.

"What makes you think he was any more stuck than me? Or Doc? Or Crab? Or anyone else who settles here in this delightful little corner of the world?"

Caleb watched Jonah's eyes shift and settle on the wall of books above Caleb's head. "I don't know. In his journals he talks about being stuck in this town, and about how much he doesn't want that for me. How he wants to get me out of here. How important it is for me to be able to take care of myself, have security, and afford the things I need."

"Jonah—you know I loved your dad. He was my son. I loved him every bit as much as any father has ever loved one of their own. But I thank the stars that your heart is more like mine—and your mother's—than it is his."

Those blue eyes locked on his and Caleb saw the curiosity swirling in there.

"Burke talks a fair amount in those journals of his about how much he misses the city, too, right?"

"Yes, he does."

"Did you ever consider why he left it in the first place? If he loved it so much, why didn't he stay there?"

Jonah's brow furrowed in thought. "I assumed he came back because Nana had died."

Caleb shook his head. "Nope—your grandmother died months before he and your mother moved back. And I tell you—as sorry as I was to lose her, I'm glad she didn't live to see the mess he'd created—the lives he destroyed."

"Lives he destroyed? Gramps, what do you mean?"

"Jonah, he was *stuck* in Rankins because he was running from the law. I was doing my best to try and unravel it all for him when he and your mother were killed in that plane crash."

Caleb watched the shock transform Jonah's face.

Finally he spoke. "Gramps—what?"

"Your dad was a criminal, Jonah. There's no way for me to spin it—and I don't think I should. You're a grown man and I was wrong to keep it from you all these years. I'm so sorry, son. I'm sorry that it happened, and I'm sorry that I wasn't honest with you from the start. But mostly I'm sorry for how it shaped you— for the choices I believe you made for him instead of yourself."

JONAH DIDN'T THINK he'd ever experienced emotions like he was having now. To say that his foundation was shaken was an understatement.

Maybe Gramps was on to something about being too close to the situation with Shay and Adele. He could see that now, how badly he'd wanted to fix everything for Shay—to take away her pain and maybe make up for some of what he'd failed to do ten years ago.

But, his own father...? How had he not seen this?

"What did he do?" He found himself asking the question even though he knew the answer was going to hurt. It felt a lot like driving by a car accident and trying not to look; you just wanted to assure yourself that this horrible, terrifying thing wasn't happening to you...

"Stole about ten million dollars from clients and lost it all."

Jonah knew his dad had been a real estate developer, but he'd never really known any details about his business.

"It was a phony land investment deal. You know your dad went to college in California. That's where he met your mom. Audrey was a good woman, Jonah—I want you to know that. She wasn't aware of any of this until it was too late. Broke her heart, too. Anyway, he decided to stay in California after he graduated because he loved city life. Like you, he rarely came home. Until he got into trouble."

"Gramps, I, I'm...Why didn't you ever tell me?"

Caleb ran a hand over his jaw like he did when he was mulling something over. "I should

have. I see that now. But how do you tell a
nine-year-old or a twelve-year-old or even a
seventeen-year-old boy who lost both of his parents in such a devastating and tragic way that
his dad was a crook? And then when you got
older…I don't know, I thought it best to let you
have your fantasy of your dad as a good guy.
What could it hurt? But then I began to see how
much it affected you, Jonah. Too much. You've
spent too much time trying to have the life your
dad wanted instead of the life you want."

Jonah thought about how hard he had tried to
live up to his dad's expectations. How he'd tried
to take the letters from those journals and apply
them to his life; 'Dear Jonah, I can't stress to
you enough the importance of wealth. In spite
of what some people say, Jonah, money *can*
buy you happiness if you know how to use it…'

Passages ran through his head—how important it was to have financial means, not only
to buy material things, but for the prestige that
wealth brought. Had his wealth brought him
prestige? He wasn't even sure what that meant
now—prestige? He supposed it had earned him
a certain status back in Chicago, but prestige
meant something entirely different here in
Rankins.

He believed Gramps, Shay, Doc, Bering,

Agnes, Mrs. Milner—these were the kinds of people who enjoyed good standing in this town, and not because of how much money they made, but because of the people they were; generous, loyal, honest, and full of integrity.

He realized now that his dad likely hadn't had any of those qualities. He wasn't sure how many he had himself, and that was the toughest realization of all. He'd spent his life trying to be a certain person—but he was also recognizing that all of that ambition and drive had been wasted on trying to acquire the wrong things, and fostering many of the wrong traits.

"I'm so sorry, Jonah."

Jonah stared at the man who truly deserved his love and adoration. The man who had, throughout Jonah's childhood, shown by his example what mattered in life. His father had stressed the importance of "wealth" equating it with "success." Gramps had hoped Jonah would discover what was really important on his own. And then, when he hadn't—when he'd seen how much Jonah had diverted from that foundation that he'd lain—he'd done his best to steer him right again. Sure, his method had been a bit…unorthodox. But it had worked.

Jonah was so grateful to this man, so incredibly lucky to have him. A lump of emotion welled in his chest and he made a vow to not waste another minute of his life caring about the things that, in the end, really didn't matter.

"Gramps, I'm sorry, too. I feel like an idiot for not seeing through my dad's nonsense. Now I can so clearly see his journals for what they are—the desperate ramblings of a man—a criminal, trying to justify his crimes."

"I should have shared this with you years ago, Jonah."

"Maybe, but I don't know that I would have heard it the same years ago, Gramps. I probably would have still wanted to see for myself if Dad was right. So thank you. Thank you for... tricking me into coming home. I like who I am when I'm here."

Gramps's face radiated with another big smile. "Are you saying what I think you're saying, Jonah?"

"If you'll have me. Gramps, if you want a law partner, then yes."

Nodding his head, Gramps removed a handkerchief from his pocket. He wiped his eyes and then his nose. It took a few long seconds before he could speak. "Yes. Yes, I sure would like that, Jonah."

And in that moment Jonah knew this was the best career decision he'd ever made.

Gramps cleared his throat. "So, how are you going to fix things with Shay?"

"I'm not sure if I can, Gramps. I think she'll probably forgive me, but I don't know that she'll ever trust me. Really trust me like she needs to if we're going to try again. And then there's another problem. It's not a problem for me, it's just that she believes it is. Anyway, it's shaped her choices as much as Dad's journals shaped mine."

"You're talking about her not being able to have kids?"

"You know about that?"

"I suspected."

Jonah narrowed his eyes and thought that he'd probably more than "suspected." He didn't bother to clarify, but he knew that Doc had been the physician who initially treated Shay in Rankins after her miscarriage.

"It's a huge issue for her. Shay has always wanted kids. The fact that she can't is heartbreaking, Gramps. And she can't seem to get past it."

"It may sound harsh, Jonah, but the truth is, there are worse things in life. Much, much worse—and besides, no one gives you any guarantee about what you're going to get when you sign up to be a parent. I loved your dad, but I didn't like who he turned out to be all that much."

"How do I make Shay see this? How do I make her see that I don't care if we can't have kids? We would still have each other—and you. And she's got more than enough family for all of us. In fact, they seem to be coming out of the woodwork lately."

Gramps let out a chuckle. "If you're open to it, I may have an idea or two."

"Don't listen to him, Jonah," Doc called out as he strolled into the office. Neither one of them had heard him come in through the front door—not even Francis who was snoozing under the desk at Jonah's feet. "We all know the trouble his ideas can get us into."

"You're a sneaky old coot—you know that?"

"If I wasn't, you'd be in here talking Jonah into something just as foolish as I let you talk me into on an almost daily basis."

"That doesn't even make sense. Now, sit down. We need to help Jonah come up with a plan."

Doc's face lit with eagerness. "Is this about Shay?"

"Yes, it is. Now listen…"

"A letter?" Doc said a little while later after

Caleb had revealed his plan. "That's your big idea?"

"Yes!" Gramps scowled at Doc. "A good old-fashioned letter where Jonah pours his heart out to Shay—letters are prominently featured in a lot of romance stories, you know?"

"Do tell. You're an expert in romance novels now in addition to the law?"

"Women like letters. They like words. Sometimes—and you might want to pay attention here, Doc—men aren't so great with words."

Doc chuckled.

That was certainly true, Jonah thought, his mouth had gotten him into plenty of trouble where Shay was concerned—and Adele and Laurel, too, for that matter. And speaking of words...

Doc raised a finger and seemed ready to shout eureka. "He should give her a gift— something special and meaningful and romantic. Women like romantic baubles, too."

Gramps rolled his eyes. "Baubles?"

"You know jewels and...what not."

Gramps snuffled out a laugh. "What not? Is that what you've been giving to Bernice these days?"

Doc shrugged a shoulder. "Bernice happens

to like flowers. It wouldn't do you any harm to send Mary Beth a bouquet now and then."

"I'll have you know that Mary Beth doesn't particularly care for flowers. She says they make her sad because they look so pretty at first, but then they die too fast. She likes candy. She is one of those rare and precious women who doesn't have a love-hate relationship with chocolate—she just has the love."

Jonah sat forward and said, "These are both great ideas, fellas. I'll write the letter and I already have the perfect—hopefully—bauble. But I might need something even more drastic."

The potential implication of what he was about to suggest nauseated him. He felt it might explain a lot for Shay—it certainly had for him now that he'd seen the information through older, more mature eyes, but what if the content only confirmed her belief that he was self-centered and materialistic by nature—that these unattractive traits were genetic or worse?

Gramps and Doc were staring at him expectantly.

"I'm thinking I should let her read Dad's journals, too—if that's okay with you Gramps?"

CHAPTER TWENTY

SHAY WALKED ALONG the waterfront toward the spot where she'd told Jonah she'd meet him. She couldn't believe August had already arrived. More than a month had passed since they'd learned of Adele's identity; more than a month since she'd rushed to the edge of that emotional cliff and nearly leapt into something crazy with Jonah.

She and Jonah had reached a place in their relationship where they could be friends. The sniping, the arguing, and the recriminations had disappeared, and they'd rediscovered the mutual respect they once shared. And she liked the way Jonah had used the rest of his remaining stay in Rankins; spending time with Caleb, with Bering, Tag and other friends, fishing and hiking, and even doing a little babysitting for the Wattes.

Adele had been accepted into the James fold and was busy absorbing her heritage, asking questions, and learning how to be a part of a family. Shay had hired her as the Faraway Restaurant's manager and she was excelling in the position.

Jonah had taken Adele to lunch, and while not privy to all that had transpired, she knew Jonah had apologized for his assumptions. Jonah told her that Adele had refused to allow herself to be held blameless, insisting that she should have revealed her identity sooner.

Adele had then told Shay how lucky she was to have someone love her as much as Jonah so obviously did. Burke's journals had added yet another angle to Shay's feelings for Jonah. And it all made finally letting him go for good even more difficult.

Shay spotted Jonah seated at a picnic table— backwards, his long legs stretched out in front of him, elbows resting on the table behind him. Francis sat calmly by his side as if she too were enjoying the view.

The waterfront was being transformed for Gary and Ingrid's anniversary party later that evening—pots of flowers had been set about and strings of twinkle lights were hanging here and there. A group of men were assembling a temporary dance floor on a green expanse of lawn.

Shay went over to where Jonah sat staring into the waters of the bay. Francis rose to greet her.

Jonah smiled. "Hi."

"Hey," she said, patting Francis before climbing up to sit on the table. She placed her feet on the bench beside Jonah and leaned forward to rest her forearms on her knees.

"This view," he said. "I can't seem to get enough of it these days—ever since I've been back. Something just pulls me here. Well, Francis nudges me along, too. She's gotten to the point where she just stares me down. I put these shoes on and she knows we're going for a walk. I don't wear them anymore unless I know I can bring her with me."

Shay chuckled. "Francis has you wrapped around her furry paw. You always loved going out on the bay."

"She does," he admitted. "With you," he added. "I liked going out on the bay with you— the privacy we had out there on the water—the sense that we were really alone for a little while. That can be an elusive feeling in this town."

She smiled. "I liked that, too."

Jonah's eyes searched her face.

"Jonah, I read your letter, and I read your dad's journals. It's awful and mind-boggling— you must be reeling. I can't believe no one ever found out about what he did."

"I have Gramps to thank for that. And Doc,

too—apparently he knew and never said a word to anyone." He gave his head a shake. "Those two—they are really something. Like brothers—at least how I imagine brothers would be."

Shay wanted to reach over and take his hand but she stopped herself.

"Jonah, I'm so sorry."

"It's crazy," he said. "How much of my life I've lived based on those stupid journals. And it was all a lie." His voice was filled with disgust. "My father was a criminal. Why couldn't I see that before?"

"I don't think your dad's love for you was a lie. And I think he wanted what he thought was best for you. He was definitely mixed up about the things that are important in life—the things that truly make a man, or a person for that matter."

"Where did that greed come from?"

Shay watched a bird swoop down close to the water. She wondered what he was fishing for and wished that she and Jonah were out there fishing at this moment, too.

"I don't know. Where do anyone's faults come from?"

He inhaled a long breath, exhaled, and then turned to look at her. "I'm afraid, Shay. I'm afraid that I'm like him. And I'm afraid that you probably think even worse of me now…"

His words were filled with so much pain, and his troubled face echoed every word. Shay winced.

"You do. You've told me so many times, Shay. Selfish, career-obsessed, neglectful of Gramps and my friends, disdainful of this town… And the way I treated Adele…"

This time she did take his hand. She laid it in her lap and placed her palm on his, relishing the feel of his warm skin on hers, how it made her feel safe.

"No, that's not why I was flinching, Jonah. I was flinching at the pain in your eyes. When you let me see it—then I know it's bad. Those journals do explain a lot about you. I understand your motivations so much better now. Thank you for that—for sharing them with me, but some of this stuff I'd already figured out on my own.

"Jonah, I want you to know that a lot of the things I've said to you over the years came out of my own anger and bitterness. I'm so sorry for that. You were right about me being every bit as obsessed with the Faraway Inn as you have been with your law career. I was just so… self-righteous about it because I thought my reasons were so much more pure than yours. That I didn't have a choice, when in fact you were right—I did. I just couldn't see that I did.

"But you have to know that you're nothing like your dad, Jonah. Even when you tried to be—you couldn't be—not really. All the gifts you've bought for Gramps, the charities that you've given to, the pro bono work. The things you've done right here in Rankins this summer? Do you think your dad would have done any of those things? Or been proud of you for doing those things?"

"No."

"And putting your life on hold to come home for your gramps—not because you were hiding from your mistakes or running from the law and expecting someone else to clean up the mess you made? That speaks to who you are, Jonah—your love for your gramps."

He ran his free hand over his unshaven jaw. Shay's heart ached to think that he'd been worried that those journals would make her think worse of him.

"And I know what you were trying to do for me with regards to Adele, and how you handled Konrad? I think the world of you for fighting for me, Jonah, and I won't ever forget it."

"It's just… My world has pretty much been turned upside down. The things that I want…"

"Jonah, you still have all of the things you want—a successful career, money, an expensive apartment—your car. None of that has changed. And just because you have these things doesn't make you a bad person, or mean that you're like your dad. You earned everything you have, Jonah. You. You didn't lie or steal or cheat to get where you are. And that you should be proud of. I am. Your gramps is."

His gaze froze her in place and yet made her insides—and her resolve—begin to melt.

"For me it has though. The things I want are totally different than what I thought. Now that I'm…free, I guess, to want them."

She broke eye contact because she couldn't let him head in this direction. "Okay, well, I'm sure that whatever it is you do want now can be yours, too."

He stared silently out over the water. He squeezed her hand and Shay's heart began to beat fast and hard.

"What if what I want is you, Shay?"

"Jonah, no… You're just feeling adrift right now because your life view has changed so dramatically. But that doesn't change who you are as a person. You're still an attorney—

an excellent attorney. You're still going back to Chicago. That's where you're happy. And I'm staying here. This is where I belong—in Rankins."

His eyes were so clear and full of emotion. "I haven't been happy in a long time, Shay. I can see that now. And I doubt you have been happy, either—not really. I've spent my life trying to please a dead man, convincing myself that it would please me, too. And you've been married to the inn, using it as some kind of a replacement for the love you think you don't deserve because of the children you can't have."

"Jonah, I've—" She started to deny it, but she knew his words were true. She had attempted to use the inn to fill that empty space inside of her. She'd been unsuccessful, she realized that, too, but she didn't regret pouring her heart into the inn. Because it had helped, the Faraway Inn had given her a reason to live. But now, she was making plans to step back a little and, like Hannah, appreciate the things about herself that weren't tied to her career.

She wasn't sure she'd ever reach the place where she was completely comfortable with not having children, and in spite of what Janie had said, she could never ask someone else to do the same, but she was going to try and learn to live with it and not hide from it anymore.

"That may be true to a degree, Jonah, but it's not so simple for me. I *can't* have the life I want. But you *can* have any life you want."

"I want a family and I want a life with you. That's what I want."

A samurai's sword could not have cut her as surely or as painfully as these words. "Jonah, stop. It's cruel to say that to me. I can't have children—you know that. It's not that I don't want children."

"A family doesn't have to be a mom, a dad, and two-point-three kids, Shay. A family can be two people—or twenty-two."

"But you deserve the chance to have the twenty-two if that's what you want."

Jonah shrugged. "But, Shay, there are no guarantees in life. At any minute our lives could be taken from us—you know that. We both know that. We've both suffered plenty of loss, and Gramps's antics, however unorthodox and imprudent they may have been, showed us that, too."

"But you should have options, Jonah. If you marry me you won't have the option."

"I've spent the last ten years with that option

right in front of me and I've never exercised it, Shay. Why do you think that is?"

She glanced away. "I don't know," she answered, her voice choked with emotion.

"Oh, I think you do."

"Jonah, please stop."

But he wouldn't stop. Nope, instead he chose to continue slicing away with his words.

"Because my heart chose you about twenty years ago and as much as I told my head that I was over you—my stubborn heart did not agree. And now, finally, I'm listening to my heart. And it's not just my heart—it's my head, too. I'm making a choice. I'm choosing what I want—for me. I choose you, Shay. Kids or no kids. Six cats or ten cats…I would like a dog though. Francis has really done a number on me."

Shay could only stare at him. His beautiful blue eyes were full of love and she could see it and oh, how it hurt. It looked so like the way he used to love her when she was free to let him love her. She could feel the tears threatening, but knew if she were to try to speak a word, or even move a muscle, the floodgates would open. And she had to make Jonah see reason. He couldn't look at her like that anymore—or say these kinds of words that made her want things, too.

"No," she whispered. "I won't let you do this, Jonah."

"Shay—"

She somehow found the strength to untangle her hand from his and stand. "You need to go back to Chicago where you belong, Jonah. Right now you're reacting to everything that has happened here in Rankins. This place might be small but it can be its own little force of nature. Once you're in the city, your perspective will change again. Good bye, Jonah, and good luck."

THAT'S IT, JONAH THOUGHT, as he watched her leave.

No, that wasn't *it*, actually. But he had had enough of her…pontificating. And she thought he could get lost in his language of legalese? Ha, Shay spoke fluent martyrdom.

He stood up and jogged after her. She hadn't made it far. He reached out, took her hand and gave it a tug. She turned and he could see the tears streaming down her face.

"Are you through?" he asked.

"What do you mean am I through?"

"With that speech, where, once again, you get to make my decisions for me? Tell me how I must feel. How I should feel even—and the

choices I should make. Then you get to run
away and hide because you're scared."

She gasped and Jonah was happy to see a
flash of anger in her eyes. He was right. And
she might not like hearing it, but she was going
to.

"How dare you—"

"Shay, listen to me. You're not the first
woman in the world to be faced with this. So
you can't have children? Okay. That may be
cruel and unfair, but you have so many other
blessings in your life—your family is at the top
of that list. And a man standing in front of you
right now, wearing his heart on his sleeve, and
telling you that he doesn't care that you can't
have children. It's getting awkward now talking
about myself in the third person, so I'm going
to stop and add that I don't even like kids."

She couldn't help but smile at his speech,
and at his final, obvious, desperate lie. "Yes,
you do."

"Yes, I do. But maybe *I* can't have children
either—have you thought of that?"

"We already know that you can—"

He held up a hand. "I'm not finished. Maybe
that was my only chance—you don't know.
And even if we could have kids, there would
be no guarantees that we'd even like them. I

mean, you're really temperamental and stubborn and a little dramatic at times—I'm just being honest. And I'm arrogant, condescending, and maybe even a little…over-confident. What I'm saying here is that our children could be criminals like my dad or…or…arsonists. Imagine an arsonist in the family with your arsonphobia?"

Shay snuffled out a laugh through her tears. "Did you make that word up?"

"No, honestly, a fear of fire is called arsonphobia."

She shook her head, and started to argue—stubborn, argumentative woman that she was.

"Shay, think about it for a minute. Take the Crispins for example. Stu and Wanda are nice people—by all accounts, wonderful, caring, generous parents. They have three children—Linda, who refuses to speak to them because they didn't get her that big-screen TV at Christmas, Stan—a forty-year-old body-builder who can lift a car over his head with one hand but for some reason can't hold down a job. And who can forget Gordie? He emptied out their retirement account and took off to the Caribbean. Interpol is after him."

"Jonah, I believe that you mean what you're saying right now—and I love you for it. But I can't. I know that someday you'll change your mind and you'll resent me for not being able to give you what you want. I have to say no, Jonah. I don't have a choice."

His rolled his eyes, but slowly this time, so she could get a nice long look at his frustration. "You do have a choice, Shay. You can choose me back."

"Jonah, I can't do that to you."

"Then do it for me, Shay. I love you. Only you. It's always been you."

She gathered what strength she had left and told him, "I love you, too, Jonah. So much. But I'm saying it because I want you to know it, not because it changes anything."

OLD JONAH'S GRIN could light a darkened auditorium, Shay thought. She speculated whether it was possible Old Jonah and Attorney Jonah could somehow combine to make *her* Jonah.

"Oh, yes it does," he said. Then he wrapped his arms around her and branded the side of her neck with a kiss that seemed to dissolve what little determination she had left.

She rested her hands on his shoulders and looked up at him. "But, Jonah, what if…sometimes love isn't enough? It wasn't enough for us ten years ago and—"

"That might be true, but in our case it is. Our love is enough. Think about it, Shay. All these years we've been so far away from each other and living these pseudo-lives—both of us striving for our own versions of success, trying to fill the emptiness that the other took away…"

"The only thing that could fill that empty space in my heart is you, Jonah."

He scooped her up in his arms so fast that she let out a yelp of surprise. But when his lips found hers, Shay once again felt that delicious, addicting combination of spark and comfort that only Jonah could provide—along with the irresistible desire to let him back into her heart, and her life, in one fell swoop.

She was breathless when he finally set her down.

"Okay, I have one more card to play."

"What?"

"Gramps and Doc would be disappointed if I didn't follow through with the entire plan."

"Plan?"

Jonah grinned. "Yes, they helped me devise a plan to win you back." He reached into his sweatshirt pocket and when he pulled his hand out, his fingers were fisted around something. "Here, I have this for you…a bauble."

Shay laughed. "A what?"

She held out a hand and Jonah placed a small box in her palm. She recognized the tiny carved box immediately. Kella Jakobs carved boxes for all of her best jewelry and although this one looked a little worn, Kella's work was unmistakable. Shay's free hand flew over her mouth to stifle a sob. She swallowed it down but tears were clouding her vision. She blinked them away because it was time—finally it was her time—to be happy.

"I ordered this ten years ago on the day of Gary and Ingrid's reception. I was so happy that day because it felt like the last thing to do before we could get married and officially start our life together. It took Kella a while to make it, so by the time it was ready things between us had already…"

She opened the box and saw a ring nestled in the soft velvet. She removed the gold band and studied the intricate carving decorating its surface. Shay had always adored Kella's artwork and the idea that Jonah had been thoughtful enough to commission her to create Shay's wedding band…"It's beautiful, Jonah. So…perfect. I can't believe you had this made and then you kept it all these years?"

Jonah smiled proudly. "Not only have I kept it, Shay, I've kept it in my pocket."

Shay stared at the ring for several seconds, and then brought her eyes up to meet his. "That day at your gramps's house—you said something odd...about something and your pocket?"

"That ring has literally worn holes in pockets."

"No. What?"

"Yep." He chuckled. "Every single day for nearly ten years that ring has ridden around with me in my pocket and every single night it has sat on the nightstand by my bed."

"Jonah..." she whispered.

"My way of keeping a piece of us with me always. Do you still believe that I forgot about you, Shay?"

In awe, she shook her head gently.

"No more miles, no more distance between us, okay? That inn of yours is the only faraway I want between us for the rest of our lives. And can we talk about adoption at least? There are a lot of babies that need loving homes."

Silence. "Shay, say something."

"I can't."

"What do you mean you can't?"

"Attorney-client privilege prevents me from disclosing my true feelings. Or maybe it's the Fifth Amendment? I'm not sure. I may have to obtain some legal counsel before I can answer."

He looked happy; his expression both playful and intense.

"Put the ring on, Shay. Put the ring on and then let me take you to Gary and Ingrid's party tonight so the entire town can see that yes, we are back together. I'll announce it during my speech and we can save everyone the trouble of having to gossip about it." He nodded encouragingly.

So she did.

And she let all the love she was feeling, all the love she'd tried to bury for the last ten excruciating years show on her face. She knew he could see it because his lips were already curling up into a satisfied smile, but, strangely enough, those tough-talking, overconfident, attorney lips didn't bother her nearly as much now that they were headed toward hers.

* * * * *

Look for more SEASONS OF ALASKA
*romances from author Carol Ross
coming in the fall of 2015 in
Harlequin Heartwarming!*

LARGER-PRINT BOOKS!

GET 2 FREE LARGER-PRINT NOVELS PLUS 2 FREE MYSTERY GIFTS

Love Inspired®

Larger-print novels are now available...

LILPDIR13R

LARGER-PRINT BOOKS!

GET 2 FREE
LARGER-PRINT NOVELS
PLUS 2 FREE
MYSTERY GIFTS

Love Inspired®
SUSPENSE
RIVETING INSPIRATIONAL ROMANCE

Larger-print novels are now available...